SEDUCED BY DEATH

VEGAS IMMORTALS: DEATH & THE LAST
VAMPIRE

HOLLY ROBERDS

BOOKS BY HOLLY ROBERDS

Book 5 - End Game

* For recommended reading order, visit www.hollyroberds.com

To my family, friends, and fans who always believe in me, even when I forget to.

1

VIVIEN

"Hold on to your tail, Cupcake!" I shouted over the roar of my motorcycle as we barreled down the road.

The small reaper puppy yipped behind me. I sped up, trying to get closer to the guy roaring on his black bike ahead of us.

Initially, I'd wanted a motorcycle with a sidecar for Cupcake, but the Kawasaki Ninja allowed me to weave in and out of the packed night traffic of Las Vegas. And seeing as Cupcake was an incorporeal dog who would grow up to reap souls, I didn't have to worry about her safety on the sport bike. The fact that it was fuchsia also drew me like a moth to flame.

Cupcake's tiny body perched behind me, pink tongue hanging out as the wind whipped by us. Chancing a look back, I noted no one got hurt. I would have smelled the blood. The perks of being a vampire.

"Fuck a duck," I muttered, as the black motorcycle we chased cruised through the tail end of a yellow light.

Though it turned red, and traffic began to cross from either side, I couldn't let him get away.

My lungs filled with air I didn't need as I braced myself. We shot through the intersection, causing cars to screech to abrupt halts. The smash of steel rang out, and horns blared in an angry chorus.

I set my attention on the motorcyclist again. A scabbard slung over his back. The glint of a sword hilt peeked out at me.

Why did this dick nozzle want me to chase him down the Strip on a Friday night? Even in autumn, people were out en masse, partying like the world was going to end.

And if I didn't catch this guy, the world could very well come to a screeching halt.

He'd gotten far enough ahead that I was in danger of losing him. I needed to close the gap. My vampiric senses scanned the surroundings, taking everything in, making calculations. Yellow flashing lights caught my attention from the side of the road.

My body registered before my brain that I was about to do something tremendously stupid. An enabling yip of encouragement came from behind me. Cupcake was on board with it. I cut in front of the cars to my right.

Don't do it.

The growl of warning inside my head sounded exactly like a certain scary man I knew. I swatted it away. We'd been hanging out too much if he now lived rent free in my mind.

That being said, while vampires were immortal, they could be smashed into a painful bloody pulp.

I twisted the throttle, taking full advantage of the fifty feet of clear shoulder, avoiding the orange cones. Connected to a long truck bed were a couple of trailer ramps. The construction crew used them to unload the bulldozer that was now hard at work on the road. The workers' faces contorted with horror and disbelief as I roared by them.

My wheels hit the slope, and I hoped I'd reached a fast-enough speed to pull this off. Suddenly, we were sailing through the air. Time slowed into thick honey as Cupcake and I flew over lines of cars. Bright neon lights blinked down on us from the billboards overhead. The smell of cigarette smoke and someone's heavy cologne wafted out of an open car window. I regretted not wearing a cape for this epic stunt.

Unable to help myself, I screamed out, "I'm king of the world!"

The black motorcyclist looked back over his shoulder, witness to my glorious daredevilry as we closed in on him.

It seemed a great way to savor the moment. Just like Jack did in *Titanic*. Then I remembered young Leo said that before the ship famously crashed and killed most of its passengers. A fact that rushed up as quickly as the blue sedan. I hit the roof hard, denting it with a sound crunch. Muscles tensed, I worked to navigate down the slant of the hood. When the tire bounced on the asphalt, my teeth clacked against each other. A metallic taste covered my tongue, but the bike continued up the street.

An unhinged giggle of disbelief escaped me.

We'd made it.

Cupcake yipped behind me, and I could feel her squirm against my back. Her tail must have been wagging double time.

My gamble had gotten us significantly closer to our target.

When the motorcyclist turned his head to see us gaining, he missed the car pulling out onto the road. The black bike smashed into the van, sending the rider rolling in the opposite direction.

"Whoa, shit," I breathed. That was a hell of a hit to take.

But then he was up and running.

I heaved a dramatic sigh. "Runners, am I right?" I asked Cupcake.

She gave me a yip of affirmation that she knew what I meant.

As I navigated my bike around the angry drivers who'd gotten out of their cars, I followed my mark. He darted into the Parisienne Hotel as a group was leaving. I took advantage of them, opening the doors, and drove in, giving a polite thank you as I passed by. The man holding the door openly gaped at me.

If only I'd been wearing a cowboy hat I could tip in his direction.

My target continued to half-run, half-stagger as he looked over his shoulder at me. The sword still hung over his back.

The thought of letting this douche canoe get away with that weapon turned my stomach into a sloshy mess of ice and fear. Grim was death itself, yet that weapon could kill him. The thought of losing him made the frozen anxiety churn, and a sweat broke out on my brow. I couldn't lose him.

Despite my smooth entrance, the casino floor was jam-packed with gamblers and late-night partiers. I wouldn't get any farther like this. I parked and shut off the bike. I pushed my hot pink riding glasses up onto my head as Cupcake and I hopped off and started running after him.

No one would get out of my damn way. By the time we

chased him to the elevators, the doors closed. In that last second of visibility, the motorcyclist flipped me the bird.

That little fucker.

As annoying as this was, deep down, I was riding a high. Before someone had turned me into a vampire, I was a bounty hunter. Tracking down and chasing skips gave me a thrill, and a purpose. Though that life lay far behind me, the taste of it flooded my mouth as I jumped on the elevator next to the one he'd disappeared on. Cupcake stayed hot on my heels.

Closing my eyes, I focused all my heightened senses on the scent of the motorcyclist.

I sure could have used these bloodhound abilities when I'd been bounty hunting before. In the past, this is where I would have lost him. He could get off any floor of this hotel, and it'd take me far too long to catch up.

But the faint ding of his elevator reached my sensitive ears, and I knew exactly where he'd gotten off.

My lips split into a smile.

The breeze up on the rooftop bar blew cool. I was grateful to be wearing Cookie Monster—my favorite bright blue faux fur coat. Colored lights illuminated the white couches where partygoers lounged. Music bumped through the club inside but faded out on the patio so people could talk. Glass surrounded the outdoor area to serve as protective fencing without obstructing the view.

I didn't know how the motorcyclist got in, but my name was all but etched into the VIP lists across the strip.

A man in jeans, with ruffled hair, and a gray, sweat-stained shirt, stood at the corner edge of the rooftop bar. I tapped his shoulder.

"Excuse me," I said. "I think you have something I need."

He whipped around, his eyes wild with sudden terror.

The motorcyclist had shed his helmet and bodysuit some-where up here. But in doing so, his scent became only stronger, making it easy to pinpoint who he was even though I hadn't seen him out of his black cycle suit.

Thin-framed, with a long face, he was practically a teenager. He stuck out like a sore thumb in his rumpled clothes, amidst all the popped collars and flashy rhinestone dresses. The smell of vodka, pheromones, and perfume filled the air, while the guy in front of me stank of fear and something strange I couldn't identify.

Behind him, the crisscross of metal rose into the night. A replica of the Eiffel Tower gave partiers a unique view. He'd trapped himself in this corner, and there was nowhere left for him to run.

"Where is the sword?" I asked, holding out a hand. He must have stowed it away with his helmet and race suit.

The surprise in his eyes flattened as he shook his head.

I dropped my arm. "Listen, the chase was fun while it lasted, but let's get one thing straight. If someone wants your shit on Craigslist, the polite course of action is actually let them buy it."

Cupcake gave a little yip of agreement that was posi-tively adorable. Too bad I was the only one who could hear it.

Instead of answering, the guy jumped up onto the ledge, a foot balanced atop the glass partition.

Conversation hushed around me as people nearby took notice. Though they likely thought this was some kind of impromptu Vegas side show.

"Whoa." I raised my hands. "No need to get dramatic."

"You cannot stop a god," he said, matter-of-fact.

I wanted to point out that's literally what I could do with the sword, but he teetered precariously on the ledge. "Why don't you come down from there and tell me more," I suggested in a soothing tone.

He jerked when I took a step forward. I stopped in my tracks, hands held up to reassure him I would stay put. The surrounding crowd watched with fascination.

"What's your name?" I asked, touching my chest. "Mine is Vivien."

He only shook his head, gaze darting over the edge of the tremendous drop.

This dude was going to jump.

So I did what I had to. I reached out with my vampiric mind control. I almost never used it, but I could feel my power wrapping around him.

"Step down," I instructed, lowering my arms now that I had him under control.

His eyes fluttered close, and his shoulders relaxed a couple of inches, succumbing to my will.

I hated using this power. Someone's will should always be their own. But this was to save a life. I'd make an exception for this dumb-butt, so he didn't hurt himself.

Then his eyes snapped open, a green glow emanating from them.

Aw blood balls. He'd been worshiping a god.

"I vow allegiance to the one true god," he said.

Before I could ask him which god, the blanket of power I'd wrapped around him fractured.

With that, he jumped. A collective gasp, along with a couple of strangled screams, came from behind me as he hurtled over the glass partition.

I darted forward to grab him, but his body already cleared the edge. At the last second, I grabbed the back of his shirt, but I lacked the leverage to easily pull him back over, and he hung there like dead weight.

I just needed a minute to get a better grip to drag him up.

Come on, vampire strength.

His pale eyes turned up to meet mine, without a trace of fear in them. "You can't go back and change the beginning, but you can start where you are and change the ending."

Then he lifted his arms, slipped out of his shirt, and plummeted downward.

I wanted to shut my eyes. Keep from seeing him hit the ground, but I couldn't force them to close.

His body smashed into the walkway with a sickening sound. He landed in front of a group of girls, and a chorus of shrieks rose into the air. His head twisted on impact, so he faced upward. Even from here, I could see the red-stained teeth and sightless eyes. Blood seeped out in a pool around his broken limbs.

The screams and rush of everything around me faded into the background as I backed away. A strange numbness washed over me. People ran to the edge, peering over with wet eyes and shocked expressions. Multiple calls to 911 echoed in my ears.

At first, I thought I should do something too, but there was nothing left. The kid was dead.

I turned away and walked back into the club. The crying and exclamations were muffled, as if I were underwater.

You'd think as a vampire, it would be no big deal to me. But it's not like it is in story books. I didn't turn and become a monster. Heightened senses, strength, speed, and a need to drink blood, sure, but a desire to kill? The media got it wrong. I didn't lose my soul when I turned. It hardened and crystallized in my body. There would be no afterlife for me. No ticket to heaven. If someone snuffed me out, my soul would be destroyed, along with my body.

The kid painted on the pavement at least had a shot of getting into the heavenly gates.

Still, it didn't make me feel better. The vision of him hitting the ground played over in a sickening loop.

My limbs grew stiff, and I struggled to take in what just happened, even as I scented the hiding place of the motorcycle suit and helmet. He'd stashed it behind a lounging couch. Reaching further under, my fingers closed on the scabbard.

You can't go back and change the beginning, but you can start where you are and change the ending.

It wasn't the first time I'd heard the C. S. Lewis quote. It had been written on a piece of paper and packaged in a box, along with a god's head. Presumably, the blade I held now was the same one that killed Seth. Though a major dick nozzle, I still hadn't wanted Seth dead. Even when he did his best to torture me and kill my boyfriend.

That would have been one hell of a feat too, considering my boyfriend was literally death. The grim reaper, the god of the dead, and coincidentally, the owner of the most exclusive hotel on the Vegas Strip, Sinopolis.

But whoever killed Seth intended to change the world order. The quote confirmed one of the gods was no longer satisfied with the status quo, giving reign of this world to the humans. They would upset the balance even if that meant breaking the law of Osiris and taking a worshiper, imbuing that person with power.

Somehow, I made it back to my motorcycle, though I didn't remember the journey down. Red and blue lights filled the streets as a crowd gathered.

The sheathed blade lay across my palms, a strangely light object to cost someone their life.

The numbness gave way to a sick feeling.

Cupcake leapt into my lap, forcing me to lift the sword up to make room. The reaper puppy whined, then yipped until I brushed a hand over her soft, black fur. Her golden eyes peered up at me with sympathy, and the nausea subsided a little.

"Come on, girl," I said. "Let's go home."

2

GRIM

A soul kneeled before me. His eyes were downcast as he trembled in fear. Torches flickered along the limestone walls and great pillars in the hall of judgment. Murals in bright colors depicting the weighing of the heart lined the antechamber, looking as fresh as if painted yesterday. The scent of lotus flowers and cedarwood surrounded me, though this place reeked of archaic power and the old ways.

Timothy stood off to the side with his tablet. Five thousand years ago, we performed the rites with fine white linen cloth wrapped around our waists, and brightly colored headdresses. Those who worshipped us would anoint me and Timothy in sweet-smelling oils before we began.

But now, Timothy preferred expensive cologne and statement three-piece suits. Today's suit was a deep teal color, covered in velvet paisley designs. He'd always had a taste for more fashion-forward styles.

I hardly recalled his old features. After spending many centuries in the east, primarily China and Korea, his features had reshaped Asiatic. His thick, dark hair was gelled to perfection. Despite the changes, he still maintained his essence of elegance and acuity. Nothing escaped his notice. He filed every little detail.

I spent much time traveling the earth as well, but I retained my dark Egyptian traits. I appreciated the feel of fine materials but hadn't veered away from the color black since the 14th century, the dark years of plague. Back when they referred to me as the black death, the grim reaper.

To this day, I retained the namesake, feeling the title Grim suited me.

But no matter our appearance or style preferences, the job remained the same. Judgment.

"Please," the man begged at the base of my dais.

They always begged.

"Have you lived an ethical life?" I asked, standing in front of the stone chair etched with hieroglyphics.

Dark blue eyes searched the ground around my feet. While he thought, I observed the thinning hair on his head and the rough stubble peppered with white. I could practically taste the conflict in his soul. He'd committed iniquitous deeds in his lifetime. Things he regretted and tried to make up for after the fact.

Hands clasped together, he met my gaze, searching my eyes for clemency. "I don't know."

I exchanged a look with Timothy.

This was a rare one. Usually, the soul would stumble over their adamant conviction they were innocent and ethical throughout the course of their life. Not that their answer mattered. Still, I asked the question, allowing them to prepare for their sentence, whatever it might be.

I felt Vivien the moment she entered the stone antechamber. My eyes flicked up to watch her cross the room along the far wall, sitting down on the floor. Cupcake climbed into her lap, settling in. They would wait patiently until we were done. The blood in my veins rushed faster, and heat spread through me.

Auburn hair fell in wild waves past her shoulders, wind-blown from her bike, no doubt. The juxtaposition of her presence in this place did not escape me. Where I ruled my domain with an iron fist, I was keenly aware I could not control the woman who just waltzed in. But I learned I'd never want to. Her ability to surprise me with her passionate beauty and fierce heart was the only force I'd ever bent to. Though she'd bent before me in other alluring manners... that sent my blood rushing south.

I pushed Vivien from my mind, so I could focus on the task at hand.

"Let us see about your soul, then, shall we?" Turning around, I faced the wall behind me. A mural depicting a set of golden scales covered the expanse of sandstone blocks. Power flowed off me, awakening magic older than even me. They shimmered and emerged as a set of three-dimensional, corporeal scales, floating in midair before me.

I'd shed my suit coat and rolled up the sleeves of my shirt. I bore my left arm out to the side, making a fist. Ink swelled to the surface of my forearm as the feather of Ma'at appeared. I pinched at the tattoo until I plucked it away from my flesh. The soft feather I now held emitted a gentle yet strong power, a power stronger than Timothy and I combined. After setting it on one scale, I turned back to the kneeling soul. His face had gone slack from awe.

Timothy's tablet rose from his hands, glowing turquoise blue. Magic hieroglyphs streamed from the space between his eyes and into the device as he recorded the judgment.

I descended the few steps from my dais and reached into the man's ribcage. First, he blinked at me, then at the hand that disappeared into him. When it emerged, my fingers wrapped around the bright red organ. The man frantically patted at his chest, searching for an open wound, forgetting he'd already crossed over into the realm of spirit.

"We shall see if you have lived a life good enough to be admitted into the glorious afterlife. Or"—my voice lowered — "if you are only fit to be consumed by Amit."

I set his heart on the empty scale. Back and forth, it rocked. Tension filled the room as the scales measured.

The feather was divine order, truth, and morality. It embodied a state of grace that humans can destroy with their deeds of greed and hatred. It was my job to make sure that never happened.

The feather determines if a person shall be bestowed eternal life. And as the god of death, I was the guardian of the doorway to that glorious afterlife.

At last, the scale settled, until the one holding the man's heart rose higher than the feather.

"What does that mean?" the man wrung his hands, fear in his voice.

The feather floated to my inner forearm, disappearing into my skin, while a gold light surrounded his heart. The massive set of scales, along with his organ, receded into the wall. Now the painting reflected his heart lifting higher than the other side.

"It means," I said, turning around. "That I can now escort you to the heavenly afterlife."

With a resounding boom, the wall disappeared, revealing lush green reeds and bright blue sky. A breeze of fresh air and sweet grasses swept through the antechamber. I leaned down, offering the man my hand.

Tears of relief and gratitude glittered in his eyes as he took it. I pulled him up to his feet, then escorted him across the boundary to where the grizzled ferryman waited with his boat, and his long steering staff at the ready.

"Hraf-haf will chaperon you to the other side," I explained. "There you'll find peace, salvation, and eternal life." The old man nodded at me. He would take it from here.

When I returned to the antechamber, the wall reappeared, the man's heart now gone, scales reset.

I crossed to Vivien, while unfastening another button at the top of my shirt. She scrambled up, Cupcake leaping off her lap. I pulled her up against me, then dipped down for a deep kiss. My blood simmered as my body instantly craved more of her.

Though she kissed me back, there was a stiffness that usually wasn't there. I knew I should investigate the cause, but I'd already fallen into the taste of her. The scent of leather and sugar surrounded me, along with her unique feminine signature. As my tongue pushed past her teeth, she melted against me.

I'd seen her this morning, but my skin felt starved for hers. She sparked an insatiable desire in me, which possessed me, body and soul.

"What's wrong?" I asked.

"That was one hell of a production," she said with a weak smile, changing the subject, gesturing behind me.

"Right. I forget you've only witnessed the tail end of a judgment, and it left you with the impression I was a ruthless monster."

A woman I'd judged had ended up in Amit's chamber instead of the afterlife. The enormous crocodile god devoured the woman's dark soul. Out of jealousy, she'd poisoned her stepdaughter, to secure her husband's affections all to herself. Though she threw herself into charities and philanthropic work, it did not make up for the terrible deed she'd committed.

I'd further cowed her down in anger, as I personally possessed a particular loathing for those who harmed children.

Vivien threaded her fingers through the hair at the base of my skull. "Oh, you are definitely a ruthless monster. But in all the best ways." Then she reached for my left arm, twisting it around. "Also, you have a tattoo? Wait, where'd it go?"

My fist closed and tightened until the black ink swelled up again to the surface.

"Look at you, Mr. Badass. Inked up and what not," she said, impressed. "Didn't know uptight old guys like yourself got tatted."

I shook my head, but the side of my lips curved up. Only she would make light of our five-thousand-year age difference as if we were a normal couple.

"Do you like it? Shall I keep it visible?" I would do anything she asked of me.

"Hell yeah, keep it visible," she encouraged. "I can't wait to tell my bestie that you've got ink."

"Perhaps you could not, seeing as Miranda is my employee and head of security here at Sinopolis. I'd like to preserve some amount of respect."

"Okaaay," she said in an exaggerated tone with an ingenuous wink. "I definitely agree not to tell my best friend all the intimate details of our wild sex life, or about your tattoo."

I suppressed the need to sigh. What else should I expect? Even when I'd commanded her through supernatural means not to reveal the knowledge that gods walked amongst humans, Vivien still managed to clue in Miranda. With a game of charades, of all things.

"I can't win, can I?" I asked, as I held her tighter against me.

Her expression turned sensual as her eyes hooded. "Oh, I think there are plenty of ways you can win." One hand slid down my chest to play with the edge of my belt. My skin zinged with electric need, as my blood heated with desire and I hardened. For her, I was always ready, always needing more.

The way this woman made me forget myself...

"Ahem." A sound from behind me.

"Apologies, Timothy," I said, readjusting myself against the shield of Vivien before turning back around.

"No problem, sire," he said.

"Okay," Vivien teed her hands for a time out. "I thought as Grim's aide, you were one step above a butler, Timmy. But we haven't talked about this whole mystic mamba jamba you've got going."

She referred to the glowing hieroglyphs that emanated from him into the tablet, taking record of the judgment.

He rolled his eyes. "As I've told you many times before. Grim is not Batman and I am not Alfred."

"So why do you always call him sire?"

Vivien could test anyone's patience with her childlike harangue of questions.

"It's a sign of respect," he shot back. Anyone who saw them arguing like this might suppose them to be enemies instead of friends. But I'd learned, the more biting their banter, the greater the care between them.

She tapped a finger against her lips. "So, you are even more of an uptight control freak than Grim. Because as a god, you want to clean up all the messes, and coordinate details."

Timothy's chest puffed out. "That is exactly it. I enjoy keeping everything tidy and organized. It makes the transcription of events much easier to document. I am the scribe. One of my most important duties is to record all history, as well as Grim's judgments."

"Right." She snapped her fingers. "I've read about this. Like how his original god-name is Anubis, yours is Tot."

"Thoth," I corrected gently.

Her brows furrowed in annoyance as she threw up her hands. "Well, excuse me. I've been reading books on Egyptian mythology, but I'm wondering why I should even try. Sometimes the information is wrong. All those historians, mythologists, or whatever you call them, they all think Amit, the giant croc-god, the soul devourer, is a girl, but he's actually a boy."

"At one point, Amit was female," Timothy said.

Vivien's expression flattened. "Seriously?"

I answered this time. "Around, I believe it was the ninth, or was it the tenth century?" I asked Timothy. "Amit decided to try out being a male."

Timothy's eyes glowed turquoise for a moment as he retrieved the information as official scribe and history keeper. "The tenth, sire."

Her frustration returned. "Boning up on all this Egyptian history to keep up with you old fogies isn't easy. Especially since I'm mainly interested in a different kind of boning these days—"

"And on that note, I believe we are done here," Timothy said, his words clipped, ready to flee.

"Hold up, I think you are going to want to see this too," Vivien said, stopping him. The stiff demeanor I'd first noticed when she arrived returned. Something was definitely amiss.

She ran back to the corner where she'd been sitting. She came back with a sheathed sword.

"Is that what I think it is?" I asked.

"Let's hope it is," she said, her tone grave.

Timothy held out his hands. "May I?" Excitement made his voice tense, though from fear or anticipation, I couldn't be sure.

She placed the covered weapon in his hands. Timothy carefully pulled out the weapon. The ornate bronze hilt curved down on either side of the sword while ancient etchings decorated the length of the blade.

"Looks like something King Arthur would swing around," Vivien said, her voice quiet.

"Another race who feared us, and wanted a means to keep the gods in check, forged the Blade of Bane in medieval times."

Vivien stilled. "What do you mean, another race? There are gods, humans, and vampires. Or I'm the only vampire now, I guess..."

I took the sword from Timothy as he gave his history lesson.

Timothy shook his head. "There is far more to this world than you could imagine. Layers upon layers of beings other than the three you mentioned."

I tested the weight of the sword in my hands. I ran a finger along the sharp edge, careful not to cut myself. As Seth found out, the edge of this blade inflicted real and permanent damage to a god. The grayed flesh at his neckline had assured me he would not come back to life. I knew instantly the blade responsible, though it had been lost for centuries.

"If you tell me werewolves exist too, I'll faint dead away." Vivien lifted the back of her hand to her forehead.

Timothy cracked a smile at that. "Well, now you're just tempting me."

I interjected, still examining the blade. "The race who forged the Blade of Bane is what we refer to as the fae. Like gods, they are immortal, but only if they do not undertake serious bodily harm. They possess a more delicate constitution, like that of a human. Stab me in the heart, I will survive and regenerate. They would not. The fae possess magics and talent as varied as they are secret. They managed to stay far out of the gods' way in history, but times of war compelled them to seek security should they need it. Thus, they created the Blade of Bane." I turned and deftly sliced the sword through the air. "However, this is not that weapon. This is a replica of the original design."

Timothy looked down at his tablet, his face tightening. It was bad for all of us that this had resurfaced.

"How can you tell?" Vivien asked.

"Because the authentic god-killing blade is quite light. I've held the sword before, and this clunky, unbalanced piece of steel has all the flourish, but none of the mastery imbued by an expert swords-maker."

Her shoulders slumped, hope fading from her eyes. "You're telling me I ran all over the city tracking down a fake sword? And that he..." She trailed off. Vivien crossed her arms over her chest and took a step back.

I dropped the sword to my side and stepped forward, cupping her face. "What? What happened?" I asked gently.

"If someone has been worshiping a god, what happens to their soul when they die? Do they have to go through you for judgment?"

Her hand covered mine and played with the skull ring I

wore. I hadn't worn it since the late eighteenth century, but lately I'd been drawn to the gold ring with ruby red eyes.

"Their fealty and service guarantee them automatic entry into the afterlife. Why?" Seth took worshippers. It was forbidden, and Osiris would have punished him severely.

With an almost imperceptible shake of her head, Vivien told me she wasn't ready to talk about it right now. "I—I need some sugar." She tripped over her own words.

A devilish grin curled my lips.

"Not that kind," she said, smacking my chest. But I caught her hand and turned it so I could drop a kiss on the inside of her wrist. Her pupils expanded into dark pools as she shivered. "Well, maybe that kind."

I hadn't noticed when Timothy left, but now that work was done, I swept her up into my arms before she could change her mind.

3

VIVIEN

We didn't even make it up to the room. As soon as Grim carried me into the lift, he had me splayed against the tufted wall. My ass rested on the handrail that curved along the elevator, my legs balanced around his hips as he pushed into me, rocking us both toward insanity through our clothes.

When did I lose my top? I was down to my cherry red lace bra.

I had a weakness for lingerie, and I especially liked what it did to Grim. Though I was convinced I could wear a paper sack and the man would get a stiffy for me.

I helped myself, unfastening his pants and slipping a hand inside. My fingers wrapped around his incredible girth. Grim stopped kissing my neck to drop his forehead into the crook of my shoulder.

"Fuck, I need you," he groaned.

"You're so big," I breathed, enjoying the feel of his silky skin stretched taut over his hardness.

Lifting his face to meet my eye, the amber irises now glowed gold. "And you're so beautiful. My fierce warrior woman, handling all the hunting, while I stay tethered to my godly duties. How can I ever show my appreciation?" Then he leaned down to lave his tongue against the sheer lace of my bra. Zings of pleasure shot through me and down to my core, making me squirm. Appeasing me, he covered my peak with his entire mouth, sucking until I moaned with need. The fabric added a layer of friction, but I wanted to rip it off to feel his hot, wet tongue.

He pressed a large hand against my lower belly, stoking the smoldering heat between my legs into a blazing fire.

"I think... I mean, if you're up for it..." I stuttered.

He hummed to let me know he was listening, but the vibration shot directly into my breast and pinged down to my very needy center, making it even harder to think.

"I was thinking we could try that, uh, trick again."

He paused his ministrations this time, lifting his head. The glow of his eyes had simmered to a molten, liquid gold as he searched my face. "Are you certain?"

I nodded. "Yeah, I want to."

We'd done this only twice before, as the trust required had stretched me to my limits.

"Just to be absolutely clear," he said, "You're giving me permission to use our blood bond to exert my will over yours."

I wanted to roll my eyes at how explicit he was being, but I knew why. If I were being honest with myself, it scared me a little.

"I am a willing and consenting vampire." Despite my answer, I swallowed hard.

"Then we are going to need more room," he said, promise lingering in his words.

He reached over to press a button. The lift had already

arrived at the penthouse at the top of the pyramid hotel, and
the doors must have opened and closed.

We stepped into our apartment.

God, that was weird. *Our* apartment.

As soon as I fled my aunt and uncle's house at eighteen,
running as fast as my skinny legs could take me, I was determined to always live alone. Freedom was not something I'd
known growing up under my relatives' roof, and I preferred
to reside in a dirty hovel, chasing after skips, if it could be on
my terms.

Until now.

Though it still felt like Grim's apartment, rather than
mine. The penthouse was at the very tiptop of the pyramid.

Neon lights from the Strip streamed in through the
slanted, floor-to-ceiling windows. Grim began slipping the
rest of the buttons out of his shirt as he walked backward,
pulling me with him farther into the penthouse.

I followed him into the bedroom. It was like walking into
a gothic boudoir. I felt his magic pulsate, and suddenly the
candelabras lit up along the walls, casting light on the black
moulded walls and gold finishes. Nifty trick. His masculine
scent permeated the room, mingling with the aroma of
freshly laundered sheets and something dark and tempting.

Thick purple curtains hung on the walls, though there
were no windows. The ornate bed could have fit a half-
dozen people, and I remembered first seeing it and imag-
ining all the orgies he'd likely hosted here. But now I knew
it as the place where we explored each other, pushing one
another to the absolute limit before breaking together. I
could no longer count the times I'd clutched and clawed at
those black silk sheets.

We stopped at the foot of the bed. The shirt slid down
his arms, revealing his sculpted body. Broad shoulders

framed his wide chest before tapering down to his defined abs. Though he spent his days judging souls from a throne, his body appeared combat-ready, ready to go to war at a moment's notice.

The Greeks thought they knew beauty when they carved marble into the likeness of gods, but Grim left them all in the dust.

My brain raced like a hungry school child in a candy shop, trying to focus on my favorite part of him.

His rounded shoulders.

No, wait!

His perfectly lickable six pack.

No, but what about the dip at the base of his neck, between those handlebar collarbones?

Your favorite part hasn't been exposed yet, my brain whispered.

I shucked my boots and leather pants, about to push down my matching red panties, when Grim stopped me.

"I would like to start now, if that's alright." His tone was low and steady, as if he were approaching a wild animal.

I was nervous as hell to hand the reins over to him, but I dropped my arms and nodded. Traipsing around in my underwear never made me self-conscious before, but standing here stripped down, I felt vulnerable and exposed.

Those honey eyes glowed again as he called his power forward. When he spoke, his words seemed to come from inside my head, from inside the marrow of my bones, until I was absolutely compelled to do as he commanded.

"Touch your neck."

I couldn't have disobeyed if I tried. Once a vampire drank from a god, a blood bond formed, giving gods the power to bend them to their will. I was Grim's first blood bond, having abstained all those years ago, we were still learning our own way through this connection.

My fingertips touched the column of my neck.

With bare feet and exposed chest, Grim padded around me.

No, he stalked around me like a predator. His eyes were alight with a hunger that tripled the thrum of my nerves, but it was too late now.

"I want you to slowly run them down and over your breasts."

He stopped behind me. My hands followed his direction, sliding over the soft swells of my chest and over the lace of the bra.

His hot breath fanned against my ear, causing goose-bumps to rise along my neck. "Slip one of your hands inside your bra. I want you to feel the silken texture of your skin. The perfect weight of your breasts, that delicious peak I'm dying to wrap my lips around."

My desire turned molten and pooled between my thighs.

"I want you to feel every inch of what an absolutely gorgeous creature you are."

My mouth dried as he directed me, without ever touching me. Still, part of me wanted to stop this. I'd learned freedom was the most important thing a person could possess, and I'd just handed it over to Death himself.

My thumbs brushed over my straining peaks and a jolt ran through me, as though it were his fingers playing with me. Electricity raced along my skin. I didn't know if it was his power or simply how I brought awareness to my own body.

Though the weight of his power pushed down on me, making it hard to speak, I managed to get a few words out. "This isn't how I thought this would go."

In the past, he'd used his power to command me into two of the most intense, out-of-the-blue orgasms I'd ever known. The first time he did it to demonstrate to me the potential perks of our blood bond. And the second time, it was to punish me for going commando in a form-fitting dress. We'd gone to the Wolf Club and I may have strategically bent over in front of him. His eyes blazed, focused on only me, even as people crowded around him requesting selfies and autographs.

Grim's command had blossomed in my mind. *Come.* My arm had shot out to steady myself against the bar as my legs crossed to keep from falling to the floor. My vision went black as shudders of release rolled through me, leaving the insides of my thighs sticky. The throng of people around us paused as I convulsed but were none the wiser. Though Grim had claimed he felt bad and I wanted to be livid with him, it was...fun. But he knew how I felt about being controlled.

"You thought I was going to simply tell you to come for me?" Grim asked, bringing me back to the present. Warm lips pressed against my bare shoulder in a teasing kiss as he toyed with the strap of my bra. "That I would command you to fuck me like an animal?"

That's exactly what I thought.

Slowly, he drew the strap down one arm, then the other. My fingers still massaged and played with my breasts. He hadn't commanded me to stop. "If you are going to entrust your body, your will to me, I'm going to use it the way it was always meant to."

Though he was speaking out loud, his voice also reverberated inside my head again. "Touch yourself where you want it most, over those sinful little panties you insist on wearing."

My fingers skimmed down my stomach, following an invisible line, downward. Not that I'd ever tried drugs, but I imagined this is what ecstasy would be like. Every nerve ending was on high alert, noticing every tiny sensation, sinking pleasure and desire into my brain.

"I'm going to show you exactly how amazing you are." He brushed the hair away from the nape of my neck and over my shoulder, somehow making me feel more exposed. "How responsive, how passionate you are. Make you desire yourself almost as much as I do." He kissed up the back of my neck.

I reached the ache between my legs, the fabric already damp.

I shivered as he pushed the sheer cups of my bra down. The air hit my bare skin. The pressure in my nipples coiled tighter. Still behind me, Grim played my sensitive tips with an expert touch.

I choked out something incoherent. I wasn't even sure what I was trying to say, but I knew I was desperate for penetration. My inner muscles clenched as I obediently continued to only rub through my panties.

Grim watched over my shoulder. I leaned against his strong, warm chest, my head rolled back onto his shoulder. My body turned boneless. Moans broke from my throat. I couldn't think. I registered the stiffness pressed against my back from his erection.

"Look at what feeling you are capable of, Vivien," he said. "Only you can do this. No one can make you feel anything you can't already feel yourself. You are capable of such intensity, and I want you to feel all of it."

Whatever he did next didn't come in words, but I felt his power. A heat blossomed in my already-sensitive clit, a phantom pressure like I'd never known before. I bit back a gasp as his lips curled against my ear. More phantom tendrils licked down my throat, between my breasts, and down my stomach.

My fingers slid up and down against my wet center faster, pressing harder into the lace. Oh sweet fucking god, any moment I was going to lose it.

"But you will not come, not until I let you." His words snapped like a cold whip.

His power yanked me back from the crest. I moaned in agony, and my knees shook.

"Do you know how long you could do this for? Stay on the edge, in this space between stimulation and completion?" His words were dark and dangerous. "Do you think I could keep you here for hours? Maybe days? Until you are dripping in sweat, melted between your legs, and out of your mind with need?"

His words would have sent me into orgasm alone, but his magic held me back.

"Pl-please," I begged. I never begged, but that didn't matter at this moment. Another phantom pressure against my sensitive bud left me gasping for air I didn't need.

One of his hands finally slipped down under my panties on my hip, but he didn't push them down. "Do you want to feel all of it? All of what you are capable of?"

I did want to feel it. I desperately needed it.

But my words couldn't surface this time. I couldn't beg him again. His power had bound me too tightly, and I was utterly and completely his.

Fear threatened to climb up into my consciousness.

He must have sensed it somehow. Grim cooed in my ear, "I've got you. You're safe."

He held me there for minutes that seemed to span hours.

"You may touch yourself under the panties," he said, finally pushing the lace down. Though I wasn't restrained, it felt like it. Panties wrapped around my upper thighs, bra pushed down just under my breasts, his fingers digging into my hips. They felt as illicit as if he'd tied me up in rope.

My hand greedily hit the target, fingers pumping in and out. My cries increased as my pleasure did. On my tiptoes, I struggled to get my digits deep enough from my standing position, but Grim had wrapped his hands around my arms, holding me up against him, preventing me from going deeper.

I neared desperation, frantic for release. I was so close, yet so far from satisfaction, as my inner muscles clenched, wanting so much more.

Grim's words reverberated in my head, near demonic whispers of sin and lust. "What you want—they named it after me. They call it le petite mort. The little death." His lips curved against my neck in a wicked grin.

There was nothing little about what rioted through me, or the hardness pressed at my back, but I couldn't form words, caught in Grim's spell.

This bordered on torture, but part of me never wanted it to stop. I'd never been so inside of a moment. Time didn't matter. Nothing else mattered except the feeling of my own skin.

"Vivien," he said, in that low, near-animalistic growl. His desire pressed against my back.

I could only let out an incoherent "Ungh." Perspiration covered my body and dampened my hair.

It did feel as though I were approaching some kind of death. On a precipice, part of me wanted to back away and regain control over my senses. But I'd handed all the control over to Grim and there was no going back.

Come, he commanded at last.

My orgasm hit me like a freight train. I'd already been running up to it, but bam. My body shuddered as it broke free of the near-agonizing buildup. Grim's hand squeezed my arms like two vices as I bucked against him, keening and moaning.

"Good girl," he said softly into my ear, as I sobbed from the relief.

It kept rolling through me, drenching my thighs, as my inner muscles clenched and spasmed.

Then his magic released me as I finished riding it out. Before I could collapse, he scooped me into his arms.

For the second time, I begged. "Please, fuck, I need you now. I need you inside me, please." My voice shook, words nearly incoherent.

Crossing to the bed, he laid me down. When he covered me with his body, I found he'd shed the rest of his clothes. When had that happened? His rich-caramel colored skin pressed against mine, and nothing had ever felt so right. I ran my hands through his thick dark hair, already messy though he hadn't fucked me yet.

Something sharp slid along the side of my ribcage. My bra loosened as he cut through it. I didn't need to look to know his hand transformed into a black claw. They sliced through my panties next. I'd complained about losing all my underwear to his little shifter trick, since he could transform into an eight-foot, terrifying jackal monster—his god-like-ness. But he got away with it by always supplying me with all the replacement lingerie I needed.

But I wasn't going to complain about anything right now as the real monster, the one between his legs, brushed against my slick opening. His tip glistened with pent-up release. As much fun as he had, it must have been torture for him, too. When he pushed into me, my back arched as I struggled to take him all in.

Body already primed, I greedily wrapped my legs around him, embracing the pain and pleasure. My fingers raked down his straining triceps. I needed him to move, but he held back.

"I love you, Vivien," he said. Some of his hair fell over his forehead, as he regarded me with almost painful devotion through honey-colored eyes. In that moment, I saw glimpses of a boy, desperate to be loved.

Though my heart was dead, I could have sworn it pumped a beat.

The words climbed up my throat, then a fist closed around it. Fear and uncertainty won yet again as it beat the words back down.

The little men who ran things in my brain popped up to see if there was anything they could do about it.

Sir, the system is flowing backwards. Should we push some buttons? Hit some levers? Do something to help her say it back?

Jenkins, I've told you before. We just keep the lights on. Those kinds of big decisions are above our paygrade.

But will she ever say it, sir?

Well, if these two get to live for an eternity, at some point I have to believe she will work up the cajones to tell him how she feels.

I'm not as optimistic, sir.

Grim didn't push, though I could see how much he craved to hear the words from me.

I'd fight until I was bloodied to protect him, make sure the Blade of Bane never cut into his body. I would not let him go the way Seth did.

But to fully surrender my heart, leaving nothing for myself... I couldn't do it. I wasn't brave enough.

Hurt flashed across his eyes in a millisecond before he closed his emotions off from me. Before I could react, Grim began to thrust. It was a punishing rhythm, though who he was punishing, I couldn't be sure.

Friction and desire consumed me like a fire. Pleasure swallowed us up in a cloud as we strained for more. He pounded into me until all the pain, guilt, and unsaid words fell away. Our cries for release rose into the air.

It took almost no time for us both to slam into our release. Emotional and physical tension were pushed past the breaking point. We shook and strained as our bodies hurtled into oblivion. I screamed until I was hoarse, while he let out a roar that shook the mirrors on the wall.

When he rolled off me, we both just lay there, staring at the ceiling, reeling from the intensity.

"Wow," I said, though it came out as a whisper.

Grim rolled onto his side, tucking an arm under his head, making his muscles bulge. "Are you okay?"

"Yeah. I mean, I think so. I don't think my brain has returned to my body yet."

He didn't laugh, just continued to regard me with concern.

"I'm okay," I said in a quiet voice. And I was.

"You're too far away," Grim grumbled, dragging me across the half a foot until he nestled against him. In moments, he'd stilled and his breath turned heavy and deep.

He still insisted it was impossible for a god to snore, no matter how much I vowed he did.

I skimmed my fingers through his hair, enjoying the texture. The experience he'd just given me had been incredible, and while part of me wondered how else we could explore this control, I was still scared of giving it to him again.

He'd completely taken the wheel and driven my will, but he'd chosen to make it all about me.

But if I gave into him fully, loving him, there wouldn't be a "me" anymore.

I so desperately wanted to let myself love him but as soon as I did, I would do whatever it took to keep that love. Even if it meant bending me to be someone I wasn't.

It would start small, like trying not to say things that annoyed him, or dressing in a way I thought was more appropriate, to be seen at his side. If there were parts of me he found displeasing, the urge to fold them up and tuck them away would be overwhelming. No matter how I'd try to resist, I'd still twist myself up like a pretzel to appease him, even if he had no intention of doing it to me.

Even though I knew I'd never win the love of my aunt, I hadn't been able to keep myself from trying. Maybe if I finally did the right things, my aunt wouldn't look at me with that sour disappointment and tell me I was a pustule she was making do with. Maybe if I acted perfectly at the senator's house for a fundraiser, I wouldn't get smacked around when we got home. Maybe she would protect me from my uncle, and he'd stop visiting me in the middle of the night.

After getting out on my own, I freed myself to be loud, rebellious, and followed my gut any which way it would take me without any regard for what someone else would think of me. People often found me immature, rude, ridiculous, but I told myself it was how I knew I was doing things on my terms.

But allowing myself to love Grim...

The truth was my need for love was so intense and

desperate, it had created a dark cavern in my soul which had turned into a bottomless pit. If I kept myself from fully loving Grim, I never risked fully receiving his heart.

Because if I got the love I so craved, I'd do anything to keep it. And that terrified me to the marrow of my bones.

4

GRIM

I don't know what woke me up. Usually, I did not fall into such a deep sleep, but it happened more and more since Vivien took up residence in my bed. I instinctively reached out for Vivien. Instead, my hand met empty sheets.

Sexually sated, I was more relaxed than I could remember being in my entire existence. Even my toes felt as though they'd pressed into the warm, black sands of Egypt.

Then something coiled around my chest and squeezed with malicious intent. The memory of Vivien's expression when I'd mentioned I loved her returned to me. Abject terror flashed through her eyes, spearing me through without a sound. She trusted me with her body, her will, but not with her heart.

When I first said it, she seemed so eager, wishing to respond in kind. But she could not do so. Vivien claimed she needed space, and I could give it to her. Our blood bond would last.

We had the luxury of eternity, but endless time could also be agony, depending on how it's spent. An agony of waiting, of always wanting more and never getting it. And though I owned her body, and she'd even given me her free will, I wanted Vivien's heart.

Fuck that. I wanted all of her. And every moment I didn't possess all of Vivien, a deep, keening anguish plagued me.

Something clattered from the direction of the kitchen, pulling me out of my mental spiral. I pulled on a pair of silk boxers and padded toward the sound.

Vivien was banging around. The smell of burnt sugar hung in the air, but a pan of fresh, uncharred cupcakes sat cooling on the counter. Cupcake sat, curled in a doggie bed between the living room and kitchen. Her golden eyes tracked Vivien's manic movements. I stopped to ruffle the pup's ears. Not long ago, the idea of treating my reapers like common canines would have been preposterous. But Vivien proved to be a mighty force, and apparently all the reapers adored her affectionate nature. I couldn't blame my envoys. I also found her attention positively addicting.

Vivien had on her favorite bright blue faux fur coat. She'd named it Cookie Monster and referred to it as if it were a close, personal friend. Under her jacket, she wore a black T-shirt with some punk rock band on it, and shorts that barely covered her cheeks.

I would have gone over and stolen a pinch of her luscious ass, but I knew better than to get in the way when she was in this mode. Several times, I'd seen her struck by rush of manic energy, and the few times I'd tried to calm her down ended up in physical violence, and some very rude name calling she apologized for in the aftermath.

Apparently, I wasn't really a "controlling dumb-butt, cookie saboteur." She had rained kisses on me, hoping to erase the memory of her outburst. But I'd learned my lesson and stayed out of the way rather than invoke her wrath.

Instead, I went to my espresso machine and started it up.

When I returned to sit at the countertop across from her with my demitasse, she'd moved onto icing one of the cupcakes. My trepidation melted away as I watched her. I never imagined life could be like this. I'd heard the phrase 'domestic bliss' but I'd never understood it until the last few months. There was no banality to our lives, but the certainty she would be in my bed every day, that I'd find the kitchen a sugary mess, and her cheeky smile gave me a new level of satisfaction I hadn't known possible.

Though she knew I was there, she remained focused on her task. A bit of her pink tongue poked out as her forehead wrinkled in concentration. I fell a little more in love with her right there.

But something bothered her. I could feel it, and it took everything in me to not push. I had to wait and hope she'd tell me.

Finally, she paused her pastry decorating, shoulders dropping as she sighed. "He jumped off the roof of the Parisienne Hotel."

"Who did?"

Still, she didn't meet my eye. "The guy who duped me with the fake sword. After I found the Craigslist ad, I kept sending him messages that I wanted to buy it. But he never responded, so I went to Echo."

Echo was an older, Samoan woman who also was an expert hacker. She used to help Vivien when she was a human bounty hunter. When I'd met Echo, I suspected her of being more than just human, but hadn't mentioned that to Vivien.

Vivien picked up the frosted cupcake, pretending to examine it before setting it back down. "When I showed up at his apartment, he grabbed the sword and ran like hell."

I turned my body toward her more, trying to gauge her reactions. "Then he jumped off a roof?"

She nodded, her emerald-green eyes lifting to meet mine finally. So much conflict and pain lay in them. "He was practically a kid. I chased him up to the top of the Parisienne. I tried to influence his mind to get him to step down from the ledge."

Something kicked me in the gut. I knew how hard it must have been for her to do that. Freedom mattered to her almost more than anything, and she never used that power if she could help it. Even though she'd broken her own rule to save someone from themselves, I knew she hated herself for it.

She went on, her brow furrowing. "But then he broke my hold. Someone else already controlled him."

I set down my cup and rolled my shoulders back. "What do you mean?"

"I mean," she said, scooping up her perfectly iced cupcake, coming around the island to sit next to me. "He'd been worshiping a god."

My alarm mounted. "Are you sure?"

Was that why she asked about what happened to the soul of a worshiper?

She placed the cupcake in front of her on the counter, studying the pink frosting. Or rather, she looked through it, her mind's eye elsewhere. "Yeah. Some dickhead god is breaking all the rules. Taking worshippers, killing other gods, and they don't care who gets hurt."

I swiveled the stool until my legs were on the outside of her chair. Holding one of her hands in mine, I gently rotated her seat toward me. Still, she didn't meet my eye.

"It's not your fault," I said.

"I know."

"Do you?" I asked, ducking my head to get her to look at me.

Finally meeting my eye, she ran a hand through her hair, inadvertently smearing icing into it. I suppressed my smile since it was not the appropriate time. The boy's death clearly agitated her.

"I know, it's not my fault." She sighed. "But my head's all messed up after seeing that guy go splat on the sidewalk. And he died for what? A stupid fake sword?"

I licked my fingers and ran them along the iced strands of her hair. "Gods are accustomed to playing games of power and deception."

"Well, I fucking hate it." She crossed her arms across her chest and pouted. "In three months, we're no closer to figuring out who this psycho is. I mean, I could guess, but even I know I'm biased against your a-hole brethren. There is no actual evidence. I feel like I'm trapped in some game of mousetrap, and I can't get to the piece of cheese."

It was true. While I saw to my duties of judging souls, Vivien had been hunting for the Blade of Bane. She'd spent time in the library, trying to trace its path through history. Eventually she gave up and went to Timothy for the "Cliffs-Notes," as she called it. He shared that the last sighting of the weapon had been during the Renaissance era. A demigod had been found slain, but no one mourned the loss. His reputation had been cruel, particularly toward animals. After that, the Blade of Bane disappeared.

After pumping Timothy for information, Vivien turned to the internet for leads. Then she prowled the Strip at night, when I was busy. Vivien suspected the blade was being held in one of the hotels. But as the days came and went, her frustration mounted.

"Eventually, they will show their hand," I assured her.

"Whoever started creating vampires, whoever killed Seth and revived the god slayer, has an agenda. They can't play games forever."

She eyed me. "Yeah, but they can go for a really long time."

"True. Gods have been known to play games for centuries."

"I can't wait that long. I'll lose my tiny mind." To prove her point, she pulled at the roots of her hair, re-icing it.

My thumbs stroked over her bare thighs. "Stop thinking like a mortal. Impatience will make your existence a misery."

I told myself the same thing with each passing day that she didn't return my sentiment. Still, not having all of her neared torture.

"Are you saying that because once we figure this out, Osiris will kill me?" She asked the question plainly. Her eyes jerked down as a snout poked at her leg. Cupcake rose up onto her hind legs so that Vivien could scratch the pup's head. The reaper had sensed her distress and come to Vivien's aid.

"I won't let that happen," I said, the words coming out low and dangerous.

Vivien scratched behind Cupcake's ear. "Osiris said I was the only vampire allowed to exist because I could help figure out who is behind this conspiracy bull. But the second we Scooby Doo this shit, he'll come for me. I know he's your dad. I got the 411. I've been reading up on it too, but I've also met the dude. Even I'm not stupid enough to pretend I'm not afraid of Osiris."

I cupped her face, getting her full attention. She paused her ministrations on Cupcake. "Listen to me, Vivien, I swear to you. Osiris will never take you from me."

Her voice dropped to almost a whisper. "I believe you." She shivered.

"Shit. You're cold. And you haven't eaten since yesterday." I pushed back my chair and stood up, pulling her to her feet as well.

Vivien's eyebrows shot up. "Did you just curse?"

"What can I say? You are a terrible influence."

"Mwuahahaha," she cackled dramatically, back to her normal self. "I honestly thought it would take at least a couple of decades to see the effects of my evil influence."

"You either underestimate how powerful you are, or how adaptable gods can be. Now stop stalling. Where do you want to eat?"

She stared longingly at the iced confection still sitting on the counter.

"Later," I promised.

Knowing she'd done her job, Cupcake trotted back to her doggie bed and curled up again.

Vivien huffed. "Fine. Couch, then."

With that, I hoisted her over my shoulder. She yelped in surprise. In the past, she would have clawed, beaten, and bitten to get out of the hold. But now, she relaxed against my possessive need to carry her around.

But I didn't feel completely right about getting away with it, so I laid a sound smack against that perfect ass. "Hey!" she protested. "I'll bite you," she threatened.

"That's the idea, badass." I sat down on the couch and slid her down my body until she was sitting on my lap, knees on either side of my thighs. "Dinner is served," I said, tilting my head, offering her the expanse of my neck. Her lap covered mine, radiating heat, and fitting so perfect against my body.

"My favorite," she exclaimed, then bit into me with a

sharp pinch. The pain was always brief. I found it easy to surrender to her. My hands massaged her cold thighs. There was something so strangely intimate and erotic about her sucking my blood. I'd tried my best to be professional and aloof about it, but once we'd fallen into a routine, the intimacy of the act only increased.

I grew dizzy, and my eyes drifted shut. She squirmed on top of me, making the most sinful sounds as she drank. Her fingers tugged the short hairs at the base of my skull, and I growled. Blood divided in my body, rushing up into her mouth and down to my lap. Her legs warmed under my touch.

When she didn't feed for long periods of time, she became unbearably cold. I should have figured out she needed to eat when I saw her wearing Cookie Monster. The more she drank from me, the farther the coat slid down her arms, as she no longer required its warmth.

My hands had settled on her hips, grinding her down against me. Tension corded through my muscles, and desire gripped me. Wetness spread through her sheer shorts and to my boxers. The scent of her arousal surrounded me, and my mouth watered. I was already too close to the edge. Oh gods, I would do anything for this woman. I'd rake down the stars and fashion them into a collar she could wrap around my neck if she just let me kiss her, worship her.

Vivien pulled away when she'd drank her fill. Green eyes glazed, and hair tousled like I'd already taken her seven ways from Sunday. Leaning down again, she reverently licked over the puncture marks, cleaning up the wounds even as we rocked against each other. The bites would heal soon enough, and it secretly aroused me to see the marks she left behind. I was hers, body and soul. I didn't care who knew it.

My voice came out in a rasp. "Did my dirty girl get her dinner? Maybe she wants dessert now?"

Her hot, slick tongue doubled the desire snaking through my body.

"Mmmhmm," she hummed against me. Her eyes swept up to meet mine. "What's for dessert?"

I grabbed the back her head, jerking her up against me in an almost violent move. "How about my thick cock, followed by a dose of my cum down your throat."

Her eyes flew open in shock, then lowered in a smoldering stare that made my blood boil.

My hips surged up, trapping her sensitive bud with my hardness. Her mouth always fell into a perfect 'o' when I found the spot that made the thoughts disappear from her brain in a puff of smoke. Vivien moaned and threw her head back as she gripped my shoulders. All her concentration was on that perfect pearl I ground against with deliberate attention. The dampness between us spread faster.

"That's my girl. All drenched, and ready for me."

Her pupils nearly swallowed the green in her eyes.

Fuck, I was ready. I needed to slide past her perfect lips, into the inferno of her mouth where that wicked tongue knew all the ways to undo me.

Brushing my lips against the delicate shell of her ear, I gave a low chuckle. "And of course, I'll lap you up like a bowl of ice cream. And I won't stop until you hit that perfect orgasm that melts your kneecaps and make you forget your own name."

She shuddered against me, responding to my words.

A presence pulled my attention away from our shameless grinding. When I looked past Vivien, I found Ardnassak staring at me with glowing gold eyes. My reaper dog arrived, calling me to duty.

Vivien twisted around to see we weren't alone.

I heaved a heavy sigh. "No rest for the wicked." I lifted her off my lap and set her next to me.

I jerked my head, signaling Ardnassak to go ahead of me. The reaper disappeared.

Damn. Vivien was more than understanding about the importance of my duties. But I was coming to resent them. Was it so much to ask to spend a century or two simply pulling Vivien apart and putting her back together? Finding every last possible point of pleasure I could wring out of her body,

Vivien snorted and rested her elbow along the back of the couch. "I don't think we were about to get rest. Besides, I have more hunting to do." Despite her bravado, her thighs trembled and her voice shook.

Vivien used her fingers to clean the corners of her mouth of any errant blood.

"Don't do that," I said to her in a commanding voice.

She froze. "Do what?"

"Don't lick and touch your lips like that." My words came out in a warning. I found the movement impossibly seductive. I was already on the brink. It wouldn't take much to snap my resolve.

Her eyes turned devilish as she darted out her pink tongue again, swiping it against her lips before catching the tip of her finger in her mouth.

Fucking damn. My hand shot into the opening of my boxers to grab the base of my length with a growl.

"You intend on being a brat, I see." I squeezed harder, trying to gain some semblance of control though a snarl curled my lips.

Her finger emerged from those silky lips with a loud pop. "I thought you had somewhere to be." Everything about her dared me to do something about it. Vivien never learned her lesson about toying with Death.

"I do, but I always have time to punish a brat. Don't make me teach you a lesson." I stalked to where she sat on the couch, towering over her.

This time, her middle finger disappeared into her mouth in a slow taunting movement.

Before she could mouth off another smart thing, I commanded her with my power, "On your knees."

Surprise flickered in her eyes, even as she obeyed my direction in a quick, jerky movement.

The silk boxers slid down my thighs with a whisper of fabric and her top flew over her head, leaving her perfect breasts bare.

The next command came without words. Her finger fell from her mouth as she replaced it with my hard length. That hot, sinful mouth swallowed me over and over, farther down each time, until she took me to the base. My head fell back, and I grasped her silken hair, fighting for that thin shred of control I had left.

I was pushing my luck. Vivien very well might kick my ass after this, but she'd been a brat, and I said I'd teach her a lesson.

She looked up at me from under her eyelashes, desire and triumph blazing in her eyes. Her lips curled up as much as they could, as if she had won. I wasn't sure if she was winning, but I'd make sure no one lost in this game.

My hips bucked hard, when her guttural moan vibrated around me. She knew exactly what that did to me. Then she added that impossible trick with her tongue to the mix. The little devil.

I sent another command, and her hand tweaked her

own nipple. A sound half protest, half pleasure emitted from her throat.

With a mere thought, a bead of my power formed, and I sent it to her neglected breast. The bit of heat danced around her sensitive tip, until it drew impossible tight. She gasped. Then I sent the hot bead skittering down along the split of her lower lips, in delicate, fleeting sweeps.

Her ass wriggled and bucked, her moans loud and pleading. Though her mouth was full, she was begging me. I knew exactly what she wanted. For me to fill her aching, wet pussy. Without words, she was begging me to slide my hard dick into her and fuck with abandon.

My release came hard and fast, without warning. With a guttural growl, my fingers gripped her hair as my knees threatened to buckle. She greedily swallowed, making sounds that could split me in two.

I immediately dropped the power I held over her. When Vivien pulled back, she pouted at me, though there was still that sparkle of mischief in her eye. She was already thinking of some way to get back at me for that little stunt.

I couldn't wait to find out how.

My thumb brushed over the corner of her mouth, like she had earlier. "*Now* you can clean up that wicked mouth of yours." I leaned down and replaced my thumb with my lips for a quick kiss. Then I headed toward the bedroom to change.

"Really?" She shouted after me. "You're just going to walk away after that? Leave me all...melty and wanty here?"

I turned around in time to see her gesture to her nether regions. She'd stripped off her shorts, and I could see her sex and thighs glistening with need.

"I am very busy and important and have somewhere to be," I said, doing my best to suppress my smile.

Her pout morphed into a full scowl. I'd made my dirty girl angry.

Vivien stormed past me into our bedroom.

With an overly dramatic sigh, I said, "Well, I guess I can multitask while I'm at work."

She turned to me with her arms crossed, at the edge of our bed.

I reached out with my power and grabbed her, though we were several feet apart. "You want me to take care of you, baby?" I drew out the last word. Already, I was lighting up her nerve endings with heat and pleasure. Her eyes turned glassy and her mouth parted, as she went limp.

With only a slight push, she fell back onto the bed. Leaning over her, but without actually touching her, my breath fanned out over her lips. This time I sent a bead of power to each pink peak of her breasts, while three danced wildly along her swollen pussy and tapped at her bright red clit. She jerked, eyes fluttering.

My hand curved around her elegant neck, letting her know who was in charge right now. "You are going to lie here for me, and you won't get up until you've come. Ten. Times." Her lids flew up at that, eyes trying and failing to focus on me as sensation rioted through her. "You won't get up until these sheets are soaked, and your throat is hoarse from screaming." I pressed the command into her body, then dropped a lingering kiss on that seductive pearl at the crest of her sex before standing up. "Have fun."

She cried out behind me, her knees shaking as she came.

"One," I counted out loud, laughing, even as I disappeared into the bathroom to shower and get off to work.

5

VIVIEN

"Stop trying to scare me. It's not going to happen," Miranda said before sipping on her quad espresso shot.

"How the hell did you know I was there?" I demanded, plopping down in the seat across from her. "I am a scary, light-footed vampire. This is utter bullshit."

Most mornings, I met Miranda at Perkatory—the coffee stand in Sinopolis. The best part of being a vampire in Vegas is there were no windows in the hotels. Windowless passageways adjoined most of the resorts. When I'd been drinking animal blood, I'd go down hard when the sun came up. But the more regularly I drank Grim's blood, the less sleep I needed. I'd come to depend on our morning coffee date as it was my pre-bedtime wind-down, while Miranda was getting started for her day.

In fact, it was a fucking miracle I could leave the penthouse at all after Grim's last stunt. True to his word, my body followed his command to the letter. Ten mind-splitting orgasms, ruined sheets, and I not only screamed myself hoarse, but my legs turned into useless pool noodles. I'm not sure how long I laid there in the aftermath, feeling as though I'd died and gone to heaven after all.

Using my body like that was the hottest goddamn thing I'd ever experienced, and I already couldn't wait to pay him back for it. Grim definitely had some surprise anal beads coming in his future. And yet, that still felt like I'd hardly level the playing field.

Who knew a relationship built on complete trust could be so...so hot?

I took a good five minutes to relay the juicy details to Miranda who leaned in but stared off in the distance as if trying to watch it like a movie in her head. She muttered a few curses at the appropriate moments.

When I got to the part where he commanded to lay there until number ten, I stopped. "Is this too much information? I'm still not used to the whole girlfriend share thing."

Miranda fanned herself with her ID badge. "God no. Not only is that hot as hell, who else gets to kiss and tell about an actual god. Are you sure he is the god of death? He sounds more like the god of sex."

"I'm digging the braids," I said, appreciating the purple woven throughout. The color complemented her dark-brown skin.

Before I could touch one of her braids, Miranda's hand shot out ninja-quick and smacked it away. I could have used my vampire reflexes to grab it anyway, but Miranda taught me that a black woman's hair was no joke. Even though I was immortal, she promised certain death if I ever messed with her do.

The barista walked over, my usual order in his hand. A frothy, frozen coffee that was more sugar than caffeine. An absurd amount of sprinkles blanketed the whipped cream.

"So does t-that make t-twelve to zero?" The barista stuttered, referring to the number of times I'd failed to scare or surprise Miranda.

Aaron reminded me of Patrick Swayze in *Point Break* with his shaggy, sun-bleached hair, bronze skin, and turquoise blue eyes. His stutter was a constant companion, but I never asked him why he had it. If he wanted to share, he could.

"How does she do it?" I asked Aaron. Then I squinted one eye at Miranda. "Are you some kind of supernatural being?"

Miranda shot a deliberate glance at Aaron. He didn't know about vampires and gods, and she didn't appreciate how loose I was about dropping the hints around our friend. But what normal dude would assume we were ever serious about that stuff?

"Special forces," Aaron reminded me. It was true. Miranda was a certified grade A badass.

"I still think it's some kind of mom power," I countered. "How is Jamal doing?"

"I signed him up for a fall baseball season because he can't get enough right now. His pitching arm is almost unstoppable now." She couldn't help the sideways smile and pride from slipping into her voice.

I clapped my hands. "Oh, if they have a night game, I'm totally there! I'll bring pompoms and scream the loudest."

Aaron would have continued to hang with us, but a line formed as the hungover masses in their luxury sweat suits and overpriced sunglasses lined up. Top shelf liquor and various drug residues oozed from their pores, assailing my senses with sour yeast.

"So, did you get it?" Miranda asked, leaning an elbow on our little café table.

I shook my head, staring into my drink. "No. I mean, I got it, but it was a fake. And it ended bloody at the Parisi-enne." I played with the cheap cupcake charm on my neck-lace. It was a gift from the owner of the bakery I used to live above, and the best gift I'd received in my adult life, until Grim started showering me in motorcycles and reaper puppies.

Her eyes widened. "That was you? Everyone is talking about it."

I nodded and rolled the cup back and forth in my hands. It wasn't like every day ended with someone jumping off a building in Vegas. Though admittedly, it happened more often than other places, considering people got desperate after making poor life choices in Sin City.

"I couldn't stop him. Worst yet"—I leaned in and lowered my voice—"he'd been worshiping a god."

"That's a big no-no, right?" she asked.

"Oh yeah," I affirmed, before sucking on my frothy caffeine fix. Though eating and drinking anything other than blood did nothing to keep me alive, I was living the dream. Eating and drinking anything I wanted without ever gaining weight. I took advantage of that as often as possible.

"Well, what is Mr. Scarapelli going to do about it?" She referred to Grim more formally, as he was her boss. He lured her away from a neighboring hotel to be head of security, and she was damned good at it.

"Nothing." I chewed on my straw, a habit that used to get me smacked around when I was a kid.

She arched an eyebrow. "Nothing?"

"Nothing," I affirmed.

"Isn't he"—she lowered her voice—"the god of death?"

"Sure, but that doesn't mean we can go around cracking

heads until we get answers. Or at least that's what he tells me."

She leaned back in her chair, frustration radiating off her. "There must be something we can do."

"This is what I like about you Miranda, you are a woman of action like me. We don't just sit on our laurels. Who is Laurel anyway? What lazy-ass kind of life did she lead that inspired someone to coin that phrase?"

"The kind of life that likely led to the invention of delivery food," Miranda offered.

"Well, I can't knock that," I said, cheers-ing her with my cup.

That was the other reason I loved her. We rode a similar bizarro brainwave most of the time.

Miranda rhythmically tapped the table and furrowed her brows. "So if this guy was worshiping a god, doesn't he need an altar or something?"

"All he needs to do is pray to the god using the original god's name. Their ancient Egyptian one."

She blew a raspberry. "There are tons of people who worship Egyptian gods and goddesses."

"Some, yes, but not a ton. Not like it used to be in the ancient days. And gods can't solicit for alms. I'm sure Mary Jane in witchy Salem took it upon herself to pray to my boyfriend, but she's a drop in the bucket of power for him. Seth did a big no-no by taking those followers under his wing. As you saw, he also reached back and bestowed his worshippers with powers."

"Yes," Miranda said in a flat tone, "I vaguely recall how they turned into massive snake monsters and tried to eat us."

I shook my cup at her. "We sure do know how to party hard."

Miranda ignored my cheeky comment. A line formed between her eyes as she dove into deep thought. "Maybe he is following the god on social media. Since all of them run the hotels on the Strip, and you know they love the attention."

I sighed dramatically, flopping my head back. "I already checked. He follows a lot of them. Too many to narrow down. He was definitely a high-roller groupie."

Still, she didn't let it go. "What about his house? Maybe there's a clue about who his favorite was?"

I raised a finger, about to protest. It curled back down when I realized I didn't have a counterpoint. "Well, that's just a damned good idea. But don't you think the cops have swept through his house and cleared evidence?"

Her fingers ceased tapping her brows dipping further. "It's a suicide. They don't need to investigate. If there are tiny statuettes or pictures of Egyptian gods, no one is going to look twice."

"Except for us..." I finished, in awe of her genius. "I'm in awe of your genius."

"That's fair." She shrugged, taking another sip of her coffee with a sly smile.

The sun was up now, but I knew the first thing I was doing as soon as I could set foot outside. It was date night with Grim, but this wouldn't take me long.

The memory of how irritated he'd been the last time I'd been late sprung to mind. He'd tried to squash down his ire, but I couldn't escape the lecture.

Simply because we have all the time in the world as immortals, it doesn't mean we shouldn't treat it with respect.

I wasn't being disrespectful. I just had shit to do and got delayed. Not everyone lived by a perfect schedule.

A familiar figure caught the corner of my eye. "Well, this is unusual," I announced.

Miranda followed my gaze to see Timothy walking toward the Perkatory line.

"I thought he usually gets his coffee later in the day," Miranda said.

"He does. Maybe he just couldn't wait to get his fix," I said, not referring to caffeine at all.

Timothy must have been really absorbed because he didn't even notice us sitting there. Another café employee had taken on the register while Aaron worked the steamers and pulled shots of espresso. Once Aaron caught sight of Timothy waiting in line, he waved him over.

Timothy approached the pickup counter with a crooked smile. He ran a hand through his coiffed-up hair, as if he could make it any more perfect. Not only did Timothy have brains and amazing fashion sense, he carried the alluring confidence only a god could manage.

Per usual, Aaron shot him a dazzling, white-toothed grin that even I could see promised fun, adventurous sex. Timothy's eyes actually smoldered, shooting back a quiet dark promise of his own.

They exchanged some words we couldn't hear, but I'd seen it enough to know Aaron wouldn't be the only one stuttering.

When he handed over Timothy's drink, their hands touched.

Both Miranda and I shared a collective gasp, as if we were two fangirls vying for our favorite characters to get together on a popular tv show.

Their touch lingered, and I swear my heart almost started beating again. Then Timothy stepped back with his order, and Aaron returned to work.

"Woof," I said, as it was the only emotionally appropriate word to carry the weight of tension we just witnessed.

"You can say that again," Miranda said.

Timothy caught sight of us staring right at him. Knowing there was no escaping now, he walked over to join us. "Ladies."

Miranda pulled out the empty chair between us while I gestured to it.

"Have a seat," Miranda said.

"We insist," I agreed.

With the cautious regard a rabbit would give a couple of foxes, Timothy sat down.

"When are you going to ask him out?" Miranda asked first.

"Oh, good one," I said. "I was going to ask if I could be maid of honor, or best woman. Whatever works."

"You can't ask that," Miranda shot back. "He might want me to fill that position. I've planned a ton of kid's parties. I throw an excellent shower."

"Ladies," Timothy interrupted loudly, setting his cup on the table with a surprising clack despite being made of paper. "He has already asked me to dinner."

Miranda and I had to suppress our squeals of excitement so Aaron wouldn't overhear. Instead, they came out as unseemly snorts.

"Where are you going?"

"What are you going to wear?"

I wasn't sure who asked what, but Miranda and I didn't care as long as we got answers.

"I turned him down," Timothy said, not meeting our gaze, before demurely sipping his soy half-caf whatever nonsense. As if he weren't breaking three hearts instead of one.

"You what?" Miranda said in a tone dangerously close to that of a disapproving mom.

"Careful how you answer, she may ground you," I warned. Then added, "or shoot you."

Timothy pursed his lips. "What did you think I would say?" he asked, his words clipped and cold. "You know what I am. There would be no point."

"Grim and I are making it work," I pointed out.

"You are an immortal vampire. You have a blood bond with each other. While Aaron is human. He knows nothing about our world."

"You could tell him," I offered.

He pinched the bridge of his nose as if I gave him an instant headache. "Unlike you, I don't share forbidden information whenever it's convenient. Besides, even if on the very rare likelihood he took it well, it wouldn't make a difference. Gods and mortals mixing have been historically catastrophic."

I smacked his shoulder, tired of his excuses. "Then why not just go out and have some fun? What could a couple of dinners hurt? A couple hot, wild, sweaty nights with the gorgeous barista boy? Barista man? Barista man-boy?" I nodded, satisfied with the last title.

Something in Timothy's expression fell. He tried to recover, but he wasn't fast enough.

"You can't, can you?" Miranda asked softly. "You're in love with him."

"Don't be ridiculous," he said, though his denial was weak all the way around. I could tell even he wasn't buying it, but Timothy was grasping at straws that it wasn't true. "Even if in some parallel dimension we were to try, he's the complete opposite of me. He thrives on chaos, adventure, and never has a plan. Those are all terrible qualities in a partner."

"Oh honey," Miranda breathed, patting Timothy's hand.

"Gods aren't made for relationships with humans," he said more seriously. "There's a million reasons why it would never work. But for a brief moment, I can come here and enjoy his ridiculously gorgeous smile and get treated to a free drink, though we all know I could buy a million of them without blinking. Simply because he thinks I'm worth special attention."

Timothy left out that he tipped five times what the original latte would have cost, anyway.

"You are worth special attention," I said to Timothy, meaning every word of it.

"Thank you." He gave a wry smile. "I can't choose the situation, but I can choose to make these small moments enough."

My respect for Timothy grew to an almost unbearable degree.

"Well then," he said with finality, "back to work." With that, he was up and off to help Grim sort souls.

Miranda and I sat there, stewing in our mutual heartbreak for him.

"W-what'd I miss?" Aaron asked, showing back up, having dealt with the line. His eyes lingered in the direction Timothy disappeared to.

I opened my mouth to spill all of Timothy's secrets, but Miranda shot me a stern look. My mouth snapped shut again. Even I knew I shouldn't get involved in that mess, no matter how badly I wanted it to work for the two of them.

Besides, I had a house to break into tonight.

6

GRIM

The bing of the elevator heralded Vivien's return. Late for our date night again, I couldn't say I was surprised. I'd been dressed and ready for an hour and a half. This was a new record, even for her.

I emerged from the library, a book still in hand. The sight I was greeted with was unprecedented. "Are you okay?" I asked.

Vivien stalked into the penthouse. Cupcake trotted in next to her, ears down and eyes mournful. A bright red gash ran along her snout.

Vivien fared worse than the reaper pup. Scratches marred Vivien's arms and cheeks. Her clothes were tattered, and her hair looked like it had been in a wind tunnel.

I'd been about to rush to her, to make sure she was okay, but her glower kept me at bay as irritation flowed off her in powerful waves. I'd learned the hard way to give her space when she was in this mood. And she didn't appear severely harmed.

Breezing past me, she lifted a finger. "Let me change first."

She disappeared into our room to get changed. Cupcake followed dutifully behind her. When Vivien reemerged alone, she wore a tight leather dress with lace panels running down the sides of her ribcage, and little metal spikes lining her bosom. She'd brushed through her hair, so it flowed in luminous waves once again.

The scratches were already healing. Unable to help myself, I pulled her to me and dropped kisses against the red lines along her collarbone. Her body softened against mine.

"What have you been up to?" I asked. "You look like you got in a cat fight."

She stiffened in my arms. Then extracting herself, she grabbed Cookie Monster and slung it over her arm before walking into the elevator. She punched the button for the lobby in a punishing jab.

"As it so happens, that's exactly what went down," she said, her voice sharp.

I blinked, next to her. "What?"

Folding her arms under her breasts, she pushed them up, like an offering. I wondered if she did it on purpose to distract me. The need to lick and suck at the ample swells already caused me to harden. My hunger for her was insatiable.

But I needed to focus. To help with that, I took a step back and leaned against the elevator railing. "Tell me what happened," I demanded in a low voice.

She ran her fingers through her hair, still openly agitated. "I went to the jumper's apartment. His name was Kyle Smith, and I figured maybe I could get some clues about who he'd been worshiping."

"And did you?" I asked carefully.

"No." She stomped her heeled foot as the lift opened.

Taking her arm, I led her forward. Lights flashed as people mobbed us with cell phones and cameras. My jaw tightened as I navigated Vivien through the throng of people. Miranda had also sent a few of her guards to keep the crowd at bay.

I was already a celebrity in the eyes of the public, though they could not understand their attraction to me. The truth was that they all carried a death wish, and it drew them to me like moths to a flame. Nearby, a gang of women, and even a couple men, bounced up and down in T-shirts with my face printed on them. Across their chests in big pink letters were the words "Grim's Groupies." I recognized the name. It was a popular online fan group.

I was used to the rubbernecking when I walked into a room. But with Vivien at my side, especially in one of her provocative outfits, people couldn't take their eyes off us.

"What are the scratch marks from? Is he hurting you?" a paparazzo yelled out.

Another jumped on the line of questioning. "Is it from your adventurous sex life?"

I usually never responded, but my temper flared at the questions. If they wanted to run my name through blatant falsehoods to sell a couple of entertaining magazines, that was one thing. But to drag Vivien down into their petty muck...

The man who asked if I'd hurt Vivien lowered his camera, and I locked eyes with him. My death mask flickered through. Nothing but a skull and black sucking darkness. I sunk my power into him, overwhelming him with the sensation of his own oblivion.

The whites of his eyes widened, and his lips trembled as he stood, struck under my influence.

I wanted him to feel exactly how small and insignificant

he was in comparison to the universe. How transient his life was. I could taste the taint on his soul, like a sour patina. It was not yet determined if he deserved entry into the afterlife, but if he continued on the path of disregard of others, he'd certainly earn a spot in Amit's belly.

A groan of pain and fear slipped from between his lips.

Vivien dropped her arm to interlace her fingers with mine. "Down boy," she mumbled. I pulled her closer to me, her spikes pressing into my suit. The pressure points soothed me, somehow.

She broke my attention from the man, so we left him a trembling, groaning mess. No one took note of his state as the crowd continued to hound us.

Vivien chose to smile at the flashing cameras. Or more like, bared her teeth at them. I half-expected her fangs to elongate. But instead, she flipped them the bird.

The valet opened the door to my black Bugatti Chiron, and I gave Vivien a hand in. Vivien had resisted my gentlemanly mannerisms for a while, until I explained I was the most old-fashioned person she'd met. And it was a small way I enjoyed showing respect for her, as well as using the excuse to touch her. After that, she stopped making a fuss about being able to open doors on her own.

I strode around the car, getting in the driver's seat. Vivien had already punched in the directions for the ride. I closed the door, and the live wire that was Vegas nightlife, silenced. The engine came alive with a velvet purr, and I pulled away from the flashing camera lights. I waited to continue my questioning until we'd merged onto the interstate. "Tell me about the catfight. Who was it with?"

"I didn't catch the name," she seethed. "He wasn't wearing a collar."

"You're serious," I said, still not believing it. "You literally fought a cat."

"Yeah, it was this massive Maine Coon cat. It was the biggest, fluffiest, most ornery feline I'd ever met."

I struggled to keep a straight face.

She cast her glower at me. "It's not funny."

"I'd think a vampire would be faster and stronger than a cat. We'd best not let it get out that your kryptonite is a domestic animal." I bit the inside of my cheek.

She punched me in the shoulder. "Hey, that thing was anything but domesticated. I didn't use my super vampire abilities because I didn't want to hurt him. He probably wasn't used to intruders, but the little monster legit attacked me. No matter what I or Cupcake did, the fluffy beast would fly at my face, claws stretched out. Eventually, Cupcake and I managed to lock him in a closet. Poor Cupcake took a few blows too."

"We'll make sure Cupcake gets extra attention when we get back." The pup enjoyed belly scratches, and I planned to spend ample time rewarding Cupcake's bravery. Then I asked, "So you found nothing in the man's apartment?"

Vivien's eyes turned down, and she shrugged. "Not really. I found out he had a normal life as of two weeks ago. He changed when that damn sword got posted online. He worked as a bag boy at a grocery store. Then suddenly, poof, he goes off the radar. He doesn't show up at work, doesn't answer his phone, stops talking to his friends or family. I was hoping to turn up some kind of evidence of a payoff from one of the gods."

I shook my head. "You wouldn't find a material payoff. Worshippers feed off the love of their god. Like in ancient Egypt, this man who jumped, he was more likely to bring gifts to those he adored."

She thought about that for a moment. "If only there'd been an altar or something like that to tip me off. But his place was cleared out. Even his computer was wiped. Someone covered up."

"Your instincts were right to investigate." Sometimes I worried I'd given her more than she could handle. But Osiris had tasked her with assisting on this matter, and she took that seriously. He'd appointed us with discovering who was trying to upset the balance among immortals. He must have known her skills as a former bounty hunter would be of use in this situation.

Vivien slumped down into her seat, crossing her arms over her chest. "If I hadn't been all screwed up after watching him jump, if I hadn't been so hot to get the fake sword to you, I might have made it in time to recover some information."

I wished I weren't driving so I could touch her, draw her face to mine. "You may be immortal, you may be a vampire, but you are not immune to trauma. Death has been at the center of my existence, but I keenly recognize that is not the case for everyone. It must have been disturbing."

Her throat visibly bobbed as she swallowed hard. "Disturbing. That's the right word."

"I'm sorry you had to go through that." The silence spanned as Vivien sank into her feelings next to me. Before she could spiral too much, I asked, "So where are we dining?"

Vivien had put the directions into the GPS, but I'd no earthly idea where we were headed or what the plan was. Before her, existence had been nothing but routine and duty. But since I met her, she had filled every day with light and life.

A mischievous smile spread across her face, chasing away the shadows. "Who says we're going to dinner?"

"I just assumed..."

Usually, our date nights centered around food, as that was Vivien's passion. For someone who drank blood for sustenance, she had not given up on being a foodie.

I pulled the car into a parking lot, as the GPS indicated we reached our destination. We arrived at a mecca of strip malls with varying businesses and restaurants, and I couldn't begin to guess which she had in mind. She directed me to park at the far end of the lot, prolonging the mystery.

Last time she chose, we ended up at an indoor paintball arena that was open after dark. Even after we decimated the group of teenagers matched against us, the kids gathered to take selfies with me and the woman they'd adoringly referred to as Ninja Warrior Punk Queen. She begged me to call her that in bed ever since.

"Okay," Vivien ran her fingers along center console. "So food is an element, but we are more here for the floor show than for the food."

"We are attending a show?" I asked, opening the door. I walked around and opened hers, offering a hand to help her out of the car.

"In a way," she said, turning me to face the all-black building. Even the windows were darkened.

Reading the sign above the building's entrance, I didn't understand right away. "Noshing Noir?"

"Everyone has been so nosey about our lives, paparazzi and crazy posts trying to figure out who the hell I am, I figured we wouldn't have to worry about being seen here."

"Because no one has ever heard of this hole-in-the-wall place before?" I asked, wrapping an arm around her waist while slipping my other hand in my pocket.

"No, you big snob." She smacked my chest. "It's a dining-in-the-dark restaurant. The waitstaff wears night vision goggles in a pitch-black room. It forces people to really focus with their other senses."

"Vivien...we can both see in the dark."

There was that devilish grin again. "Exactly. We can see, but no one will see us. It's going to be a blast."

I couldn't help but let out a low, throaty laugh. "Have I told you how infectious your enthusiasm is?"

"Aw baby, you mean it?" She rested her head against my chest. "Like how infectious? Ebola-level?"

I simply shook my head, not rising to the bait. We entered and after a bit of stuttering from the flabbergasted hostess, she led us into the dining room, night vision goggles on her face.

Indeed, Vivien had drawn me into a novel experience. The things people did when they didn't think they were being watched was astounding. Most of the others in the restaurant were couples on date nights themselves. A young woman didn't bother to hide her disgust as her date waxed poetic about how much money he made at his job, and how he knew the owner of the restaurant. She flipped him the bird and flapped her hand to mock his nonstop prattling.

"Kay, I don't think I can do this," a man said. The hushed anxiety came from the couple next to us. They'd been seated only moments ago, but I could sense the tension.

The man reached across the table in search of her hand, but she gripped the napkin in her lap.

"I know, Michael," she said, anxiety making her voice tight. "I thought this would be fun, mix things up, but I'm feeling a little claustrophobic."

Vivien and I exchanged a look, able to perfectly see and hear.

"Babe, are you okay?" Vivien said, loud enough to be overheard. "Your hand is clammy. Are you afraid of the dark? You should have told me before we came inside."

I raised an eyebrow at her. I knew what she was doing, but didn't appreciate the role she cast me in. "Yes, darling. I don't care for the darkness. This is uncomfortable."

The couple turned their heads in our direction, though they could not see us. Still, the tables were close enough that it was easy to converse with them.

"Is this your first time too?" Kay asked, sitting closer to Vivien.

Vivien smiled. "Yeah, I thought it would be a fun night out, but I think my date is a little nervous."

Kay nodded. "I get that. This is a bit too intense. We're thinking about leaving."

"Give it a couple more minutes," Vivien coaxed. "It's disorienting, but maybe a drink will calm you both. In fact, have a drink with us, and help me keep my date calm."

"Oh no, we couldn't," Michael started.

"We insist," I said. "As my lovely girlfriend said, we would love to treat you both to a drink, and I could use the company to relax."

I ordered an excellent bottle of wine for their table as well. In no time, Vivien was deep in conversation with both of them, while I sat back and enjoyed the unique position of being able to observe without being scrutinized.

The hiss of a zipper drew my attention to the couple on the other side of us. The waitstaff was nowhere in sight, but the couple couldn't have known that. Still, it didn't stop the woman from pulling out her date's erection. Slowly, but surely, she found her way under the table to wrap her mouth around him.

Vivien spat her wine and began coughing.

"Are you okay?" Kay asked, genuine concern in her voice. "See? Eating in the dark is a choking hazard."

"I'm fine," Vivien insisted, watching the amorous couple. "But I agree with you on the choking hazard thing," she muttered.

The woman continued her vigorous attentions to her date under the table while he shoved his fist into his mouth, doing his best not to make a sound. His face screwed up as he reached his climax. Then she was back up in her chair before the waitstaff returned.

Vivien looked back and forth between them and me with an open look of amazement. I did not care for the spark that appeared in her eye. Then she reached over to my lap.

"Don't even think about it," I warned. Her fingers stilled on my belt.

"What was that?" Michael asked, thinking I'd addressed him.

"I don't think we can come this far without having dessert," I said, smoothing over my reprimand.

Vivien gave me an impetuous look, licking her lips like a hungry predator. Her dress of leather, lace, and spikes was made of sin itself. And while we were engaging the couple next to us now, my brain thought only of reclining the driver's seat in my Bugatti and positioning her over my face to greet whatever equally sinful lingerie she wore underneath. Or maybe I'd park the car somewhere remote and bend her over the hood. The scratches on the car from her dress would be worth it, to take her in the open night air.

The server returned with their night vision goggles, saving me from Vivien's wicked designs. Though I still had to reach down and reposition myself, as my desire pounded with insistence.

Not long after, we finished our meal and left, along with the couple we'd met. We all took a moment to adjust, emerging from total darkness into the light of the lobby.

The couple tried not to react when they finally brought us into focus.

"Oh, I recognize you two," Kay said, her eyes rounding. She tugged on her husband's arm as she spoke to me. "You own the hotel, Sinopolis."

I realized how pleasant it was to talk with people without them being aware of my status. It felt so terribly normal. Now that casual air all but disappeared.

"I do," I said. Pulling out a black business card from my pocket, I handed it over to Michael, who was closest. "And if you two would ever like to get dinner again, we'd be happy to do so. Our treat."

Vivien squeezed my arm.

"I didn't realize I was underdressed," Kay said, appraising Vivien's outfit.

"Don't be silly," Vivien said, waving a hand. "I love your earrings, and I still can't get over how amazing your perfume smells." She had a way of gushing over other people that disarmed them.

"How long have you two been together?" Michael asked.

Kay smacked Michael's chest even as her cheeks reddened. "Don't put them on the spot like that, Michael. It's rude."

Michael shrugged. "What? It's just a question people ask."

"It's fine. About four months." Vivien licked her lips. She tried to play it cool, but I could sense her growing uneasy. "Though it feels longer."

Kay shed her self-consciousness about the questions

and jumped in. "Oh, I know the feeling. After only a few days, I knew Michael was the only one for me." She laid a hand over his heart, pressing against his side. "And I can tell you two have that special spark like we had. Not everyone has it, but you can tell when some couples are meant to be."

When I thought of the future, traveling through the ages with Vivien, my chest tightened with anticipation. That deep hunger inside me made itself known again.

Michael covered Kay's hand with his own and dropped a kiss on her head with an affectionate smile.

My hunger doubled down, even as Vivien shifted back and forth on her heels in obvious discomfort.

I was careful not to move. Not to make any expression that might spook Vivien.

I would do anything to possess Vivien's heart, to have all of her. But she wasn't ready to give it to me. And there was nothing I could do about it. The pleasantness of the evening crumbled into dust as the uncertainty of my position with Vivien plagued me again.

After saying our goodbyes, Vivien and I headed toward the car. I'd parked it on the far end of the lot, and it had filled up since we arrived.

"You're upset," Vivien said in a quiet voice.

"Of course not." But even I could hear the stiffness in my tone.

"I'm not holding back because I want to hurt you," she said, defensiveness creeping in.

"Then you are holding back because you are unsure," I stated.

She stopped cold, forcing me to do so as well. "You think I want someone else?"

Slowly, I turned toward her. "I think you like to keep your options open."

"Maybe I do, but that's not a bad thing. I've avoided relationships and serious attachments since my parents died."

I slipped my hands into my pockets, attempting to remain reasonable. "And how long shall I wait for you, while you have one foot out the door?"

"What are you talking about? I live with you. I'm not moving out anytime soon," she said, flinging her arms out in frustration.

My words turned into a growl, despite myself. I pulled my hands back out of my pockets, feeling constrained. "I love you, Vivien, and you claim to want to say it back to me, but it's what you do that counts. Not what you promise. Day in and out, I hear souls plead with me, claiming that they meant to do better or different, but in the end they are judged by what they do."

Her green eyes flashed a warning. "Are you seriously comparing me to one of the fucked-up souls you judge? Am I on par with a child-murderer because I won't tell you what you want to hear? Is that what you're telling me?"

I took a calm breath, speaking in a controlled manner once more. "Saying you will do something and actually committing are two entirely different things. Thinking I'll be satisfied with your intent, without expecting me to want more, is...unrealistic."

The fight deflated out of her, but she turned back on the defensive. Her eyes glittered with unshed tears of frustration as she hugged herself. "God, I just need more time. It's all I ask for. And that should be the easiest ask, considering you and I have forever."

My hands alternately flexed and balled into fists. "That's exactly the issue, Vivien. We have all the time in the world, which means pain and uncertainty can last as long. Your uncertainty. My pain."

"I don't mean to cause you pain," she said, her voice turning small.

I wrapped my arms around her. "I know you don't. But do you mean to say that if we were mortal, you would tell me you feel the same? Because if that were the case, I'd trade my godhood in an instant. Just to have all of you." I laid my head in the crook of her neck.

I felt her swallow against me.

My intent hadn't been to guilt her. Even if she said it now, the words I so dearly wanted to hear, I'd feel I'd coerced her into it. Not that I felt in danger of making her do anything she didn't want to do.

Still, I needed to end the conversation before more harm was done. So I stuffed the feelings deep down inside and straightened. Vivien continued to rub her bare arms, and I realized she didn't have Cookie Monster with her.

"Wait here, I'll get your coat. You must have left it inside."

She waved me off. "No, I'll go get it. Just pick me up at the front of the restaurant."

What she really wanted was space. I bowed my head and turned, heading toward the car.

I paused when I reached the door, taking a moment to run my hands through my hair. If someone told me, six months ago, I'd be losing my mind over a vampire vixen, I would have had a raucous laugh.

Yet here I was. Twisted up inside. Needing Vivien's declaration of love like a weak mortal consumed by ego and desire. Acting like I'd die without it.

But the true danger was *living* without her love. Hellfire was preferable to that.

My finger pressed against the identification lock on the door handle.

I had less than a moment to hear the click and rising buzz. My jaw tightened and my hand clenched tighter around the handle right before the vehicle exploded.

7

VIVIEN

I made it halfway to the restaurant when a crack of thunder followed by a wave of heat against my back sent me flying. Time escaped me, and I found myself splayed against a car, the hood crushed in under my body.

I checked to make sure all parts were still attached, but blood seeped out of my nose and slid down my forehead. What the actual fuck just happened? My brain took far too long to compute an explosion had thrown me.

Panic gripped me as I realized the direction the blast had come from.

"Grim." My cry for him came out in a strangled word as I rolled off the car.

Oh, shit shit shit. I ran toward the blazing fire.

The air shimmered from the heat around the crackling flames. I had to throw an arm up to shield my face from them.

"Grim," I cried out, finding my voice this time. I screamed his name a few more times.

Oh fuck, he couldn't be dead. *He's a god.*

Even as I tried to reassure myself that he'd survived, my

insides twisted with agony and grief. A sob choked me, so I couldn't call out for him anymore.

I staggered back, unable to take the heat any longer. Should I check the ground for body parts? Did I gather them in a pile and hope he'd repair himself?

The very thought made my stomach somersault in vicious spins. I began to lose my footing, staggering to the left until I could hold myself against a slightly charred hood.

Metal crunched and groaned in the conflagration. I squinted, trying to bring the movement into focus. A shadowy figure moved inside the flames.

Grim emerged, his clothes burned away. Smoke twirled off his bare, rounded shoulders. An aura of what I could only describe as divinity shimmered around him. His bronze skin and dark hair gleamed as though he'd been polished in the fire. His golden eyes glowed with a fierce rage, making him one scary motherfucker. Any human who witnessed the naked, almighty god would melt into a puddle of incoherence and fear.

Then his eyes landed on me, and his expression morphed into one of worry and love. In moments, I found myself in his arms. Sirens wailed in the distance.

"Oh, sweet baby hamsters, I thought you..." I couldn't finish the phrase as the invisible grip around my throat had yet to release.

"Are you alright?" he asked, pulling back, running his hands over me, checking for wounds. A hardness flickered in his expression when his fingers brushed against the cut on my forehead.

"Am I alright?" I asked, incredulous. "You were the one at the center of an explosion." I could hear the hysteria climbing up in my voice.

Say it. Say you love him. Tell him. It's right there, ready to spring off your tongue.

Except the panic and fear shoved it right back down into the deepest cavern.

Tucking my hair behind my ears, he stared deeply into my eyes. "I'm fine. You didn't lose me."

The sirens grew louder. "We need to get out of here," Grim said. "Do you have your phone?"

I numbly handed it over to him so he could call Timothy.

We fled from the fire as people emerged from the restaurant and surrounding businesses to see what happened. We tucked ourselves back in an alleyway while emergency services put out the blaze.

I clung to Grim, unable to stop touching him. He didn't push me away. Instead, he held me close and ran his fingers over my hair, muttering soothing words about how it was over, and everything was okay now.

Time passed in what felt like forever and also mere minutes. My mind crowded with the prospect of what almost happened. But it didn't. Grim was alive. He was okay. He couldn't die.

The limo showed up, and we climbed in. Timothy sat on the side bench. His cheeks were drawn with displeasure. Timothy hadn't brought an extra set of clothes, but Grim's unclothed state didn't seem to bother either of them. Grim and Timothy discussed the attack, but I wasn't listening.

What once had been a forgotten memory resurfaced in a crisp clear picture. My parents dying in that car crash. The man in the suit who showed up to walk them to the afterlife. While it had bewildered Grim that I could see him, he was even more surprised when I vowed to walk with him someday. Only now could I see the brilliance of my child mind.

If I attached myself to such a figure, I could never lose him. But tonight, I'd known every aching, screaming bit of loss for a few moments when I'd thought he'd gone up with the car.

We arrived in the private underground lot. My brain fuzzed as Timothy and Grim discussed the plan for damage control before we got out of the vehicle. Then Timothy took off in the limo again.

Grim and I got in the lift that led up into the library of the penthouse. The doors slid open, parting the book-shelves, and we were back in the safety of our place. Mahogany shelves full of tomes loomed over us, and the smell of books and leather surrounded me.

Once inside, I turned, facing up toward Grim. Still nude, there wasn't even a trace of soot on him from the fire.

"I'm not okay," I said, not knowing what else to say. Tear tracks dried on my cheeks, and my eyes stopped stinging, but I'd dropped into a far scarier place. A place where Grim left me all alone. Where I faced eternity by myself.

His brows dipped together in concern and love. "What can I do?" he asked, gently.

"I need—I need to feel you," I said. Then I grabbed the back of his neck and crashed my mouth against his. Needing to touch every part of him, I hungrily tasted him. A smoky flavor mixed with his masculine one, and I kissed him deeper, trying to erase the fire.

He was here. Here with me. Nothing would take him from me. I had to make myself believe it.

Grim didn't shy away from my onslaught, meeting me with as much passion. The velvet skin of his shaft hardened against my thigh.

An emptiness yawned inside me, threatening to eat me

up. A black hole of fear and desolation. I needed to fill it. He needed to fill me, or I would die.

I broke long enough to turn and shove the papers and books off his antique executive desk. They hit the floor with a crash, but I was already sitting on the edge of it, pulling Grim toward me. Understanding innately, he backed me farther onto the surface. Grim pushed my leather dress up around my hips while positioning me at the edge of the desk.

"No panties," he mused, eyes hooded. He took himself in hand, the tip already glistening with his desire.

Panic and need crawled up my throat faster as what felt like a hysterical breakdown threatened to beat him to the punch. My desperate urge to be filled had already turned my center liquid.

My bronze god wasted no time entering me. He stretched me, filling me in the way I needed. My body clenched around him, as if never wanting to release him. I cried out, a million emotions rioting through me—fear, desire, and the word I refused to let touch my tongue, though it squeezed my heart with painful bindings.

This felt right. He felt like home. Wherever Grim was, it's where I belonged, and I never belonged anywhere before.

A hand cupped my face and I saw so much love and reverence in his eyes. I saw a mirror image of the same hunger that gnawed at the pit of me. We'd both been alone for far too long. No one really seeing us, only seeing what they wanted to see.

My aunt and uncle saw a girl they could use to complete the image of the perfect family, to hide the ugliness inside them. Qwynn saw power, and possession. And the world saw him as darkness, as salvation, as the end.

But I saw Grim, and he saw me. We could be messy, combative, and petty. But no matter what, I could always be myself and completely accepted the way I was. I'd become addicted to that.

Grim's body rocked and my hips met his rhythm, stroke for stroke. My legs wrapped around his hips as he pulled me closer, driving deeper into me. The friction of his hard strokes sent shockwaves of pleasure radiating through me, sending me higher and higher. His forehead rested against mine and our eyes stayed locked. Molten gold moved like liquid in his powerful eyes, occasionally sparking. He was mine. The god of death himself loved me, and he would have to live for me. I couldn't accept anything less.

"More," I gasped.

Grim obeyed, straightening to speed up, thrusting deeper and harder. My fingers clawed for purchase—in his hair, along with the straining bulges of his arm muscles, his strong shoulders.

"I'm here," he rasped. "I'm not going anywhere."

Even as my body tightened around him, pushing toward the breaking point, the lump in my throat doubled.

Say it. Say it now. Say you love him.

The crushing weight pressed on my heart until I couldn't tell if saying the words would release me from the unbearable pressure or kill me.

Still, the words couldn't make their way past the blockade of thick, binding emotion.

"I love you, Vivien," he said, as if reading my thoughts. "I will never let you go."

My body broke with a sudden violence that sent shockwaves pulsating and rolling through my body with an all-consuming force. Grim's face screwed up, helpless against the sensation as my muscles clamped down on his hard length.

I needed this, all of him inside me, and I needed to feel connected to Grim in every possible way. My fangs elongated, and I sunk them into that perfect space between his shoulder and collarbone. Grim's blood hit my tongue. I went flying through the universe as I spasmed, while he continued to pound into me, prolonging my pleasure.

Eventually, maybe after a couple minutes or years, my body calmed and I came back to earth. Then a second orgasm, more intense than the first, crashed into me. I convulsed under its unrelenting power, incoherent and drowning in Grim and our connection.

His fingers dug into my hips with bruising pressure as he succumbed to his release with me. It rolled through the room, a physical force, like a thunderclap. The silent pulse slammed into the marrow of my bones. He cried out, face fierce with desperation as he shot into me.

Blinking a couple times, I found myself lying back on the desk, legs still curled up around his hips. I'd never drunk from him during sex before, but it had done the trick, calming the quaking fear at my core.

Grim lay across my chest, but was still standing at the end of the desk. I felt him soften inside me. I intentionally clenched my muscles around him and he jerked.

"Brat," he mumbled into my body.

And just like that, our argument from earlier tonight evaporated. I knew it wasn't over. I knew he still waited, wanting more from me. But right now, in this moment, what we had was enough.

"Doesn't that hurt?" I asked. His face rested on the spikes surrounding the bosom of my dress.

Lifting his head, he gave me a view of the little indents

around his cheek. "I think I can survive a couple of your spikes," he said.

Right. He'd just walked away from a car bomb. A shiver went through me.

"The couch," I directed.

Grim understood, scooped my ass into his hands, picking me up. Still inside me, he dropped on the over-sized couch. The soft leather of the brown, tufted chesterfield caressed my bare legs as I clung to his neck, now sitting on top of him. He didn't give any sign he'd let go of me, either.

I stopped to take a moment, pulling my dress over my head. The cool air of the room slapped my naked body, so I pressed myself against his muscular chest. The comforting heat of his skin reassured me in a primal way. Though my blood ran hot from the sex and drinking from a god, Grim grabbed one of the faux fur throws and wrapped it around my body.

"Better?" he asked, stroking my hair as I snuggled into him.

I nodded into his neck. "Yes," I whispered.

"I told you," he said gently. "I can't die."

"Unless I drink too much of your blood and decide to kill you with crazy power."

"Do you plan on sucking me dry and murdering me any time soon? I have some arrangements I'd like to make," he joked.

"Unless someone chops your head off with a sword that can kill gods."

"We'll find it before that happens," he reassured me.

"Two ways for you to die is too many," I said, pulling back to look him in his face. My fingers played with dark hair at the base of his neck.

"Two..." he started, then drifted off as if there was more to tell.

Alarm raced through me in hot flashes. He was going to tell me something bad. Something I didn't want to hear. I felt so very fragile, like I could fall to pieces in his arms. For once, I didn't want to know. I couldn't handle it.

Grim seemed to change his mind about what he was going to say and tightened his arms around me. "You are the one who could have been hurt. If you hadn't forgotten your coat."

It was true. While I was immortal, fire, beheading, or having my heart ripped out could still end me.

"Why would someone try to blow up your car? A human enemy?" I asked, fury snaking through me. "Someone who wouldn't know you'd live through it?"

He shook his head, pushing my hair back over my ear, before tracing his thumb down my jaw. "No. Someone is trying to distract us. Throw us off balance."

"I'll rip their jugular out," I snarled. An animalistic need to protect what was mine tore through me at whoever this faceless enemy was. I couldn't tell if it came from the vampire part or the human part of me. But the fury was primal.

"I know you will," he said. His confidence in me was profound. A god needed me. Leaned on me. "I trust you."

I knew what a big deal that was. Especially after what his ex-wife, Qwynn, had done. She'd resented his commitment to the duty of reaping and sorting souls. To become the center of his world, she'd dragged him down into opium-den orgies to keep him from surfacing to do his job.

After reading up on ancient Egyptian mythology, I learned her original name was Qadesh, and she was the goddess of sexual ecstasy. So while I understood she wanted to keep her in his slut cave forever—we may share the same feelings on that point—I wasn't driven to jealousy the way she had been. Can we say co-dependent much? And then she'd betrayed him. In the Victorian age, people acquired the bodies of mummies and threw unwrapping parties. Then they would eat the mummy flesh, thinking it would grant them long life and health.

Apart from the fact that's absolutely disgusting, and this comes from a gal who sucks on blood clots, to Grim it's an abomination. Qwynn eventually revealed her hand when she served him the desiccated flesh of a mummy, revealing she was behind the unwrapping parties. She had done something sacrilegious to Grim on purpose, to see if he would love her more than his own values. She destroyed their union the moment she did it. The jealous biatch still tried to reel him in, but she could try all she wanted.

Grim nuzzled my neck breaking into my thoughts about his past. "It seems only right to move to this to the bedroom and have a dozen cupcakes delivered."

I nodded against him, feeling a spark of interest at the prospect of sugar. "Not to mention there is another Cupcake in need of head scratches for facing that evil cat with me."

Instead of letting me walk, Grim cradled me in his arms. The soft blanket was still wrapped around me. I leaned against his large, muscular shoulder. They carried the weight of the world, literally. He deserved the joy of the world, not the weight of it.

As soon as this sick feeling in my gut passed, I'd give him what he wanted.

I'd find a way to tell him those three little words.

But first, I'd have a couple cupcakes.

8

GRIM

Vivien refused to fall asleep even as daylight came. She paced through the apartment like a caged-up lion. I decided to put off a day of judgment to stay with her, since she seemed unbalanced. I'd done my best to tire her out by sexual means, but even after countless orgasm involving creative positions, and more than a few accessories, she still jumped out of bed.

When I eventually emerged from the shower, I found a lineup of abandoned baking ingredients strewn across the kitchen. After some searching, I discovered her in the library on one of the ladders, a stack of books on the floor. She donned Cookie Monster, as Timothy had retrieved it from the restaurant.

"What are you doing?" I asked.

She didn't turn to answer, running her fingers along the spines. "Compiling books for more research."

I tilted my head to examine the titles. More volumes on Egyptian mythology and ancient history. At the moment, I didn't have the heart to inform her the books she'd pulled weren't written in English.

"We're going out," I said, making a decision on the spot. Night still had yet to fall, but we could stay in the hotel until it did.

Vivien froze, then twisted her head toward me with an incredulous expression. The way she stood on the ladder, in those ridiculously short shorts that gave me a glimpse of her cheeks, exposing those long legs...

"If we do, someone might try to kill you again," she said, interrupting my train of thought.

I walked over to her, wrapped my hands around her waist and picked her off the ladder to set her on the floor in front of me.

"I'm not going anywhere, Vivien. Bullets and car bombs are an inconvenient annoyance."

"Annoyance?" By the pitch of her voice, I knew fear stained her.

"Yes," I said, tilting her chin up to meet my measured gaze. "Annoyance. This isn't the first time someone has tried to do away with me."

"And what if someone comes up and tries to run the Blade of Bane through you?"

"I believe you won't let that happen," I said.

"Damn right I won't," she grumbled, though her fingers clutched my bare back.

"Whoever is doing this has gone to great lengths to distract us, and keep us off kilter. So the best thing we can do is not give in. So put on the most ostentatious dress you can, and we're going to Wolf Town." I laid a gentle but firm kiss on her full, pouting mouth.

Vivien didn't like to be controlled, and she especially didn't like to be controlled through fear.

I couldn't help but think if Vivien hadn't left her jacket behind, she could have been killed. The bomb went off when I activated the driver's side door. But if she'd been any closer to the car... no, I couldn't think about that. It was one thing to blow up my car, engulf me in flames and ruin a perfectly good suit, but if Vivien had become collateral damage, this world would never know peace again.

It didn't take much time at all for her to get ready. True to form, she found an outrageous getup. Vivien wore a sheer, long-sleeve crop top and leather miniskirt. The outline of skeleton bones set against the black sheer fabric of her top.

My first instinct was to cover her body with mine, and never let another man or woman lay their eyes on this hellion. But the bones were also an homage to me, and it warmed the depths of my dark, ancient heart. It felt like the equivalent of a woman sporting the favor of her beloved knight.

The possessive feeling she aroused in me made me want to drag her into the bedroom and do more shocking, naughty things to her. But we needed to get out amongst the living.

We arrived at my club earlier than usual, but it surprised me to find our VIP booth already full. Bianca, Fallon, and Galina poised in various spots. Bianca, with her perfectly styled platinum blonde hair, in her signature color of light pink. She resembled a mix of old Hollywood and cotton candy. She'd curled up on a long couch with a glass of champagne. Fabric fell off her in swaths, resembling a style she'd favored during the classical age of Greece in 350 BC. An oracle and the goddess of love and fertility, Bianca's true name was Hathor.

Fallon wore a shiny navy suit that made his deep brown skin appear darker tonight. Hands tucked in his pockets, he looked down at the floor below. His square jaw clenched as he seemed lost in thought. No one would be able to tell his left eye of blue glowed, not with the strobing lights matching the thumping bass of the club music. The god Horus cast his shining orb of power on the mass of writhing dancers.

Galina leaned back against the banister, her body an elegant line wrapped in green satin fabric that fell to mid-thigh. Her dark hair had been slicked back, giving her the appearance of merciless sophistication. It was similar to the look she'd sported on the front of *Vanity Fair* last month. She carried the feline grace only Bast, the cat goddess, could.

"Well, this is unexpected," I said.

A genuine, warm smile spread across Bianca's face, and Vivien met it wholeheartedly with one of her own. Bianca rose from the couch, moving to kiss Vivien on both cheeks while Fallon and Galina remained where they were, only giving a nod of greeting.

"We heard you were blown up and wanted to visit our favorite grim reaper to make sure you weren't missing any fingers or ears," Fallon joked, turning to set back to the crowd, knowing very well my limbs would remain intact.

A sweaty glass containing an old-fashioned waited on the table for me. I picked it up and sipped on the full-bodied bourbon drink.

"Sorry to disappoint," I said, dryly. "Still in one piece."

Vivien sat next to Bianca, careful to avoid stepping on the pink fluff of her dress. "Is this something you are all used to? Getting stabbed, blown up, and shot at?"

"Live long enough and you'll experience a bit of everything," Galina said, waving a hand.

"Oh goodie," Vivien said. "I'm psyched to know I have so much to look forward to with this whole immortality business. What is eternity without a little maiming and torture?"

"It's not all bad," Bianca said, nudging Vivien's shoulder.

"What are you really doing here?" I asked, going to stand by Fallon.

"Did you find it?" Fallon asked, his tone serious.

I exchanged a look with Vivien. She moved to my side. My arm wrapped around her waist.

"No," she said. "It was a replica. Someone is fucking with us. Worse than that, the guy who dangled the bait ended up hurling himself off the Parisienne rather than answer my questions."

Galina straightened at that, alarm on her face. "He what?"

"Yeah," Vivien went on. "He'd been worshiping a god and when I tried to use my power to get him to come down from the ledge, he broke through it and pulled a superman."

"What a damn mess," Fallon said, dragging a hand over his face.

Galina's voice was low. "That is unfortunate."

"Yes," Bianca said quietly, "We've been dealing with the cleanup. The authorities were making a fuss about a woman matching your description slipping away before they could question you."

"What do you mean?" Vivien asked.

"Bianca owns the Parisienne," I explained.

Vivien's eyebrows rose. "Oh, I thought every time you said you were off to Paris, you were jet-setting to France?"

Bianca shrugged as she sipped her champagne. "Half and half."

Vivien's brows drew together, and her bottom lip jutted out in a pout, like it did whenever she mulled something over. "Whenever one of these crazy violent sprees happens here at Sinopolis, things get covered up like they never happened. How come it wasn't the same at your hotel?"

Tension filled the space between Bianca and Fallon. So I answered. "We employ Fallon for his abilities." I left it up to him to elaborate or not. A god's powers were private, as they could also reveal their weaknesses.

"I have many talents," Fallon said, trusting Vivien enough to explain. "But among them, the ability to heal is one of the strongest. When applied properly, I can cleanse a human's memories. So when godly business becomes violent and disruptive, that's where I come in."

"Why doesn't he do the same thing for you?" Vivien asked, turning to Bianca.

"She doesn't need my help," Fallon said in a flat voice, though his blue eyes glowed with renewed intensity.

Vivien looked like she wanted to push the issue, but I redirected the conversation.

"In summation, the sword is still out there somewhere," I said, swirling the ice in my glass. "And someone is delighting in playing with us."

Bianca shivered. "I don't like this. Someone out there with the Blade of Bane again."

"Seth was a bastard." Fallon gripped the railing, intensity sparking in both eyes. "He had it coming. And why don't you just conjure up one of your magic visions and see who is doing all this?" He wiggled his fingers at Bianca as if casting a magic spell.

Bianca frowned, resembling a pissed-off pixie. "Why don't you see who is behind this with your magic eye, oh powerful one?"

"I thought you were the authority around here. That's what everyone thinks, right?" Fallon demanded.

Bianca fluffed out some of the material of her dress. "I

think the vision depends on the accuracy of the interpreter. And I can't control what others say."

An intense stare passed between the two of them in a silent standoff.

"What's with them?" Vivien whispered.

"Several centuries of competition," I answered.

Bianca's gaze snapped to me. "I don't compete with anyone. This fool thinks that he's better than me at seeing into the future. Though our foresight works in entirely different manners."

Fallon scoffed and ran a hand over his head and walked across the lounge to put as much distance between them.

"There is another reason we are here," Galina said, her face intent as she'd watched them volley back and forth. "I've brought someone who might be able to provide some answers."

Before I could ask who, the hair rose on the back of my neck as a familiar heat crawled along my skin.

Turning, I faced a woman with thick black hair falling over her shoulder in heavy, sumptuous waves. Impossibly long lashes framed her dark eyes, while full lips promised every pleasure imaginable. Golden fabric wrapped around her curvy figure, accentuating her generous cleavage.

My ex-wife.

"Qwynn," I said, her name coming out cold and flat.

The goddess of ecstasy and sexual pleasure, she looked every inch the sinful creature she was.

But I knew she was a bottomless pit and a textbook narcissist.

Qwynn's fingers rose as if to push back the hair that dipped over my forehead. Before I could stop her, a hand snapped out and grabbed her first.

Vivien stood next to me, her fangs elongated, gripping Qwynn's wrist.

"What is she doing here?" Vivien hissed.

Galina explained, "She has been a player in this game to upset the order between gods and humanity. I brought her here so that we could learn who directed her into such treachery. Perhaps find out who possesses the god-killer."

Qwynn stared at Vivien with indifference, as if she were nothing more than a bug. "I can go if you prefer," she offered.

Realizing things were on the verge of spiraling out of control, I slid my hand onto Vivien's hip. Qwynn's eyes tracked the movement before I cut off her view by putting my back to her.

"She may have information," I said to Vivien in a soothing voice.

Osiris had trapped Qwynn in a column of extra-dimensional hellfire for what must have felt like eons to her. She'd paid for her sins, and I did not receive any further report as to her treachery. I could only assume she'd had no more useful information to give if Osiris had not extracted it from her.

But maybe Galina was right. Qwynn was our only living, direct connection to the puppet master behind all this. She could know something important without being aware of it.

Vivien vibrated with anger, her fiery gaze meeting mine. "She's responsible for forcing me to feed on Jamal. This bitch made me almost kill him."

It was true. Qwynn had been guilty of manipulating events to force Vivien to drink from Miranda's son. The price for saving Jamal entailed Vivien binding herself to me.

"Jamal is alive and safe. Miranda doesn't hold you responsible."

"She ruined my life," Vivien seethed. "If it weren't for her, I would still be human."

The blow came without warning. Suddenly, so much more made sense.

I took a step back, filling in the rest. If it weren't for Qwynn, Vivien wouldn't be a vampire. Vivien wouldn't be immortal, forced to drink my blood. She wouldn't have to deal with the gods. She wouldn't be bound to me.

How could she ever love me when she'd been forced into this life?

I was all but acutely aware of how her life had spun on its axis, and even though we filled our days with pleasure, she'd never say she loved me back.

Even if she said she loved me one day, would it be because she had no choice but to spend an eternity with me? Did it strip her of options, and I simply awaited the erosion of time on her will to give into my territorial whim?

Vivien's focus still didn't stray from Qwynn while I somersaulted over my thoughts. Finally, those sea-glass eyes met mine, and I saw the surprise register in them. I quickly cleared my expression of whatever had been there.

Vivien valued freedom more than anything, and I suddenly saw with complete clarity what a fool I'd been to think I could usurp that desire.

Bianca jumped up, putting herself in the middle of the powder keg, ready to blow.

"Okay." She clapped her hands. "Qwynn, sit over there, and Vivien come stand over here with me and Grim." She linked her arms through mine and Vivien's, leading us to the other side of the lounge.

"Do you always have to try to fix everything?" Fallon growled in Bianca's direction.

Bianca shot him a scathing look. "I thought that was your job, Mr. Mind Eraser."

Qwynn sat over by Galina, crossing one leg over the other. The movement alone had brought empires to ruin, but all of my being was focused on Vivien. The line of her body was wild with rage. If Bianca let go of Vivien, she'd likely fly across the room to tear Qwynn to pieces.

"You weren't smart enough to come up with this idea," Galina said to Qwynn. "Sure, we know you yearn for"—her cat-like eyes flicked toward me— "power. So what possessed you to bring sekhors back into the mix?"

It was true. Qwynn extracted blood from the Original to create the first sekhor in thousands of years. She'd chosen a psychopath to help her make an army of sekhors, but we'd stopped them. Osiris trapped Qwynn in a column of fire as punishment, literally putting her through hell, but he still did not learn the one responsible.

Qwynn licked her lips, slowly, deliberately, buying time. "I was first approached by a mortal who'd been worshiping. I turned down the offer in the beginning, but more vessels came to me, speaking of the grand change and all I had to gain from a new world order."

Her gaze studiously remained off me, but we all knew what she felt she'd gain. A spot by my side again.

"Did you ever try to follow them? Try to discover who was responsible?" I asked.

Qwynn lifted her Bambi eyelashes at me. Bianca tightened her grip on my arm, and I wondered if it was for my benefit or to keep Vivien at bay.

"No," she said, simply. Staring at me, she radiated every bit of longing and seduction she possessed. But I knew it wasn't me she missed. She missed having the most powerful god wrapped around her finger.

"Why the hell not?" Fallon asked.

"Because." Qwynn shrugged. "It didn't interest me."

"And one of them told you how to make sekhors again?" Galina asked, her intent focus on Qwynn.

She nodded. "Yes. I was told to find the first, and we could bring back vampires."

"They told you to take the Original's blood and create a new vampire?" I asked.

Qwynn gave another half-hearted shrug, picking at invisible lint on the chair. "A worshiper told me to wake the Original to help build an army. But I figured..."

"You figured that the Original would have all the power over the vampires then, instead of you," I finished for her in a flat, cold tone.

Galina crossed her arms and looked away in disgust. "You really are a selfish little idiot, aren't you?"

"Why on earth would you think that was a good idea?" Fallon agreed.

"Because she's a power-hungry ho," Vivien finally piped up. Shaking off Bianca, she stepped forward. "Why are you here sharing all this? What do you want now?"

Vivien had a beat on Qwynn. I realized I should have asked that question first. Nothing came without a price in her world.

Qwynn's chin set. "No one will speak to me. I am a pariah. I don't wish to spend the rest of eternity as an outcast."

"Bullshit," Vivien said, getting in Qwynn's face. "You want Grim. Or do you want me dead? Are you the one who set up the car bomb? Was it for him? Or were you trying to get me out of the way?"

She raised an eyebrow. "Do you really believe I'd dirty

my hands like that?" She lifted her fingers to show off the long, elaborately bejeweled, manicured nails.

"If you don't want your hands dirtied, then why would you be chosen to wake up the Original?" Bianca asked.

Fallon answered this time. "Because she is the only other one who knew where the Original was kept."

Qwynn's eyes slid to me. It was true. Between us there had been no secrets, or at least on my end there hadn't been. So trapped in the opium-soaked dens, reveling between each other's legs and mouths, I didn't think of the consequences until it was too late.

Never in my wildest dreams did I consider she'd remember the system of how I moved the Original every ten years to keep the staff from getting suspicious. Her sights typically remained on her target, and she'd reel them in with her wiles. Going after Sekhmet required a far larger scheme, and that was not Qwynn's style. At least when she'd been manipulated, Qwynn hadn't been stupid enough to actually wake up the Original. And I'm sure the irony of her hand in creating my perfect mate rubbed salt in her wounds.

"Well shit," Vivien said. "We need to move her. This ho could tell anyone where the Original is."

I'd taken Vivien to see the Original to discover how she'd been made, but at that point I'd been certain I would kill the fiery sekhor. She wouldn't be able to tell my secrets if she was dead. But now, I trusted her not to betray me. Just as I had trusted Qwynn.

I'd learned to rule over my romantic notions with an iron fist, but it did seem every time I let that grip slip, someone was ready to take advantage. Had I put too much faith in Vivien? Faith she'd come around to love me as I loved her?

Again, a sharp arrow pierced under my breast.

"Even if I did, it wouldn't matter," Qwynn hissed at Vivien, the aggravation finally getting to her.

"Maybe we should keep her locked up," Vivien suggested. "Then when we find the Blade of Bane, we can just lop off her head so she can't tell anyone." I knew Vivien enough to know she was deliberately goading my ex.

"No need to be nasty," Qwynn said, wrinkling her nose. "If Grim strengthened his spell, then I couldn't get near the Original again. But he's too busy fucking a blood-sucking whore like you."

Something flashed in Galina's eyes. "I've heard enough," she said in a tone that commanded the room before all hell let loose.

So had I. "Get out," I announced. When no one moved, I said, "Now. Everyone out."

Qwynn stood, adjusting her dress, sure to run her hands over her curves, shooting daggers at Vivien with her eyes.

Galina and Bianca made a hasty exit, and Fallon used his broad body to usher Qwynn out of our lounge.

Only Vivien remained.

"What are you going to do?" she asked.

"Strengthen the spell, as Qwynn suggested."

"What can I do?" she asked.

"You can..." I paused, unsure of what to say. "Go downstairs and have a drink and do some dancing."

"Excuse me?"

I adjusted my cufflinks. "You've done more than enough. You've been put under a great deal of stress. I've tasked you with trying to track down the culprit behind this insidious mess so I could focus on reaping. But you are not a god, and you need time to find grounding in your new life."

She reared back as though I'd slapped her. "What the hell is this? Are you saying you want to go on a break?"

"No," I said slowly. "I simply think you need time to adjust to your circumstances, and you haven't had time to do that. Not with chasing around false leads and being entrenched in immortal business." *And too much time in my bed*, I added in my mind. Perhaps I was no better than Qwynn, wanting Vivien all to myself with such fierce possession, that I forewent consideration of her true needs.

Vivien's words came out colder than ice as she tightened her hands into fists. "Is this because of her?"

"It is," I said with absolute honesty. Moving toward Vivien, I couldn't help but slide my fingers along the soft skin of her jaw line until I cupped her face. She looked up at me with an intense mixture of frustration and hurt. "Our relationship has been like an asteroid hitting the atmosphere. I think we both require perspective. I need you to make sure this is what you want."

One of her hands covered mine. "Of course you are what I want."

"I love you," I said, giving her yet another chance.

Her lips parted, and I knew she wanted to say it back.

But whether she wanted to say it because she felt it, or out of obligation, I didn't know.

If I didn't spend every moment doting on her, and gave her space to breathe, she might not feel the same. It felt as though my heart were being ripped from my chest to think about, but I knew I had to give her the choice.

As if reading my thoughts, she said, "I chose you when I was just a kid. I promised to walk by your side."

Indeed, when her parents died, I happened to be nearby. Young Vivien saw through me to the loneliness I bore. I escorted souls to the afterlife so they would not be afraid.

And young Vivien vowed to walk with me so I would never be alone.

I did believe that her promise set the universe in motion to bring us together again. "You were a child. A child with a big heart." I brushed her cheek with my thumb. Then I released her to step back. "But this may not be the end of the story. Perhaps this is just the beginning. I fear my constant attention does not allow you to be yourself or follow your path. I am predisposed to control, and I'm aware enough to know that I bring a level of intensity that can be smothering to others."

It pained me more than I could say. Loosening my grip on the only one I ever loved with every ounce of my being. Though part of me broke at having to let her step away from this hot fire crackling between us, I knew it was the right thing to do. Or I'd lose myself again. I'd been blinded by need and obsession for Qwynn. I hadn't seen her for what she was. I feared doing the same to Vivien, not seeing what she truly needed because of my own selfish need for her.

The pain I caused by trying to hold us in a tight, unyielding grip would only lead to more anguish.

Vivien stared at me with an inscrutable expression for several long beats.

Finally she spoke, her voice small and vulnerable. "No one has ever loved me the way that you have. No one has allowed me to be so unapologetically myself and loved me so deeply and intensely. I'm not afraid of your intensity. I'm afraid of losing you because I can't give you what you want fast enough."

Then she crossed the distance between us, her eyes glittering with unshed tears. "Please don't push me away. I promise I only need time. I'm not used to this. And as for the chase, it's what I lived for before I was turned immortal.

I can't disconnect from this, and I don't want to. And I don't want to disconnect from you. Can I please just have time? I know how it hurts you. I know every time I don't say it, I cause you pain. But I—I can't just yet. Give me more time, Grim."

More time. All too often had I been asked to give more time. More chances. And I'd learned long ago that meant more opportunities to wound and disappoint.

But this was Vivien. She never uttered an untruth. I believed in her. More than anyone before.

I covered her mouth with mine, parting her lips with my tongue so I could taste her. The relief that broke through me flooded my system. Holding her tight to my body, I knew no matter how much I tried to give her space, I couldn't. She was life to me. Without her, I could not be complete. Death needed life, just as life needed death.

She clung to me as if afraid I'd let her go.

The sensation lancing my heart entwined with the love I felt for Vivien. I nuzzled her neck and assured her. "We have all the time in the world."

Even if my eternity with her held pain and rejection, I'd have to find some way to be satisfied with whatever Vivien gave me.

9

VIVIEN

"What exactly are we doing here, again?" Miranda asked me the next evening.

I led her through the industrial warehouse. The smell of cardboard and dust on the abandoned machines hung in the air.

"You are helping me secure a valuable item," I explained for the fourth time.

Miranda ran a hand over her braids. "No matter how you keep slipping the word "secure" into your explanations, it still doesn't mean that it's part of my job as head of security at Sinopolis."

She'd said this before when I kept insisting she needed to help me "secure" sugar or caffeine. Apparently, she couldn't stay clocked in for a coffee break just because I kept phrasing it like that.

I rolled my eyes and said, "I think Grim would agree 'securing' my friendship is a valuable and necessary part of your duties, one which he is happy to compensate you for." We finally reached the freight elevator at the far end of the building, so I pulled back the gated door and gestured her in. After we were in, I closed the doors and hit the button for the basement.

"I thought you had plans tonight anyway?" Miranda asked.

"Yeah, Grim and I have another dinner date since the last one ended in a fight and a fiery explosion. But that isn't for a couple of hours."

The lift lowered with a cacophony of noisy gears and belts.

The pause between us grew heavy. I recognized the moment before she asked something super personal.

"Have you told him yet?"

There it was.

"No." My insides clenched with anxiety. Even the thought of trying to say the words and my body pushed them back down into the pit of my stomach.

"Are you guys...okay?"

I'd given her a brief lowdown of the meeting last night and touched on how Grim tried to softball taking a break. The idea he wanted to take me off the search for the Blade of Bane, and also have time apart, evoked an intense fear I still hadn't shaken off.

My lips were stiff. "I don't know. I told him I need more time, and he said he could give me that."

She shrugged a shoulder. "At least you guys have as much of that as you want."

I didn't answer. That's what I kept saying, but it didn't negate my hurting Grim every time I refused to say it.

"It's normal, you know," she said, turning to face me. I met her brown eyes. They drilled into me with meaning. "You grew up in an abusive home. That alone would give anybody trust issues, make them want to shut down and not open up again. On top of that, you died and came back a vampire and now you are dealing with all this...immortal stuff." She waved a hand. Then her voice softened. "He almost imploded a couple of months ago. Then you saw him go up in flames from a car bomb."

A reassuring feeling wrapped around my chest as she validated my deep-rooted fears.

"But," she said, her tone becoming stern, "it doesn't mean you can wait forever."

"Technically I can," I pointed out, with an eyebrow waggle.

She shook her head. "Take it from me. You need to say what matters when it's needed the most. I know you love him. He knows you love him. But if you don't give in to that love, you're making him stand out on that limb alone. Eventually, he may tire of carrying the risk for both of you and back up off that ledge if he thinks you won't join him."

The elevator came to a stop, bringing our conversation to an end. Relief swept through me. It was getting too intense. Everything lately had been too intense. She was right. It scared the shit out of me. I knew my rejection hurt him, and I hated it, but I couldn't do better right now.

I wrenched open the gates and held up a hand, telling Miranda to stay back.

Fluorescent lights flickered through the dimly lit hallway. Then several guns and a camera dropped from the ceiling on a mechanic *whirr*. They swiveled until they all pointed right at us.

My hands were up, palms out in surrender. "It's just me, Echo. Can we come in for a chat?"

The camera jerked aggressively in Miranda's direction. Miranda tensed next to me. Her face went flat as if she were falling back to military mode. The sharp scent of her fear and adrenaline surrounded me.

"Who's this?" a crotchety woman's voice demanded. "More strangers you are bringing into my home?"

"A friend," I assured. Then I said out of the corner of my mouth to Miranda, "Show her what's in the bag."

Miranda opened up the backpack with short, precise movements, and displayed the contents to the camera.

There was a pause. The only sounds were the low hum of the motors running the hydraulics in the ceiling guns and Miranda's heart, pumping hard and fast.

Then the camera and guns disappeared into the ceiling. I gave Miranda a broad smile and gestured grandly down the hallway. "After you, madame."

"I hate you," she said, zipping the bag back up.

"No, you don't," I said. "You'd be bored as hell if it weren't for me. And you have to admit, you really want to know why she let you in over a backpack with some bananas and a bag of Cooler Ranch Doritos." I began down the hall without her.

"Damn you," she said, finally tagging behind.

My charm was irresistible.

We walked down the corridor and turned right until we came to another door, shaped like a massive bank vault. It opened, and we entered a big underground warehouse. Except unlike the fulfillment center in the building overhead, this was half cozy home, and half crazy-villain observation post. They arranged a number of floral couches and chairs around a coffee table on one side.

Nineteen-year-old Aoiki, a half-Japanese, half-Samoan girl, lay down, chewing bubble gum, reading a manga book on her back. One leg dangled on the back of the couch. Her mint green hair matched the suspenders on her punk-rock schoolgirl outfit, though I don't think she was in school anymore.

She blew a big purple bubble from her gum. It popped with a snap.

"Hey Aoiki," I called.

"Hey, Vivien," she called back.

"Who the hell is Vivien?" a suspicious-sounding voice asked with a thick Samoan accent.

"I am," I said, walking toward Echo.

Monitors covered one wall, almost thirty feet up. Some featured anime, a couple were news channels, but most were live feeds from all over the city. Echo had been my secret weapon when I'd been a bounty hunter.

The bubblegum pink chair at the base of all the monitors whirled around. A stout woman in her fifties, wearing a floral mumu, gave me the stink eye.

"Remember?" I prompted. "My old name was Jane, but now it's Vivien."

"It's cool. I like it." Aoiki shot me her usual impish grin. Echo rolled her eyes and grabbed the cane resting against her desk before pointing it at Miranda with aggressive accusation.

"Who is this?" Echo demanded.

"Someone who needs to rethink her friendships," Miranda said, her lips tight as she side-eyed me.

"I'm trying to find an object and she is here to help," I said, slinging my arm over Miranda's shoulders. Damn, the woman must work out. Hard to tell under those suits, but my girl was all lean muscle.

"Payment first," Echo said in a tone that brooked no argument. Actually, her normal tone had that effect. I wondered if that was a trait that came to her naturally or if she had to practice her ball-busting cadence.

"Pull out the goods," I stage-whispered to Miranda. "I'll let you do the honors."

Miranda's dark eyes regarded me like I'd gone off the reservation. Still, she pulled out the banana and bag of Doritos from the backpack.

The moment the bag crinkled, a tiny, soft white nose poked out from under the couch where Aoiki sat. A flash of fur darted across the room until it was at Miranda's feet.

"Oh," she breathed in surprise. A small rabbit, only a couple of handfuls, stood at her feet. With a ring of black around its eyes, the breed was known as a hotot because of its coloring.

He pawed at Miranda's pants in earnest, little nose bopping up and down like crazy.

"Are you going to stand there all day, or are you going to sit down and share the goods with Darth Vader here?" I asked.

Miranda couldn't wipe away her surprised expression, but she sat down. Darth Vader instantly jumped in her lap, trying to get at the bag.

"Seriously? You want me to give the rabbit Doritos?" Miranda asked, still holding back.

"Never give a rabbit Doritos," Echo snapped. "But give a genetically engineered rabbit one and you'll be indebted to their craving for the rest of your life."

Miranda opened the pouch and shared a chip. Darth Vader crunched happily in her lap.

Reaching over, I grabbed the banana, opening it as I made kissing sounds. Two tremendous brown ears popped up from around the corner of the couch and a rabbit, five times the size of Darth Vader, walloped out. Lulu was a Flemish Giant, the biggest breed of rabbit, while Darth Vader was the tiniest breed, a dwarf rabbit. Despite color and size differences, they were positively inseparable.

"Lulu is the health nut of the two," I explained to

Miranda, putting the banana in her free hand. Lulu was the
size of a medium-small dog. She had a dopey sweetness
about her.

"Vivien-chan." A soft male voice drew my attention.

A grin practically split my face as I turned to Ryuki.
Echo's husband was a sweet, soft-spoken Japanese man who
immediately inspired the deepest need to please him to
earn the smile in his eyes. He entered from a door that led to
what I presumed was the kitchen, though I'd never been
beyond this observation room.

"See? Dad remembered her new name," Aoiki said
without looking away from her manga.

"Pfft," Echo responded in a half snort, half scoff.

The man wore khaki pants and a soft sweater vest one
might find in Mr. Roger's closet. His back already bent with
age. Ryuki shuffled forward with a tea tray. He offered it up
to me, and I gladly took the clay cup of aromatic jasmine
tea. Before he could shuffle away, I planted a big wet kiss on
his cheek, and he blushed ten ways from Sunday.

Then he offered his wife a cup of tea. Echo's expression
softened ever so slightly as he beamed at her with loving
pride. I wanted to nudge Miranda to enjoy the scene, but
she was busy, still covered in adamant rabbits.

"I need your help," I said to Echo after Ryuki moved to
join Aoiki on the couch. He pulled a special soda from his
back pocket and handed it to her.

Echo only crossed her arms and waited for more information. Her hard, dark, pebble eyes threatened to throw me
out if she thought I was wasting her time.

"We are looking for a weapon, a sword. I'm ninety percent
certain it's hidden in a hotel on the Strip. Likely concealed in
plain sight." It was just a guess, but I couldn't forget Seth's bull-

shit move of hiding Amit, the soul devourer, in plain sight at the center of a restaurant. Gods hid in plain sight every day, and there was a hubris they all shared that left me in no doubt they would delight in having something valuable dangle out in the open where no one noticed rather than lock it away in a safe.

"Why don't you go look for it yourself?" Echo groused.

"Because"—I sipped my tea to lengthen the suspense of my sentence— "you can find the unfindable. And in a fraction of the time."

A smug glint entered her eye. She may have a tough candy shell, but flattery melted her like butter in an oven.

Miranda looked up from the fluff bombs to chime in. "From what you've said, there are hundreds of"—Miranda caught herself before using the word *gods*— "suspects. How are you going to narrow it down?"

"I've got a hunch I'd bet my left boob on." I paused, then added, "But not the right one. I'd never bet rightie."

"The last time we followed your hunch, we ended up fighting a massive snake monster." Then with a nervous look at Echo and Aoiki, Miranda added, "metaphorically speaking of course."

There was nothing metaphorical about it. But neither Echo nor Aoiki batted an eye. Ryuki calmly sipped his tea. I couldn't be sure, but I got the sense they knew even more than I did. When I'd brought Grim here, he and Echo appraised each other in a way that sent bizarro energy zipping back and forth between the two of them.

"You want the Blade of Bane," Echo said, flatly.

"The whaaat?" I asked, dragging out the end of the last word to an unbelievable pitch. I was trying to buy my brain time to cover up the truth. She'd taken me by surprise. Admittedly, Echo helped me find the guy from Craigslist with the sword for sale, but nowhere did it say it was the Blade of Bane and I sure as hell hadn't let it slip.

She waved at the screen before giving me a look that assured she thought I was an idiot. "I see everything, dumb-dumb."

"Even when I touch myself?" I asked, my eyes widening.

Echo rolled her eyes while Aoiki giggled into her manga. Ryuki drank his tea as if he had heard nothing.

Miranda snorted, but she was still wrapped up in the furballs accosting her for treats.

"How the hell do you know about the god-killing blade?" I asked, knowing Grim would not be happy about this. He thought godly business stayed in the underworld of immortals.

Echo waved her thick arm at the monitors with even more vigor.

"Yes, yes, I get it. You see everything," I repeated duti-fully. "But the question is, can you find it?"

Echo's fingers drummed along her desk, as if she were deciding something. "And what will you do with it once you have it?" she asked.

"First off, keep the psychopath who has it from killing anyone else," I said, my voice went cold with anger.

"And then what? Wield it yourself? Use it for your own personal gain?"

I felt the eyes of everyone in the room on me. Even the rabbits paused to regard me. "No, it's not about that. It's about stopping someone worse from using it."

She nodded and shot a look at her family on the couch. "If I help you find this weapon, you must do something for me."

"What?" I asked, not wanting to agree to more than I was willing.

"*You* cannot wield the blade." Echo then jerked her head toward Miranda, who stood up from feeding the rabbits. She brushed off the crumbs and fur on her shirt and pants. "*She* is the only one allowed to hold it."

Miranda stilled. "Why me?"

Echo squinted at my friend. "You are not an immortal. The coming war is dangerous, and it could be catastrophic. You are mortal, and you have faced combat. You understand the weight of what it means to wield a weapon. The cost that comes when you choose to use it, and when you don't. You will bring balance."

I turned to Miranda and waited for her answer. It wasn't my decision. She had to accept the responsibility of carrying a weapon that could destroy an immortal god. What Echo said made sense.

Finally, Miranda nodded in agreement.

Relief made my shoulders sag. I hated to put this burden on Miranda. Maybe this was how Grim felt when he talked about dragging me into godly problems and putting me in danger. But I was a big girl and I couldn't walk away from what was happening. My bottomless curiosity and need to know more drove me deeper into the world I now belonged to as a vampire. Miranda had also seen behind the curtain and her sense of duty wouldn't let her walk away. I had to respect her choice, even if part of me regretted getting her in deeper.

"Now where to start?" Echo hummed more to herself.

"I may have an idea about that," I said. "Let's just say I've been in one too many cat fights lately."

10

GRIM

The candles flickered on the table. Racks of wine bottles ran up the walls of the private dining room. It was my finest restaurant and staffed the Strip's most coveted pastry chef. Tonight would provide a safe respite from the brewing trouble.

But Vivien was late. Again.

I'd grown used to it, but after last night, I was anxious to have her with me. I needed to feel the cool of her skin and then experience it warm as she drank deeply from me. The need to sink deep into her until she surrounded me and fell apart under my hands, gripped me. My hand raked through my hair as I paced the room, growing more frustrated with each passing moment. I loosened my tie, but it did nothing to ease the tension inside me.

For the hundredth time, I checked my phone. She already texted she would be late, so there was no reason to text or call her again.

Perhaps we'd forgo the meal, but order dessert, something with cream or chocolate. Perhaps I'd eat it off her stomach and then mingle it in with the sweetness between her legs. The mere thought of dipping my tongue inside her, lapping her up, heated my body with need.

"Pardon, sir," a waiter said, walking in with a tray.

I actually jolted. I never reacted like that. Before her, I was never surprised. What was Vivien doing to me? And why did I both adore and fear the effect she had on me?

"The chef asked me to deliver this to you. Something for while you wait." He set it on the table. Lifting the lid, he revealed a pile of wontons. The smell of fried dough filled the private room.

"Thank you." I nodded, then the waiter disappeared.

I shed my jacket, placed it on the back of my chair, and rolled up my sleeves. I removed the tie too and unfastened the top few buttons. It helped a little, though my skin still felt too tight.

My mouth already watered from the fantasies of eating Vivien up. So I was grateful for a distraction. The savory pastry held a hint of cinnamon. I popped another wonton almost as soon as I finished the first.

I reassured myself she'd be here any moment.

11

VIVIEN

Grim was going to kill me. I was over two hours late, and as much as he put up with my tardiness, I knew he hated it.

After finishing up with Echo, I rushed back to the apartment to change. I donned a long, form-fitting black dress with slits that traveled up all the way to my hips. To keep the skirts from flapping open in the wind, three bands of rhinestones lay across my upper thighs, holding the sucker together.

I'd been reserving this one for a special occasion, and today was definitely cause for celebration. And even if Grim was super upset with me, he'd come down pretty quick when I shared what I'd been up to.

The walk to the restaurant, Scales, dragged on. My excitement made me want to blur through Sinopolis until I got to Grim's side. But seeing as I didn't want to freak out all the normal people, I kept a human pace.

The people I passed by were decked out in expensive clothes and carried martinis as they sauntered toward the clubs or casino rooms at the back of the hotel. They paused when they saw me. A couple pulled out their phones to take pictures. Thank god the paparazzi were engaged elsewhere, otherwise I'd lose my patience and start breaking noses to get through.

The maître d' gave me a thin-lipped smile as I arrived at Scales.

"He's waiting for you," the man said in a soft but tight tone. AKA Grim's in a pissy mood because I was running late, and they resorted to plying him with food and drinks to keep him calm.

He led me to the private room, but before he could open the door, I said, "I'll take it from here."

The maître d' looked relieved even as he bowed his head and turned to go. I took a deep breath I didn't need before turning the handle.

"Honey, I'm home," I said in a cheeky tone.

As soon as I stepped into the private dining room, my world tilted.

Something was very wrong. I inhaled the odor of death as I shut the door behind me. Not Grim's scent, this was rancid, rotting, and dead.

Grim didn't seem to be in the room. Then I caught sight of his foot sticking out from the other side of the table. My purse fell from my shoulder, hitting the floor with a thud.

I raced around to find him lying on the floor, convulsing.

I kneeled by him. "Grim, baby, what's wrong?" I asked, propping his torso up. His death mask flickered as if somebody had short-circuited the controls of his body.

"Vivien," he rasped. His gorgeous caramel skin had turned a sickly gray. I grasped his hand. It was cold, too cold.

"What is it? What's happening?" My un-beating heart

stuck in my throat. Panic gripped me with icy claws. I didn't know what to do or how to help.

He can only die from the Blade of Bane or if a vampire kills him. He'll be fine.

Despite the rationale, every atom in my body knew he was coming undone before my eyes.

Black tentacles of power whipped out with ferocious strikes before pulling back into his body as if he were trying to fight what was happening.

"Poisoned," he managed to get out.

"No, no, you can't be poisoned," I said, cupping his face. "Remember? You can get blown up and be just fine. Poison can't kill you. Walk it off," I urged.

The door opened with a creak. Through the legs of the table, a pair of golden heels lazily made their way into the room until their owner came into view.

"Galina," I cried out in relief. "Help me. Grim is sick."

The goddess stared down at me. A cashmere forest-green sweater wrapped around her, falling off one perfect shoulder. She wore a pencil skirt and a sympathetic expression.

"He's not sick, he's dying," she said softly.

"No, no, no," I insisted. "He can't die. He hasn't been stabbed by the god-killing blade, and I didn't drink from him."

Galina crouched down, gently pushing back a chunk of hair from his forehead. "He's consumed the flesh of the dead."

I twisted around to see a plate half-filled with wontons. One with a bite taken out of it.

I didn't understand.

Galina gave me a pitying look, while Grim convulsed more violently before he halted.

Though they kept morphing into fathomless, dark sucking holes of oblivion, his amber eyes tracked over to mine slowly. Falling into him didn't scare me anymore. Not like it had when we met. In his oblivion, I'd found a new beginning, a new life.

A connection had been forged between us since I first drank from him. It was an unconscious tether, but I felt it become weak and thready.

I was losing him.

"You can't die," I said, my voice turning hoarse. "Death can't die." Wetness covered my face as tears crowded their way out of my eyes. Fear and anxiety battled for dominance as my brain still raced for something to do, but I couldn't leave him. All that mattered was holding onto him. He couldn't go anywhere if I held him in my arms. The second I let go, I'd lose him.

Grim lifted a hand up, touching my face, his touch as icy as my dread. His skin turned the color of lead.

Though he couldn't seem to get any more words out, his eyes shone with all the love he had for me. In them, I also saw an apology. As if he were sorry he had to go so soon.

Blood rushed in my ears like a raging storm.

Then his face emptied of expression and he hardened into stone. Even his hair solidified under my touch. Flakes drifted off him in bits, rising into the air, then faster as his body disintegrated in my arms.

"I love you," I cried out.

But I was too late. He was already gone. Dark shimmering particles hovered before me, my hands now empty. The only thing left on the floor was his golden skull ring. I realized he must have taken it off before, leaving a token behind for me.

The tether inside binding me to him broke with a quiet

snap. The wail that emerged from me released from the depths of my broken heart as it splintered under my rib cage. I gripped my face, unable to stop screaming.

12

VIVIEN

Grim said he'd give me more time. He promised I could have as much time as I needed. We had eternity to figure things out...for me to gather my strength. I hadn't been brave enough to tell him. I was now. But it was too late. I rocked back and forth, unable to free myself from the hell I was trapped in.

I don't know how long I screamed, but when I stopped, my throat was raw. It felt as though I swallowed glass. Emotion pounded me like a massive fist until I was a bloody, sobbing pulp.

I blinked away the tears, fingernails digging into the wood floor, leaving scratch marks.

Galina removed a wine bottle from one rack. A fingernail elongated into a claw she used to unwrap, then pulled out the cork. She crossed to the table, filling an empty glass.

The realization penetrated too slowly and tasted of ash when it did.

"You did this," I said. My body vibrated with grief and rage. My fingers closed around the skull ring, still warm from Grim's hand.

She sipped the wine. "I really am sorry for your loss. I know what it's like to lose someone you thought you'd spend eternity with."

Unable to get myself off the ground, I looked up at her. "Why?"

Galina drank her wine, as if weighing her next words. "I know this all seems terrible right now, but I promise, you'll see. This is all for the best."

"Why?!" I screamed this time, tightening my grip around the ring until it bit into my flesh.

The rim paused at her lips as she regarded me with an inscrutable look. She set the wine glass back down on the table without drinking from it again.

"I am here to free you and this world from tyranny. I know you thought you loved him. That's what the blood bond does. It makes you believe you are connected in an eternal, meaningful way."

If I could have moved from my spot, I would have lunged at her and clawed her eyes out. Trapped in the moment, afraid if I took any action, I'd be trapped in this nightmare for all time.

"How dare you tell me I don't know what love is." My tone was low, dangerous.

"You know what love is?" she asked, her voice suddenly sharp. Her pupils turned to slits as her magic cat eyes shone green. "Love is waiting for thousands of years to be reunited after others decided your fate. I couldn't change the beginning, but I have the strength to say enough is enough and take control of the ending."

The C. S. Lewis quote. *You can't go back and change the beginning, but you can start where you are and change the ending.*

"I should have stopped them then," she said with a snarl

that reminded me of a panther.

"Who?" I asked, still not understanding. Not knowing what all this had been for.

"Osiris, and Grim," she said, suddenly stiff, turning ice cold. "They deigned my sister was too dangerous, so they put her down." A darkness came into her eyes. It was pain and resentment that had ages to stew and steep, pushing her to near madness. "They put my sister down like a dog and hid her from me. Because they knew if I could get to her, I would have woken her up and we would have been reunited." Sadness tinged her voice, but she chased it away with the demeanor of an icy predator.

"The Original," I said, putting it together. "The Original is your sister. The one who makes vampires."

"Sekhmet," she said, closing her eyes as if reveling in the name. "Sekhmet was so powerful. It's why they call them sekhors," she explained. "Children of Sekhmet. But everyone she bit turned into a sekhor. Osiris couldn't allow it. And Grim did his bidding. So he imprisoned and stashed her away. Qwynn was the only one Grim let past his defenses, which made her the perfect puppet. Or so I thought."

She sat down, crossing a slim, tanned leg over the other as if we were having a girl's chat over dinner. I still knelt on the floor. My nails now dug into the palms of my hands, cutting through flesh. Blood slickened the ring I held and slid between my fingers in red rivulets.

"I didn't count on her changing the plan and raising sekhors on her own while leaving my sister trapped in slumber." Galina cocked her head to the side. "I suppose I should have. She's every bit the treacherous bitch the others claim her to be. She nearly killed Grim with her need for power over him, though that wasn't her objective. Qwynn was no better than a child throwing a tantrum to get attention. When I heard the story of how she offered him the flesh of a mummified pharaoh, I put two and two together about Grim's secret weakness. One's secretum mortis often possesses a kind of irony to it. Even so, I had no intention of hurting him until it became absolutely necessary. But I'm tired of waiting, Vivien. Waiting for a new order and to be reunited with my other half."

"You are the treacherous bitch," I said in a ragged whisper. "You killed Seth."

She waved a hand and leaned back. "Oh please, like you care. He planned to destroy you and Grim, but not before playing with his food. I never wanted harm to come to Grim. Our interests and goals aligned many times over the years. But between him and my sister, there is no contest. Now with him gone, the spell hiding my sister..." She snapped her fingers. "Vanished."

I wasn't impressed. She uncrossed her leg and shifted in her seat. "Believe me, this couldn't be helped. I can go to my sister and together we will begin a revolution, a new age free of oppression."

"You killed the kid who worshiped you." I tucked Grim's ring into my dress, between my breasts.

Her brows furrowed. "The boy who jumped off the roof? That was unprecedented. I simply told him to keep his distance from you, so you couldn't scent me out the way you had Seth with his followers. You must believe I never intended for him to leap, but when you cornered him, it was all he could do."

She blamed me for his death. Disbelief finally cut through the paralyzing grief. Something boiled beneath the depths of my anguish. Anger. No, not anger. It was far more powerful, wild, practically savage. It was rage.

I dove at her, ready to tear her to pieces.

Galina batted me down like a cat. I hit the wall of wine and it exploded behind me. My ribs cracked under her blow, and glass bit into my back.

Despite the tremendous crash, no one would come. The room was soundproofed. Grim had assured me of that when he'd implied his more devilish plans for the evening.

"Please don't make me do that again," she requested with stern politeness. "I don't want to hurt you."

Galina had hit me as if I were no more than a plaything. No longer did I possess the extra strength and stamina of Grim's blood. Grim's divinity had all but disappeared from my system. It had evaporated along with his body. Galina's strength far surpassed my own, and some part of me recognized she'd gone easy on me. Ruby liquid dripped into my eyes. If I fought her, I wouldn't win.

But this wasn't about winning. This was about rage and grief.

I blurred to my feet, ready to charge her again.

Before I could take two steps, Galina grabbed me like I was nothing. First, she raised me over her head before she dropped me. My upper back collided with her knee, and my neck snapped violently. The white-hot pain was indescribable. The crack of my spine breaking in two places reverberated through me, leaving a ringing in my ears. Then she tossed me on the ground like a rag doll. I couldn't move my arms or legs. She'd paralyzed me.

I sat, slumped in a pile of broken glass. Head tilted at an awkward angle, I couldn't even move my neck. Everything inside me screamed with pain, and there would be no relief. My vision blurred from tears again. "You've fucking destroyed my life. Why not just kill me?"

"I've freed you," she said, clasping her hands together

and crouching down to my level. "Don't you see? Grim owned you. You couldn't be independent of him. I know you were fond of your captor, but it doesn't change the nature of the dynamic. Even he knew that. I saw the guilt and pain in his eyes when he looked at you last night. But now you can feed from anyone." She opened her arms as if the world were my oyster.

"I loved him."

"If you say so." She stood, brushing off my feelings as if they were nothing more than dead leaves. "But you are young. You'll find love again."

She turned to go when my phone buzzed in my purse across the room.

"You think you're so clever?" I said in a raspy voice, stopping her. "But at heart, you are still just a cat. A cat who played with its food too much before eating it. You think we didn't know it was you? You let your hand slip one too many times. I could have let it slide that there was a distinct trail of stink from the truck where we'd captured Seth, before he showed up dead. I even could have let that tuna smell wafting off that poor kid you directed to die, the same odor that lingers on your skin like stinky cat chow. But the Maine coon in his apartment? The one meant to drive anyone away? Did you really think I wouldn't guess it was one of your envoys? And then dragging Qwynn in to be an ally while secretly pumping her and everyone else for information. You gods may be powerful, but your hubris gives you away. And it's the exact reason I'll succeed in killing you."

Galina turned around, her face still a mask of cold pity. "Darling, even if you could come over here and bite me, I'd use the blood bond created to destroy you in an instant."

"There's more than one way to skin a cat," I grinned, a feral, terrifying smile of someone unhinged with violence and nothing left to lose. "Because while you've been here with me, extolling on how fucking great you think you are, I've taken something from *you*, Galina."

"And what have you taken from me?" She smirked, as if humoring a child.

"The Blade of Bane," I said. I may have been a broken doll on the floor, but I still sent her a vicious grin.

From the placid rise of her eyebrows, I could tell she didn't believe me.

"You hung it in plain sight in the chandelier bar." Galina owned the Martini Hotel. At the center of her hotel was a bar that resembled a chandelier, where massive swaths of crystals surrounded the patrons as they sipped overpriced drinks.

Her expression never changed, but it frosted over.

"That's right, you crazy bitch. You are just like Seth. Once I realized you gods are all the same, I located the Blade of Bane. You used a little magic to glamor the weapon, but someone found it anyway. And though I'll give you more credit than Seth, having many security systems set up on the sword, there is one thing you could never have counted on."

"And what's that?" I could tell she didn't quite believe me.

I punctuated each word. "Genetically. Engineered. Rabbits."

When she didn't respond or react, I said, "Why don't you go check my phone?"

She paused, as if considering the request, then crossed to my purse.

I continued to talk. "It's amazing what a couple of loose rabbits in a hotel can do. It causes quite a distraction. And then without your cameras, and everyone looking the wrong way, all one needs to do is walk up and pluck the sword from its hiding place."

As Galina regarded my phone, her pupils turned to slits again, glowing brighter green now. "You little…"

I knew she was seeing a picture of the Blade of Bane to confirm the heist had gone off as planned.

"Scamp?" I filled in for her. "Don't I know it." Despite my perky taunt, my tone was dark and dangerous.

My core shook with rage, grief, and satisfaction at having taken something from her, though it was nothing compared to what she'd stolen from me. If I could lunge at her, I'd tear her to pieces with my bare hands.

Maybe I wanted her to kill me. But I wouldn't go to the afterlife. My soul was crystallized, hardened into my body, immovable. It wouldn't reunite me with Grim. And if death could die, he was out of my reach. If she killed me, it would mean absolute extermination.

Galina set my phone on the table, so close yet so far, as I still couldn't move. But soon enough, I'd heal and be able to get to it. I'd be able to go after her.

She cleared the irritation from her face and said in a solemn tone, "The sword is of no consequence now. It won't be enough to stop us. I promised myself I'd let you live, give you time to see sense. See the role you could fill, how you could guide your fellow sekhors once my sister starts turning the humans. The sorrow you feel will morph and change until you realize this new world I'm about to shape is for you, Vivien."

Galina turned to go but looked back over her shoulder. "But if you get in my way, I won't hesitate to kill you."

Then she left me in a room of shattered glass, spilled wine, and my grief and deep hunger for revenge.

13

VIVIEN

Miranda's voice floated to me through a painful haze. "Honey, you've got to get out of bed."

Fingers stroked my hair, and the sob in my chest threatened to burst. I'd been somewhere between sleep and consciousness, for I didn't even know how long. My body sensed the sun had set and night availed, but it didn't matter. I didn't want to greet the day or the night. The only movement that didn't hurt was when I caressed Grim's skull ring.

The grief, and pain of my broken back, had made things hazy as I sat amongst the jagged glass pieces in a pool of wine. Galina must have told the waitstaff not to enter, because no one found me. After far too long, I realized I'd healed enough to move. My numb fingers wrapped around my phone as I called Timothy. I don't remember what I said, but he came for me. Wrapped me up and got me to the penthouse.

Wearing one of Grim's button-up shirts, I lay in our bed, holding the black satin sheets to my nose, wanting to be surrounded by Grim's scent. But with my vampiric senses, my anxiety grew as his smell dissolved away with every passing moment. Still, I clung to the ghost of him with a white-knuckled grip.

A shadow entered the room. "The new god of death has been chosen," Timothy said. His eyes were red-rimmed, and his normally perfect tousle of hair stuck out in all directions. His burgundy suit was wrinkled and unkempt.

"Death can't die," I said in a flat voice.

The fact he could was stupid. A ridiculous notion. Impossible. Grim was fucking with me. Any minute now, he'd pop out holding a cognac and sporting a wicked smile over the great prank he'd pulled. Then I'd punish him seven ways from Sunday and never let him leave this bed again.

But the god of death was a position, not a person. And Grim had been replaced.

"Who?" Miranda asked, straightening as if preparing herself.

"Me," a new voice answered. Fallon entered the room behind Timothy. Blue eye glowing fiercely, he looked like someone told him he'd been sentenced to life in prison.

"How do you know?" Miranda asked, never ceasing the strokes along my scalp.

Fallon rolled up a sleeve and clenched his hand into a fist, rotating his forearm toward us. Black ink swelled to the surface in the shape of the feather of Ma'at.

His face flickered into the death mask I'd only ever seen on Grim. My stomach lurched. Who knew I'd come to love the face of death? That seeing it on someone else would devestate me?

"I have the power over souls," Fallon informed us. His face softened. "And over these creatures." He waved a hand, and three reapers trotted into the room. Cupcake scampered in, pushing her way through the legs of the older reaper dogs. Her pink tongue lolled out like a tiny goof where the other jackals remained: stately sentries. I recognized Anead, Secnarf, and Idurt.

I hadn't seen hide nor tail of the reapers, or Cupcake, since Grim fragmented in my arms.

This time, the sob broke. An animalistic wail emerged from my mouth. The dogs immediately jumped on the bed and covered me in a dog pile. Several more followed in until I was buried in reaper dogs.

Fallon stepped out of the room to give us a moment, while Timothy crossed over to sit on the edge of the bed. One of the reapers, Ydnic, sat next to him. Timothy held a hesitant hand out, then finally smoothed the fur along the canine's face. Timothy's shoulders relaxed a fraction.

Though Miranda couldn't see the dogs, she didn't say a word. Just kept stroking my hair.

"We've been weighing hearts for thousands of centuries. Grim and I had been through wars, plagues, and all manner of tragedies. Our work has been important as the souls came and went, but Grim and I were a constant team."

I wasn't the only one who lost. Gently pushing the dog pile away, I crawled over to wrap my arms around Timothy from behind. Miranda lay her head against his shoulder, and we stayed there in a bundle of pain and solace. Cupcake nosed her way between us until she made it onto Timothy's lap. She looked up at Timothy's face and whined before nuzzling into him.

Miranda and I had an unspoken understanding. We knew loss. Her husband, my parents. But Timothy lived in a world where he didn't have to endure the absence of someone who'd lodged themselves into the place where your heart had been. Timothy, Thoth, was a powerful god.

He'd seen time erode land and people cross the threshold to the afterlife, but this rocked him.

We stayed like that for a time. Some of the tension left my body in the embrace. I'd never had friends like this, friends who would share in heavy emotions, and I didn't realize how much their mere presence would affect me.

Finally, Miranda stood up. "As much as I want to let you stay in bed to mourn, from what I understand, we have some bigger problems about to go down." Her tone was somehow gentle yet firm. "Now I didn't go on a heist with a couple of rabbits to steal an ancient, powerful weapon, only to leave it discarded." It was true. She hadn't let the sword out of her sight since she took possession of it.

The need for vengeance reignited its light, though the heaviness in my soul dulled it. A leaden ache that only Grim's arms wrapping around me would soothe. But the spark was enough to get me to my feet. I pulled on some shorts and walked out into the living room, where Fallon waited.

As if sensing the change in mood, the reaper dogs disappeared, until only Cupcake remained. I missed the pack already.

On a day like this, as a human, I'd end up in the bakery below my crappy apartment with one of those perfect cupcakes to fill the emptiness in my heart. Grim had offered once to get me a dozen, since I couldn't visit the Cupcakery when it operated during the day, but I politely declined. I explained there was an entire experience we'd miss out on. I always loved getting to pick out my pastry in the sunny shop. The entire place smelled of sugar and the glass case was always packed with fancy and whimsical desserts

But right now, not even a hundred of those cupcakes could fill the black hole inside my being.

Fallon sat hunched over, forearms resting on his knees, with a thousand-yard stare. He acted like he'd been given a death sentence. Yes, I recognized the irony of that statement.

"Where is she?" I asked, gathering my hair up into a ponytail. Cupcake trotted in beside me as if ready to do her best to help, though she was only a pup.

Fallon's gaze tilted up at me, not moving from his pensive repose. "She did as she said she would. The concealment spell and the wards disappeared once Grim did. Nothing kept Galina from sensing her sister, so she went directly to Sekhmet at the rest home, where Grim had hidden her. Then Galina woke her up. The Original needed to feed and turned everyone there into a sekhor."

"We have to stop them," Miranda said. "We have the Blade of Bane and between you and Timothy, you can take down Galina and Sekhmet while the numbers are still even."

"That's not exactly true," Bianca said, appearing from the library. Sadness hovered around her like a gauzy film, but she floated toward us in her usual elegance. "Galina has gone to great lengths to shake the chain, enough times and with enough force that many of the gods who seek change have immediately joined her ranks. They practically lined up. Sekhmet is turning humans in sekhors, and the gods are snatching the vampires right up, forcing or coercing some sekhors to drink of their blood. They've made blood bonds, which means there are far more of them than us."

Numbness spread through my body again as the nightmare continued to only worsen. I sat on the couch, curling up into a ball, my arms wrapped around my legs. Cupcake jumped up and settled on my feet.

Miranda sucked in a deep breath, as if preparing to say something unpleasant. "I hate to say this, but I'm going to say what everyone is thinking. Maybe Vivien should drink from Fallon? That way she can help you guys kick butt. Or, if nothing else, do it for her protection?"

Without Grim's supercharged blood, I was back to being a normal vampire. Galina immediately demonstrated how far I'd fallen sans my suped-up divine strength and stamina.

Fallon and I looked at each other. I knew my face mirrored the reluctance on his. Drinking from Grim had always been an incredibly intimate experience. If I drank Fallon's blood, it wouldn't only feel like a betrayal to Grim, it would also be like frenching my brother. Ick.

"I know, not ideal," Miranda said, reading the room. "But it makes logical sense."

"It makes a kind of sense," Bianca agreed with a grimace as her fingers dug into the back of a leather chair. Fallon shot her a look I couldn't decipher. Perhaps it was a surprise, or maybe disappointment?

I loved how Miranda tried to organize things into their rightful little boxes, but that wasn't how I operated. I followed my heart. Sure, it got me into some trouble, and it certainly didn't earn me any marks in intelligence, but it was my design. And I had to follow what was right for me.

"No," I shook my head. "I can't. I'd rather go back to drinking pig's blood." Every bit of me screamed in revolt against the idea. Drink something other than the nectar from the neck of the one I wanted and needed more than anything or anyone? I felt sick at the thought. But it was still better than jumping to the next willing god. I was a one-god girl.

Fallon's shoulders fell an inch and he let out a breath, as if relieved. He didn't want to enter a blood bond with me any more than I wanted to with him. Bianca turned her face down. Did she try to her hide her relief? If I weren't so weighed down, I might have been able to decipher what was going on with the two of them.

Timothy was on his feet in a moment, straightening his suit jacket as best he could. "I'll arrange for the blood." He seemed grateful for the task.

Miranda paced behind the couch where I stayed curled up. "So if we need to stop this new vampire uprising, we need to know why Grim was the only one who could stop the sekhors in the first place?"

Fallon got to his feet again and walked over to the windows. He tucked his hands in his pockets and gazed out over the city as if looking into the past. "Grim was a biased hammer, waiting to fall. He was the only god to never take a vampire in a blood bond, before you, that is. He viewed bonds as a liability, so when the other gods came and confirmed his prejudice, he did not hesitate to clean up house. And as wielder of souls, he was the most powerful."

Bianca rounded from behind the velvet chair to sit in it, her shoulders slumped forward in defeat.

Miranda paused her nervous gait. "Now you are the wielder of souls, so doesn't that make you the most powerful?" Miranda asked.

What would I do without her? Miranda asked the smartest damned questions.

Fallon sighed and put his back to the dancing lights. "Yes, but Grim also had thousands of years to learn how to wield it. While I have inherited his power, it is a bit like handing someone a sword and expecting they know how to use it. It takes time to achieve mastery."

"We don't have time," Timothy said, returning from the kitchen with his tablet to stand next to Bianca. His eyes didn't lift from the screen.

"Not to mention, none of us know how Grim defeated

Sekhmet in the first place," Bianca added quietly. "By continually creating sekhors, she became the head of the problem. And now that she's loose again, the damage will be monumental."

Miranda kept pressing for answers. "So where is Osiris? I heard he was big, bad, and scary and going to come down and spank anyone who was behind this conspiracy?"

Timothy looked up at that, fingers hovering over the pad. "It appears Osiris has decided not to interfere."

"It's just like him," Fallon said with a dark look and a shrug. "The mysterious absentee father whenever it suits him. No explanation given."

"Perhaps he fears facing those who oppose him," Bianca suggested.

"Don't be naïve, Bi," Fallon retorted in a biting tone, removing his hands from his pockets.

Bianca crossed her arms over her chest in a protective shield, but he continued to chastise her. "He's more powerful than all of us. Who knows what the fuck he is doing? Spending time on other planets, or wrapped up in a tiny atom, he has detached from our worldly problems except on occasion. Earth is a vacation property he doesn't bother visiting but wants to know it's being cared for in case he makes his return."

As everyone brainstormed, the creaky gears in my brain slowly revved up. The little men gathered for a meeting.

What's she doing, sir?

Jenkins, I think she is trying to get back into the game.

Sir, the damage inside the body is too extensive. The workers are scrambling around the broken shards of her heart, but there's not much to be done. If she thinks too hard, her entire brain might fall out. Or worse!

Dammit, Jenkins, this is where we earn our keep. Oil the

gears, push that button. If we don't get her up and running, she may shut down for good.

"There's something I still don't understand," I said. "How can death die?" I ran my fingers through my hair before leaning down to pet Cupcake's soft head. "Grim told me there were only two ways a god could die. If a vampire drank too much blood from a god, or by the Blade of Bane. Why didn't he warn me this could happen? He told me that Qwynn served him flesh of the dead before, but he never said she'd tried to poison him." Suddenly I was angry. How could he keep this from me? He knew how worried I'd been about the Blade of Bane. I'd been like a vampire possessed trying to secure that thing, and it didn't even matter in the end.

The irony smacked me in the face. If I hadn't been so obsessed about getting the Blade of Bane to keep Grim safe, I would have been there on time. I instantly knew something was wrong with the food with my vampiric senses. Grim couldn't have noticed the way it was prepared. I probably would have said something about it to stop him from eating it, and he'd still be alive. Fury and disbelief clamped around my throat.

Everyone stopped talking, but no one supplied an answer. The cogs in my brain churned faster.

"I'm serious," I said, standing up. "I've been trying to catch up on my mythology and I've read plenty about the gods who died before. Seth killed Osiris, but Grim brought him back. There have been other instances of a god dying and coming back to life. Why can't Grim? Where did he go? He didn't get eaten by Amit, he didn't go to the Afterlife. Did he cease to exist like I would?" That couldn't be right.

"No," Timothy answered in a quiet tone. "It's true. Grim's essence has not been destroyed. Indeed, the Blade of Bane annihilated Seth, and the same would happen if a vampire drained him. What happened to Grim is..." He shot a look at Bianca and Fallon as if to ask permission or warn them of what he was about to say. "She hit him with his secretum mortis."

"Is he secreting what?" I asked, straightening. Miranda and I exchanged a disgusted expression.

"Not secreting," Bianca corrected, with a wrinkle of her nose. "Secretum mortis. It's what we call our secret weakness. Each god has a weakness, usually but not always relevant to his or her power base. You've likely heard of this in reference to Achilles' heel. And I don't believe when Qwynn offered Grim she had intended to poison him. She simply wanted him to turn his back on what he deemed sacred in deference to her, and we all know how that turned out."

Galina had said that about Qwynn, but I still needed more information.

"But Timothy said his essence hasn't been destroyed." Hope sprung inside my chest with an almost violent jerk. "So Grim's alive in a way? Can we resurrect him like Osiris?"

No one answered. The air became thick with tension. The gods were on edge.

"She's right," Miranda said. "If we resurrect Mr. Scarapelli, he can take control of the situation before it gets out of hand."

"We can't do that," Bianca said, her voice small. Her eyes pleaded with me.

"It's out of the question." Even as Fallon said it, he rubbed his lips and looked at the corner of the room as if contemplating the idea.

Timothy put his tablet down on the coffee table to elaborate. "You must understand, resurrection is a...tricky process. Which is exactly why we have the rules we have."

"What rules?" Miranda asked.

"If Grim can be brought back, why the ever-loving fuck weasels are we standing around here with our thumbs up our butts?" I demanded.

"Should he return to this life, in human form," Timothy stressed, "it could be hundreds of years or more. And only he can decide that for himself."

"Why the fuck wouldn't he come back?" I knew my tone was biting. Maybe because of the guilt and recrimination I felt over losing my window to tell Grim I loved him.

Timothy shook his head. "Wherever Grim is, he is in his raw essence. He does not have memories or feelings like he used to. It's not that he didn't love you." His eyebrows furrowed with sympathy. "It's just that in the state he is in, there is no beginning or end. There is no memory or grounding or time. He could come back confused, volatile, violent."

Seeing my deep frown, Timothy went on. "Think of it as one of your cakes. If you don't let it bake, it will make a mess. We learned long ago that when we resurrected gods too soon, their powers would be unstable, ungrounded. They could be detrimental to society as well as themselves. Eventually, one day, far from now, he may be drawn to return to this earth, but we can't interfere with that."

"Bullshit," I shot back.

"We can't, Vivien," Bianca said in a firmer tone.

"Bi, think about it, though," Fallon said. "If we could find the cradle—"

"No," she cut him off, standing abruptly. "It's absolutely out of the question. The balance of the world could be thrown on its head with the premature emergence of a god. Grim will remain in repose until he is ready to return, and none of us shall interfere with that. End of conversation. I need to get back." With that, Bianca left, disappearing in the direction of the elevator.

After checking his tablet, when it vibrated, Timothy followed after her. "I need to fetch blood for Vivien." The doors closed on the two of them, leaving Fallon, Miranda, and me.

"Fallon?" I asked. I sensed the conflict in him.

He stared after Bianca with a pensive look. "She's right. We can't."

"No," I said, my fingers curling into fists. "You won't. There's a difference."

The god's head snapped toward me, anguish plain on his face.

"You think I want this? You think I want him to be gone? You think I want to be the god of the dead?" The death mask flickered. He stilled, closing his eyes as if trying to regain control. When they opened again, the blue one glowed. "I don't want the weight of this responsibility. I don't wish to spend my days judging souls, captive to a position I can never be free of. If there was a choice, I would find the cradle and raise Grim." Desperation edged along his voice. "But I have to face the reality of my fate. And you need to face yours. We have to carry on without Grim, and be prepared for things to get a lot worse before they get better."

Miranda folded her arms as if she was suddenly cold.

I didn't dare say the words out loud, but I couldn't see how things could get any worse.

14

VIVIEN

"We'll both feel better once we have a little caffeine." Miranda sat me down at Perkatory.

I said nothing. Grief vibrated through my being as my ass hit the hard chair. All I could think was I needed to get Grim back.

The thought of waiting a hundred years or more to see him again made my insides ache. But if I could be with him, I'd wait forever.

Raise hell in the meantime, of course, but I belonged with him as he did with me.

Still, my fingers curled into my palms, digging in against the arduous inching of time between me and him.

I understood now. Grim explained forever meant having that much more time to experience the pain. And I kept him hanging on that edge of uncertainty, straining to know the depths of my feelings. Did the moments crawl along like this for him in between my weak excuses that I needed more time? I'd been a coward. And I was disgusted with myself.

Miranda disappeared over to the café line, and I sat

there growing colder by the second. Timothy went to retrieve blood for me, but the thought of drinking blood, anyone else's blood, made me positively ill.

My arms curled into my stomach as I became a small ball in my seat.

I kept trying to remind myself Grim wasn't really dead. He was asleep in some place called the cradle? And no one was going to help me find the cradle, or Grim. They'd all said it was too dangerous, and that Grim would have to choose when and if he would return.

I knew in my heart that he would come back. Grim didn't want to go. We were forever, and if that meant waiting a hundred years until he rose again, so be it. I had faith that he would return and when he did, I'd tell him I love him. That I was sorry I couldn't say it until he'd gone.

I shut my eyes hard, willing myself to believe I could wait and trust like that.

The hairs along the back of my neck and arms rose, and my blood rushed faster.

Before I knew why, I stood up and turned around in time to see five vampires stride into the lobby. Their eyes were crimson, and they all suffered from fruit punch mouth. More than that, they were all showgirls, scantily clad in rhinestones, and decorated in big, brightly-colored feathers.

The one dressed in sapphire blue grabbed a doorman and sunk her teeth into his neck. Blood spurted as he cried out.

The rest of the vampires fanned out, grabbing people and biting as if they'd stumbled upon an all-you-can-eat buffet.

In a blink, I leapt over the foliage separating Perkatory from the lobby.

"Hey," I shouted at Sapphire. "Put Raphael down."

The doorman had already passed out, but I could still hear his heart thrumming faintly.

Sapphire's head reared up from her snack, staring at me with a strange, almost alien expression.

I recognized that look.

Being turned into a vampire didn't make a person evil, and what I saw in her eyes wasn't hunger. Someone was controlling her will. Whoever was on the other end, puppeteering these vampires, wanted to inflict pain. They wanted death and fear to permeate the hotel. They wanted to stomp on Grim's ashes, and the thought made me see red.

Over my undead body.

I punched Sapphire in the face, causing her to drop Raphael. Sapphire hissed like a pissed-off cat and lunged at me.

We rolled across the black marble floor, feathers and blood in our wake. I managed to roll on top, trapping her arms with my legs, and pounded into her until she went limp. When I stood, two thin, yet surprisingly strong, glitter-covered arms wrapped around my neck from behind. She couldn't suffocate me, but she could certainly break my neck. I couldn't afford to be incapacitated. Not like that. Not again.

Vampires didn't automatically turn into ninjas, but they did get an enormous boost in strength, speed, and regeneration. And it had been at least a day or two since I last fed, leaving me weaker than usual.

At the same time the vampire in white diamonds put increasingly dangerous pressure on my neck. I spotted Timothy across the lobby. He'd returned with a to-go cup of blood I could smell even from twenty yards.

The rest of the showgirls descended on him. Timothy swatted the first one away. Violet went flying, sliding into a group of agog, posh guests. She knocked them down like bowling pins. And he connected a foot into Emerald's gut, sending her to the ground. He stepped over her body with a look of distaste twisting his lips.

Miranda rushed to usher the guests away even as Violet jumped to her feet. I continued to wrestle with the one on my back. No matter which way I staggered and smashed her against the walls behind us, she wouldn't let go.

Sapphire's eyes snapped open like an automaton. She leapt to her feet, and at the sight of Timothy, she charged. He looked more annoyed than concerned. Timothy's eyes blazed with light, then he threw out his free hand, sending a bolt of power at Sapphire that resembled a black, flaming hieroglyph. Sapphire flew backward ten yards before hitting the ground and sliding across the marble floor. She didn't get back up.

Chaos didn't even begin to describe the scene. Too many feathers and fangs.

The fifth showgirl, Ruby, snuck up behind Timothy. Before I could shout a warning, Ruby threw a rope over Timothy. It glowed green as it tightened around him. His face paled, his eyes tightening as if he were in pain. His fingers stiffened on the cup and he lurched before stilling.

The glint of steel caught my eye and Miranda pulled out the Blade of Bane, raising it over Violet. Where the hell had she been keeping the blade? No way her hoo-ha could smuggle that length.

Then again, Vegas was a veritable pool of unique and disturbing talents.

I threw my head back, smashing Diamond's nose. She stumbled as I staggered forward, stretching an arm out. "No!" I cried. "Don't kill her."

Miranda looked at me. Violet used that moment to go

berserk, fangs out in fury. I blurred forward, connecting with Violet to keep her from sinking her teeth into my friend. But the vampire took Miranda by surprise. She jerked, and the blade sunk into Violet's chest. The vampire gasped, her eyes rolling back in pain as she went limp and fell to the floor.

"No," I whispered.

I didn't have time to stop to help Violet. Ruby and Emerald yanked Timothy along using the magic rope, Diamond assisting them. I ran straight at them, but Emerald crashed into me, intercepting.

"Let him go," a security guard yelled out with a slight spanish accent. Javier had arrived. He was Miranda's second in charge at the hotel, as he had been in the Army. Javier aimed his gun at Ruby even as she dragged Timothy along. He shot her, the bullet connecting with her chest. She jerked with his blow but didn't go down. Diamond tackled Javier to the floor.

Emerald was seriously pissing me off. Her fingers raked down my face, leaving bloody claw marks in their wake. Miranda came up behind Emerald and tried to pull her off me.

It was then I noticed Aaron barreling toward Ruby. Shit. If I weren't fighting off Emerald, I would have screamed at him to run. He was going to get himself killed.

Aaron threw a punch at Ruby. Her head cracked to the side, but it snapped right back. Aaron's eyes rounded.

Oh god. Oh no.

"Get out of here," Timothy yelled, even as he strained against the rope. Veins protruded along his throat and forehead. The magic rope prevented Timothy from moving.

Ruby didn't release the rope, but she grabbed Aaron by the neck, lifting him until his feet kicked in the air. He tried to pry her fingers away, but where he was one buff surfer bro, she was a power-infused, brainwashed vampire.

"Aaron," Timothy rasped.

Ruby's fangs disappeared into Aaron's neck as Timothy cried out. Power seethed around him but couldn't extend any farther out. The rope contained it somehow.

I needed to stop this.

"Cut him free," I said to Miranda. Catching my meaning, she raced to Timothy with the Blade of Bane and sliced the rope.

A silent boom rolled through the room like thunder. Emerald and I slammed into a wall. The gun went off. Diamond slumped over Javier.

After a beat, Javier staggered to his feet, blood pouring down his shoulder from his neck. Ruby tossed Aaron aside, redirecting her attention to the armed man.

Javier shot her twice, once in the stomach and once in the head. She reeled back into Timothy and they hit the floor.

Diamond and Emerald jerked into the air as if by some invisible force. Fallon had arrived. His usually mismatched eyes turned to sucking darkness, his arm outstretched. Then, with a flick of his wrist, they sailed through the open front doors, out into the night.

Freaking finally, the feather fiends were subdued. The idea of Sekhmet and Galina commanding an army of mindless vampires made me go cold.

Timothy lay underneath Ruby, blood pooling out around him. Aaron cried out, a stuttering mess, pushing the body off Timothy. Red coated his fingers as he searched Timothy's body for the wound.

Timothy's hands grabbed Aaron's, stealing them. Their

faces were impossibly close, as Aaron hovered over Timothy, his face wretched with emotion and fear.

"I'm fine," Timothy said in a quiet voice. "It's not mine."

Even my brain struggled to understand what had happened for a few seconds. Then I recognized the scent of the blood. It was the pig's blood from the cup meant for me.

Aaron's turquoise blue eyes searched Timothy's for another moment before he grabbed the back of Timothy's head, hoisting him up into a kiss. Timothy's dark eyes flew open a moment before closing again, surrendering to the passion, fear, and longing of Aaron's mouth.

My heart somersaulted in victory, despite coming so close to death. Miranda clutched the Blade of Bane once again and held up a shaky thumbs-up. I did the same back.

We won this one. But it had been closer than I liked.

Getting to my feet, I made my way over to Timothy and Aaron, who were standing now. Miranda jogged over to Javier. She helped him put pressure on his neck wound. Fallon made his way over to them and convinced her to step aside. Placing his hand on Javier's neck, the air crackled with energy. He was healing Javier.

"W-what the f-fuck was that?" Aaron asked, his eyes dark, hand gripped tight around Timothy's waist. Timothy dazed expression made it seem as though he was stuck in the last few minutes of Aaron kissing him and hadn't caught up to real time. I figured I'd take this one and let him revel in la-la land for a little longer.

"Showgirls on drugs. PCP is a hell of a drug."

Aaron's expression flattened. He seemed displeased, like I was treating him like an idiot.

"What?" I shrugged. "You've seen the movie *Showgirls*. Competition is fierce. It takes a lot of gusto to fan those feathers and get those high kicks up."

Miranda walked over to our little group, her mouth a slash of discontent. "I sent Javier home. The other two vampires are gone. They must have made a run for it."

"I-I need to make a call," Timothy said, stuttering himself. I wasn't sure what shook him more. Almost being taken, or the kiss Aaron laid on him. I'd bet on the latter.

"Same," Miranda said, her expression sobering. I knew what she was thinking.

"Galina wouldn't go after Jamal," I said.

"You don't know that," she said, her mouth thinning with stress. She adjusted her grip on the Blade of Bane and ran. Javier followed her.

A gurgling sound caught my attention. I ran over to Violet. She wasn't healing. Miranda used the blade and apparently it could slice and dice a vampire the same way.

"What happened?" the showgirl asked. Her dark eyes were wild with fear. Her deep brown skin turned ashen as the wound in her stomach first grayed, then blackened.

Whatever hold Galina had on her had disappeared. I cradled the vampire's head. "It's okay, your healing will kick in soon. You'll be okay," I insisted.

"She bit me." The showgirl's eyes rolled with fear, like a spooked horse. "She bit all of us and drank...and then she took my mind. I couldn't get out, trapped inside. I hurt people." She gasped as if realizing the horror of what happened to her.

"It's okay," I said, pulling her heavy headdress off and smoothing back her frizzing hair. "It's not your fault."

The memory of being controlled caused a lump to form in my throat. The powerlessness as someone made me do things I never wanted. It was a violation, being forced like that.

Big, fat tears rolled down her face. "I didn't mean to. I

didn't mean—" Her words cut off as her eyes emptied of expression. Then her body turned to ash, disappearing into my arms.

I cried out in anguish. She didn't deserve that. No one deserved to be controlled and used like that. I wished I knew her name.

Aaron pulled me away. I buried my face in his chest, a blubbering mess. He smelled like tropical fruits and suntan lotion. A comforting hand ran up and down my back, never saying a word, or asking a question, though he had to be in shock from what he'd just witnessed.

I pulled away from his embrace when I felt someone approach. Fallon. Timothy trailed behind him, looking like he wanted to say something to Aaron, but I couldn't imagine he'd know what to say about this supernatural mess.

"Could you have healed her?" I asked Fallon, already knowing the answer.

"I can only heal humans," he said. "And even I cannot reverse the effects of the Blade of Bane."

Hot tears fell down my face, and I angrily wiped at them with the heel of my palms. "She was innocent. She didn't ask to be made into a vampire. This girl was used, then thrown away."

Fallon didn't say anything, and I appreciated that.

"I need some air," I mumbled, unable to stay in the spot where the vampire had expired. In moments, the three men followed me outside and into the warm night. Cars typically pulled up, picking up and dropping people off for their stay, but it was eerily quiet out here.

"The vampires were attempting to take me," Timothy said to Fallon.

"I know," Fallon said. I noticed a darkness in his eyes that hadn't been there before. "They got Bianca."

"What?" I asked.

He went on. "Galina is imprisoning anyone who opposes her. She figures if she can throw us into a deep, dark pit, by the time she lets us out, things will be so drastically different we will have to accept the new world order."

"They came for you too?" I asked.

Fallon nodded. "Yes. I got away." A lone gray feather drifted to the ground. The god had sprouted his wings to fly the hell out of there.

My body suddenly felt seized, compelled by an ancient force. Tribal drums pounded in my ears, a need to walk toward that power overwhelming me.

A hand gripped my arm and yanked me back. Timothy.

I blinked and off in the distance, I spotted two figures standing at the far end of the hotel grounds. I recognized Galina's sleek figure, and a slim, petite woman with the same raven hair stood next to her. Even from here, I could see her eyes glowing red.

Sekhmet. The Original vampire goddess.

15

VIVIEN

"Who—wh—what is that?" Aaron stuttered.

"Aaron, go back inside," Timothy said in a stern, commanding tone. But I could hear the fear underlining his words.

Aaron only squared off his stance.

Idiot.

No wonder I liked him.

Galina strode forward, gliding as if on a supernatural conveyor belt until she stood on the opposite end of the drop-off lanes for the hotel. Sekhmet blurred to Galina's side so fast that I missed the movement altogether.

I'd seen Sekhmet when she'd been in her deep sleep at the long-term care facility. In that bed, the goddess seemed so frail and young. Even now she appeared far younger than Galina, but I felt the thrum of her ancient power all around me.

Something was off in her blood-red eyes. As if she were closer to a primal animal than the sophisticated, cultured gods that stood at the ready on either side of the road. The glint in her eye reminded me of the occasional psychopath

I'd had to track down as a bounty hunter. Not evil, but disassociated with any and all humanity in themselves. I'd learned those were the most dangerous people to capture.

Galina reached over to stroke her sister's hair. Something about Galina had relaxed. She'd been waiting for eons to be reunited with her sister, and now that she'd done so, some layer of protection had fallen away. I felt like I was seeing the goddess for the first time. The mystery gave way to deep, tender love. But it didn't make her weak. No, it made her far more dangerous than ever before.

Another joined them, though he stayed back. A tall, lanky god with bleach blond hair. Tattoos peeked out from under his white clothes, on the backs of his hands and up his throat.

Idris.

He looked every bit the sexy front man of a band that could melt the panties right off their fans. I'd learned his power was music based, and his fanbase might even rival Grim's.

The demigod had once disarmed me with his mischievous grin and charm before trying to trick me into breaking my blood bond with Grim so he could control me.

"What's your skin in this game?" I asked.

A wry smile tugged at one side of his lips that didn't reach his eyes. "My mother is immortal but not a god. I don't give a flying fuck if the rest view me as trash for being a demigod." His expression darkened. "But I won't allow those in power to treat my mother like a second-class citizen. Osiris and all the others couldn't care less what my father does to her, but I do. I haven't had the influence to stop him, but you bet your fucking ass I do now." He smiled down at Sekhmet's far shorter stature, as if she was the key to all his problems.

Though he stood on the opposite side, I finally understood why he wanted power. It surprised me that his motivation was so sentimental. To protect his mom. My first instinct had been that he had a good heart, and then he double-crossed me. Now I couldn't say I disagreed with his motivations, but his tactics sucked.

If Idris had asked Grim for help, he would have done it in a heartbeat. But Grim was gone, and the gleam in his icy blue eyes told me there was no changing his mind now.

"I'm going to need you two to come with me," Galina said in a lazy tone, referring to Timothy and Fallon. Despite her cavalier appearance, I knew she was ready to throw down any second.

"You know he must be allowed to judge the souls, or chaos will rock this world," Timothy said.

"Chaos is not my concern," Galina answered. "But making sure no one interferes with this...transition is vital."

"Cripes, you really are just like a spoiled little kitty," I said, unable to keep my mouth shut.

I wanted to lunge at Galina. Claw her eyes, pummel her into a bloody pulp, make her pay for what she took from me. If Grim were here, he'd sweep the floor with her ass. His absence stabbed through my heart.

Even though Galina could swat me like a fly, it was Sekhmet's burning red eyes that kept me rooted to the spot.

I'd never been the smartest person or vampire, but this time I knew to my bones if I tangled with Sekhmet I would not win. I could feel her beckon me, and I had to push her from my mind. Once, I'd joked to Grim, asking if I should call her Mommy. But now, I felt the blood tie between us. Stronger than that between even Grim and me.

Galina's eyes narrowed at me, her pupils turning to slits. They were lucky Miranda was nowhere near with the

Blade of Bane right now. But they'd suffer the barbs of my tongue. "All the drama, all the subterfuge. You want to push a glass off a countertop just to see it smash into the floor. Poor, bored little kitty."

Fallon took advantage of my distraction and launched at Galina, fist pulled back, ready to slam into her sour-cat face.

In a second, Fallon skidded across the pavement as if hit by a cannonball. Sekhmet hovering over him, her tiny hand wrapped around his throat. An animalistic growl emanated from her chest. Then a vampire blurred to her side, then another, and another, three more, then suddenly twenty vampires were upon Fallon. Their expressions bore the blank look I'd just seen on the showgirls. Sekhmet had complete control over their minds. They appeared to be a mixture of tourists, card dealers, and even an Elvis impersonator.

I would have laughed if Fallon weren't getting his ass completely kicked. They swarmed him.

"I almost forgot to thank you, Vivien," Galina said casually. "If it weren't for you, I never would have known to call upon Idris for help, but he's been quite useful."

Dick pickles. I had been the one to tell her Idris took a shot at me to try to get some power. Why he wanted a leg up so badly, I didn't know.

Idris strode forward, his face a determined mask as he made a beeline toward Timothy. He intended to take my friend prisoner.

My muscles tensed. I knew I couldn't even tangle with a demigod without Grim's blood, but I readied myself to protect Timothy.

Aaron stepped in front of Timothy in a protective stance, having zero idea he was the least likely to survive a dog fight between immortals.

Before Idris made it halfway across the drop-off lane, someone darted in his path. A dark blur. Idris reared back. Qwynn's midnight hair was pulled into a long, full braid that reached past her shapely ass. The golden one-piece she wore dipped down past her cleavage to just above her navel, giving a healthy view of either side of her generous breasts.

Judging by the way Idris appraised her from head to toe, he was as surprised as he was aroused by her appearance. She squared off, shooting him with a spiteful stare, though he almost had a foot of height on her.

"You killed him." Qwynn's normally aloof voice shook with rage as she turned her attention to Galina. "You used me for information, then killed the only one I ever loved."

Hey. That's my line. I frowned.

"Don't be ridiculous, you've never loved anyone other than yourself," Galina said with a dismissive wave. I couldn't help but agree with Galina. Though I imagined it had been the closest Qwynn had come to real love.

Idris continued to eye Qwynn as if she were a wet dream come to life. He even adjusted himself in his pants. For blood bags' sake...

Qwynn didn't acknowledge his lascivious interest.

"Maybe I'm not the brainless pawn you think me to be, Galina," Qwynn said. With that, she raised her hands, purple magic lighting up in her palms. Idris threw his own hands up at the last second, his icy blue meeting her violent streak of purple.

The air sizzled and crackled as a burning sensation pressed against my skin from being too close to the battle.

If someone had told me Qwynn would put herself between us and him, I wouldn't have believed it, but Qwynn and Idris warred with their powers.

The vampires continued their onslaught on Fallon,

making sure he couldn't get back up. Sekhmet stepped away slowly, appraising her handiwork in keeping Fallon down.

How could there be this many vampires already? Up until last night, it had been only me, but now I was looking at fifteen vampires. Everyone she bit turned into a vampire.

I could sense the satisfaction Sekhmet felt, watching them attack Fallon. I read the praise in her eyes as her children did her bidding.

I couldn't stand it any longer. Fallon needed help. But when I started forward, Timothy's surprisingly strong grip held me back.

Another dark cannonball smashed into the vampires, sending them flying away from Fallon. Marcella helped Fallon up, then pushed him in our direction. Dark brown skin with hair as glossy as the black feathers along her dress. Marcella's eyes turned to dark fire. Her figure was five times as generous and half as tall as Galina's, but her feminine ferocity overwhelmed me. I'd once believed the goddess hated me, but she had saved me from Idris.

I caught Fallon as he wavered on his feet. His face was smashed bloody, and his right arm dangled, useless at his side.

"I thought you'd be on my side," Galina said to Marcella, a sneer curling her lip. "Grim murdered your sekhor. Your blood-bound love."

"My heart may be dead, but that doesn't mean I'll tolerate nasty, manipulative bitches like you," Marcella shot back.

Sekhmet didn't wait any longer. Throwing herself at Marcella; they disappeared in a flurry of fists. Idris slowly gained ground over Qwynn. Covered in a sheen of sweat, she gritted her teeth, trying to push back.

The odds were stacked against us. Qwynn and Marcella

would not win, and they knew it. They were going to be taken captive. But Qwynn and Marcella were queens willing to sacrifice themselves to save the king. The god of the dead. As long as the powerhouse of souls survived, there was a chance the odds could be evened.

"We need to get to safety, now." Timothy strained the words. We grabbed Fallon and retreated into Sinopolis.

With a quick, apologetic glance at Aaron, Timothy closed his eyes and tilted his chin up toward the doors.

A glowing orb appeared over his head. I'd seen this once before. Close-up, I could see the magic whirling inside it. When he shot his hands out, a rush of luminous glyphs emerged from them. They beamed out through the doors in a constant stream. The chain of the glyphs layered along the bottom of the door, slowly building in chains until lines of magic covered the entrance. He was barricading the entire hotel.

Aaron stared at Timothy in open awe. I couldn't tell if his underlying feeling was shock, fear, or if maybe he was just deeply impressed.

When he'd finished, Timothy loosened his tie. Blood still stained his suit and dotted his cheek. "They won't be able to get in now," he said, slightly out of breath.

"Are w-we trapped in here?" Aaron asked, frowning.

"No, people can come and go, but no immortal may enter or exit," Timothy said, though I saw the flash of hurt on his face. "But it's not safe for you out there."

I couldn't deal with their lovers' tiff right now. I turned to Fallon, who'd found a nice wall to rest against. "You can't stop Galina and you can't stop Sekhmet."

He shook his head. "Like I said, I am too new to this power. Learning to wield the power of souls is far more complicated and painstaking than you can imagine. Grim had millennia to hone it, and I don't know how he took down Sekhmet all those years ago." Fallon raked a hand over his face. "I've had the power for barely two days. I'm still learning how to judge a soul without either slicing them in two or sending them to the wrong place. I've no time for this war when all my attention must go to sorting the dead."

"Then we agree," I said. "We need Grim."

He looked up at me, surprise on his bruised face.

Our group went silent. I'd give them a minute. I'd give them two. But not three. It was the only way.

"We need Grim," I repeated. "He's the only one who can stop Galina and Sekhmet."

"We need Grim," Fallon finally agreed, his shoulders sagging.

Timothy started, "But Bianca said if we try to bring him back, it could mean upsetting the balance of the world."

"They took Bianca." Anger rang in Fallon's voice as it whipped about in his eyes. Standing with renewed strength, he said, "If her foresight was as good as she believes it to be, she would have seen that coming. But now she needs to be saved too. And I can't storm into Galina and Sekhmet's territory and get her back." His hands curled into fists.

"And I'm pretty sure the balance is backflipping already," I said.

"It's forbidden," Timothy said more quietly, as if contemplating what we were about to do. "Osiris would send us to the pits of hell."

"Fuck that," I said. "If we don't do something now, it's going to turn into hell on earth. I'm not asking permission anymore. I only need you to point me in the right direction."

16

VIVIEN

Fallon and Timothy crowded in next to me in the elevator. A bleak determination set about both gods' shoulders.

Aaron stayed behind, and I didn't know if he'd be there when we got back. I hoped he would be but finding Grim mattered more. Not just to me, but to the world. If I were being honest, Grim was my world, so it was one and the same.

I expected Timothy to hit the black button leading down to the antechamber where they judged souls. Instead, he waved his hand over the panel and a new button surfaced as if magic had hidden it.

"Are we sure about this?" Timothy asked Fallon.

Fallon pressed the button by way of answer. The elevator glided down.

"So you're telling me there is something below the hotel other than a secret chamber for judging and sorting souls?" A dry laugh escaped my throat. "What would you keep below that?"

The men exchanged a look that did nothing to calm the nervous ponies galloping in my guts.

The air was heavy with secrets and danger. If a couple of gods were acting like this, I should be peeing myself in fear.

Seriously, what could make them so jumpy? With Galina and Sekhmet out and about, whatever we were about to face couldn't be worse than them.

Though I didn't need to breathe, tension clouded the small space until I gasped for the fresh air when the doors slid open. Both Timothy and Fallon paused. I waited for them to go first.

We entered a narrow section of concrete floor and walls that gave us the perfect view of the massive barred cage. I immediately flashed back to my school trips to the zoo. It reminded me of the enclosure for big cats.

Cold permeated through my bones. Or maybe I needed to feed. A couple of beat-up steel chairs were nearby so someone could more comfortably sit and chat with whatever animal lay behind the bars. Except the lights were off inside the wall-to-ceiling cage, making it impossible to tell how deep the enclosure was.

"What the hell is this?" I whispered. And what the hell would Grim and Timothy keep below the antechamber holding a soul-eating crocodile? A shiver zipped down my spine as I realized I didn't really want to know.

"Don't get too close," Timothy murmured.

"Roger that," I said, my arm too stiff to salute.

Timothy crossed over to a control panel against the side wall and pressed some buttons. The lights turned red for a moment before turning back to soft white.

"What's that for?" I asked.

"So he knows he has visitors," Timothy said.

"He, who?" I really wanted to be anywhere else but in this weird half zoo, half dungeon.

Except in the clutches of Galina and Sekhmet, so I kept my shoes rooted to the spot.

If this was the way to get Grim back, I'd jump in with whatever lurked inside.

A door opened farther inside the cage. Light spilled in from the other side, backlighting the figure as he entered. It was a man. He sauntered forward with a slow, prowling gait. His feet were bare. The jeans he wore rode low on his hips, framing the deep V of muscles there. The denim was torn up as if a wolverine had raked its claws across them. Scars crisscrossed over his exposed muscled chest, some old and faded, while others were new and bright red. Had an animal done that to him? Muscular, but without the bulk, I could tell by looking at him that his body was honed for speed and violence.

The moment I set eyes on him, I recognized the power of a god, but something was off about him. Energy sizzled, raw, and untamed. My senses screamed at me to get the peanut butter fudge out of here.

But his face. His face looked as though it had been carved by angels. It was almost painful to look at him. It drew me in, like a lasso thrown around my gut that was being jerked in his direction. Under those perfect features loomed a wickedness in his eyes that promised pleasure and decimation in equal measure.

I remembered meeting Grim and the instant death wish that struck me with a physical blow. This felt similar, yet different. Grim's silky darkness was the polar opposite to the burning sun across from me.

"You rang?" he drawled. Resentment and boredom were etched on his heavenly face, reminding me of a teenager. A teenager with high cheekbones, a sharp gaze, and cut, lean muscle. Tousled hair fell into his keen eyes.

"Xander," Timothy said, uncertainty lacing his tone. "We need your help."

His harsh laugh first came out as a bark, then it rose into an unhinged cackle. The sound reminded me of a hyena.

As if knowing the unsettling effect he had, Xander turned his gaze onto me. A cold spark in his ocean blue eyes sent tiny claws raking down my spine.

I'd seen and felt Grim exude and wield tremendous power, but standing in the same vicinity as this guy felt as though I were next to a nuclear reactor.

"Who's this?" He continued to saunter forward in a wide, lazy arc. Though the bars separated us, he was stalking me.

"Grim has perished and returned to the cradle," Fallon said, forgoing introductions and cutting to the chase. "We need to resurrect him."

The hyena laughter echoed through the room again, pitchy and unsteady. Madness flared in his eyes with white-hot sparks.

I took an unconscious step back.

"You want to dig him up?" Xander asked, cocking his head. He'd stopped on the other side of the cage. He gripped the bars and stuck his face between them as if trying to press his face through. His words came quick, lurching over each other in an unsteady rhythm. "You want to dig, dig him up, pull the dirt off his grave. Rip the wrappings off his mummy." Another insane laugh echoed through the room.

"It's a bad day," Timothy said to Fallon. "We won't get anything from him when he's like this."

"What happened to him?" I took a step forward.

Xander stilled on the other side of the bars, watching me

with unerring focus. Under all that crazy was a painfully handsome god, and deeper under that was persistent, permanent pain. I recognized that pain. After living in a glass house as a child for so long, I'd gone a little crazy myself.

"He is a god, like us," Timothy said. I could tell he was trying to move the conversation away from my questions.

"Not like us," Fallon said. "He's broken."

Xander reared back with a snarl, backing up in the darkness of his cell.

Timothy shot Fallon a stern look. "He's the only one who can help us find the cradle."

"What is this cradle?" I asked. I was fairly certain it wasn't like a baby's cradle we were looking for. That would just be plain weird.

Xander spoke, nearing the bars again. "The cradle. The cradle of life." He looked down and away, shaking his head and muttering words. His fingers flexed as if he were trying to get a grip on himself. With a calming breath, he relaxed them and straightened.

Some new awareness had entered his eyes. I faced an entirely different man now. He used the moment to appraise me from my head to my toes. Though I wore Grim's button-down shirt and a pair of jeans and my ass-kicking boots, he made me feel as though I were stripped down to my cherry red panties. Then a positively wicked smile curved on his face. "You smell like leather and sugar, firecracker."

I didn't know what pissed me off more. That he referred to my scent the way Grim had, or the nickname.

"Well, you look like psycho and crazy had a baby, buttercup," I shot back.

"Oh." He mock winced. "Firecracker has some bite. Want to drop those fangs for me, love?"

I snapped, launching myself at the bars. "You want a piece of me?" I yelled.

My threshold for bullshit broke, and I was more than ready to take it out on someone. And he practically begged for it. I'd been smart enough for one day. My need for Grim howled like a raging animal.

If he were here, he'd put a calming hand on me and step in between us. Not because I couldn't handle the situation. No, it's because we balanced each other. I'd had to do the same for him in the past. He'd trust me to take the lead when he was blinded by emotion. We both couldn't be wrecking balls, but right now he wasn't here to stop me. It only fueled the raging fire in me.

Fallon caught me in his arms. "Nuh-uh, don't go any closer." I kicked the air as he carried me back several feet. He only set me down when I calmed.

Xander's dark chuckle filled the room. This time, it didn't turn into a heckling screech.

"So big daddy death is gone. And you want my help," Xander drawled again. He walked over to the wall to lean a shoulder against it. He examined his cuticles.

"But what is the cradle?" I asked, frustrated they still hadn't told me everything.

"The cradle of life," he said. "I already said that. Weren't you listening? Or are you just a pretty fangbanger?"

Timothy caught my eye and gave a quick shake of his head. Xander was deliberately trying to get under my skin. I hated that it was working.

I clicked my teeth shut and crossed my arms.

"Ah, she can listen," Xander mocked. "The cradle of life. It has existed since before time itself. Then just before the first tick of the clock, the cradle spawned"—he looked back and forth between Fallon and Timothy while opening his arms—"us."

I wanted to smack that smug smile off his perfect face.

"We need to resurrect Grim," Timothy repeated.

His eyebrows shot up, and some of his bravado hardened. "You're serious."

"We need him," I said.

All of his charisma evaporated in a moment, leaving behind an uncaring, cold immortal. He pushed away from the wall and paced in front of the bars. "You need him, firecracker? You want to go reaching into the bowels of the earth and pull out a god? And here I thought I was the crazy one."

"It's true, Xander," Timothy said quietly.

His head jerked to regard Timothy. His hard stare was met with Timothy's calm.

"Is it worth the price?" Xander sneered.

Though I saw nothing, I felt the oppressive weight of power puff up around him, filling the space. It was too big, too heavy, too...intense.

"It is," I said without hesitating. Xander regarded me again with scrutiny that made my skin break out in goose pimples.

Finally, he grabbed the bars overhead, arm and chest muscles flexing. "Why don't you come closer to ol' Xander?"

"No," Fallon warned.

Xander didn't break his stare with me. "Don't you want to know how to retrieve big bad daddy death?"

I stepped forward.

"Vivien," Timothy said in warning.

Xander's mouth curved up in a smile. Then his face contorted, and he doubled over, backing up, groaning in pain. The groan morphed into that cackling laugh. Fur sprouted on his arms and chest as his muscles swelled. There he remained, half-shifted between a man's shape and his god-likeness in a terrifying form. Fangs dripped with saliva as his wild, psychotic yet perfectly human eyes blazed at me. I could see the pain written in them as plainly as if it had been done so in blood.

He roared so loud we all clapped our hands over our ears. Timothy returned to the control panel and slammed a button. Mist sprayed from the ceiling inside the cage. It clouded around the half man, half beast until I could only see an outline of his figure. The shadow shrunk back to that of a man's and as the cloud dissipated, Xander stood there heaving. Hair damp and body slickened with sweat and whatever had just been sprayed, making his human muscles glisten.

For a moment, I thought I caught a flicker of sadness in his eyes, but he shut them tight.

"Do you love him?" Xander asked, without looking at me. His voice lacked the previous teasing tone. He almost asked as if he were curious or envious of something he could never have.

I didn't respond. My fingers found the skull ring in my pocket, and the pain of saying it too late lanced through me for the thousandth time. When I said the words, they sure as hell would not be to the wrong god. Grim deserved to hear them first.

"What is the cost?" I asked instead.

He went back to inspecting his cuticles. "Once upon a time, we revived gods soon after their essence returned to the cradle of life. But we return in unsteady forms, too powerful, too out of control. Like a supernova. In the cradle, we are pure untethered energy and returning too early makes us...crazy." Lightning arced from his eyes. "It's why we are forbidden to revive anyone anymore. We fought terrible, monstrous gods, some unable to manage their god-likeness."

"Who resurrected you?" I asked.

His face emptied of emotion, the temperature cooling several degrees.

"That's what's wrong with you, isn't it?" I pressed.

"That's enough, Vivien," Timothy said, cautioning me from asking too many questions.

He was right. I wasn't here for some random basement beast's back story. I was here to find my way to Grim.

"The cradle of life constantly moves and shifts location but I know where it is," Xander revealed rather suddenly. "I always know where it is..."

Anticipation zinged through me. I could get him. I could revive Grim and tell him that I loved him.

"But," he started before words tripped off his tongue as the crazy returned. "But but but, you can't get in without divine assistance. Not even these two fools could find the doorway."

My hope deflated like a blowup doll slamming against a safety pin.

"But I can help you," Xander whispered. Ocean eyes, now solemn, I felt both repelled and drawn to him. Power stroked the skin along my face and wrapped around me, drawing me closer, but his eyes still gleamed with madness. He staggered forward, holding onto the bars while his face rested against them.

I walked toward him, not wanting to miss a word of how to bring Grim back.

"All you have to do"—his gaze dropped to my lips— "is kiss me."

Someone else might have asked why. A smarter vampire

might have asked if there was a catch. But my gut tugged on me, leading me with the promise of getting Grim back. Before Fallon or Timothy could protest, I leaned through the bars, planting a kiss on the god's beautiful, terrifying face.

I barely registered the pressure of our lips before I vaulted back. Suddenly I was flying. Across the city, past Nevada, careening over oceans until hot sand sparkled up at me, my soul shooting toward the one magnetic point. The Giza pyramid. I slammed into stone steps, diving deep into the caverns of the pyramid until I was inside the great structure. I flew toward a wall with a painting of Anubis. I disappeared through it and found myself in an untouched chamber. No mortal had ever been inside in the doorless alcove. In the center lay a massive pool of golden light. It swirled with divine power that made me want to cry tears of joy. It reminded me of the feeling when I drank Grim's blood. Like I understood the entire universe.

Xander whispered into my ear. I didn't recognize the words, but they etched their way into my mind. He'd given me something. Like a map, or a key, I couldn't be sure, but it pulsated at the back of my brain, just out of reach from my consciousness.

My back slammed against a hard surface. I blinked, finding myself on the ground in the basement once again, staring up at the ceiling with Timothy and Fallon hovering over either side with twin looks of concern.

Holy out-of-body experience. I felt like I'd flown across the world just now.

"Well well well, firecracker," Xander muttered from the cage, even as Timothy and Fallon helped me to my feet.

"I know where to go," I said, turning and heading straight for the elevator without waiting for another damn thing. Timothy and Fallon tried to keep up chasing after me.

Xander yelled out the last words. "I hope he remembers you, firecracker. I hope he doesn't tear you to pieces. I hope he doesn't rip the world apart." Then he let out a cruel, dark laugh that soon dissolved into uncontrollable cackles.

His words floated behind me. I had all I needed.

I'm coming, Grim.

17

VIVIEN

Once we returned to the lobby of Sinopolis, Aaron pushed himself off from the wall, walking over to me. "C-can someone please explain what the f-fuck is h-happening?"

He'd played it cool until now. But I didn't blame him for having a limit. He'd witnessed vampires, gods clashing, and his crush forming a protective barrier of magical glyphs around Sinopolis to prevent immortals from going in or out.

I wanted to open my big mouth and tell him everything, but my eyes landed on Timothy. He was the one who should get Aaron up to speed.

Fallon stepped forward, his blue eye glowing. "Shall I?" He intended to wipe Aaron's memory.

"No." Timothy threw a hand out to stop him. "Wait." I could see the war inside him as he regarded Aaron, trying to decide whether to allow him in the fold or allow Fallon to erase his memories. Timothy was about the organization, keeping things tidy and in order, and he was calculating the mess he'd make if he allowed Aaron in.

Aaron met Timothy with an unfaltering stare that said, *I can handle whatever you throw at me, just try it.*

The urge to back up was overwhelming, but it would break the moment.

"It's not safe here," Timothy finally said. "And you'll need an escort to Egypt." That last bit, he said to me.

"Good idea," I said.

"Is it, though?" Fallon mumbled.

Fallon and Timothy needed to stay here. With Timothy's magical barricade, it was the safest place for them right now, with Galina and Sekhmet hunting them down.

Galina all but said she'd give me a chance to change my mind and embrace her new world. Without Grim's blood, I wasn't a threat anymore. But the minute Timothy or Fallon stepped outside, I'd bet my left boob she'd be all over them.

I turned toward Aaron and in one breath, let it all spill out. "Gods live among us. Most are right here in Vegas, including these two." I pointed at Timothy and Fallon. "A really badass god just woke up, and she's making vampires and controlling them. If we don't stop the vampire goddess and her biatch of a sister, they are going to enslave anyone who opposes them and keep turning humans into vampires against their will. Only Grim can stop this vampire goddess because he's done it before, and I'm leaving to resurrect him from the cradle of life in Egypt. You in or out?"

At first, Aaron's expression flattened as if we'd told him a bad joke. A beat, and then he looked back to where we fought the blood-sucking Vegas showgirls and did some hard calculations.

Finally, he said, "I n-need to know more, but I'm in."

I squeezed his shoulder, before turning to Timothy, who'd gone still as a statue. It seemed to be a god's reflex to impersonate stone anytime they experienced strong emotions. Grim had the same habit.

God, how I missed him. The ache inside me continued to yawn out, threatening to consume me. I needed those steady arms, and his warm amber eyes. He never held back with me in a fight or between the sheets. Even being in the same room as him created a sense of belonging I never knew possible. But without him, the air around me itched and grated.

I was done. He was coming home if I had to drag him out of that cradle by his toes.

I turned to Timothy. "How can I get out if you warded the hotel to keep any immortals from going in or out?"

He nodded. "I can open a doorway for you out the back. I already contacted the pilot for our private jet and they are standing by."

"Then the only question left is, what's the in-flight meal?"

FLYING from Vegas to Egypt on the best of days wasn't less than fifteen hours. I felt selfish for dragging him and Miranda along with me onto the plane, but neither of them balked at going.

I also wasn't afraid to admit I wanted them both far away from the Strip with so many gods and vampires running amok. Miranda assured me that Jamal was safe.

And we had plenty of time to break things down for Aaron. Occasionally, he would get up, walk up and down the spacious cabin that smelled like fresh flowers and money, then he'd sit back down with a faraway look on his face. I feared breaking his fragile mind, as it was a lot to get one's mouth around.

But I had a feeling Aaron had gotten his mouth around a lot bigger.

HA!

Ever since visiting the scary monster in the hotel's basement, I had a choice. I'd made a plan and hope soared in me that I'd soon be with Grim again.

They said he could come back wrong, too powerful, it could be bad news. But I didn't care. I knew who he was and no matter what state he was in, I could bring him back. Any little bit of him was better than nothing. I didn't love Grim because he was perfect, convenient, or because he gave me swanky digs and out of this world, mind-blowing orgasms. No. It came down to the impossibly simple point that I loved his very existence. And the lack of it brought me unending pain.

"Are you sure this is going to go how you plan?" Miranda asked. She leaned over from the seat next to me. Jamal was with his grandmother and they took an impromptu road trip after Miranda's strong insistence. Miranda wanted them far from danger, but she couldn't stay out of the fight. It wasn't in her nature.

"He fought Sekhmet once before and put her down. He can do it again," I assured her, even though I didn't know how.

I picked up the reusable, bling-covered Perkatory cup and sucked on the hot pink straw. Human blood hit my tongue and my body warmed. Though it satiated me, it was nothing compared to the blood of a god. It was the equivalent of having to change my diet from ambrosia to cheap diner food. It did the trick, but my taste buds longed for the sensual experience, not to mention the intimacy of the act with Grim. I ached for so much more.

"Is that really why you are doing this?" Miranda asked gently.

"I have to tell him, Miranda," I said, putting down the cup, my voice thick with emotion. "I let fear hold me back, thinking that I'd lose myself if I loved him. Now, I see how stupid that was."

Miranda licked her lips as if trying to be extra careful with her next words. "Is it? We do a lot for love, to find it, to make it work, and to keep it. In the Army, I learned fear sometimes keeps you safe. That's its job."

Taken aback by my best friend's anti-pep talk, I asked, "Are you saying I should be afraid?"

"I'm saying I hope you are right. I hope bringing him back is the right thing to do. That it's not like Bianca said, and something catastrophic will happen. Or that he comes back...different."

"I thought you were on my side," I whined.

She reached over and touched my arm. "I am on your side. I just don't want to see you hurt."

I had to muscle my way past the defensive feelings, past the resistance to what she was saying. It was then I realized she wasn't talking about me. The fear was hers, and she was just ascribing it to me. Was it because we were on the verge of a war with immortals and a new world order? Or because the idea of handing over her heart to someone scared the ever-loving tacos out of her too?

I knew Miranda hadn't been married long before she became a widow, and she hadn't given anyone a second look since I'd known her. I'd asked her once if she was maybe asexual, she shot back, "What I am, is busy."

But I gathered she purposefully avoided those feelings.

In fact, I realized she resolved to live vicariously through me and Timothy and our torrid affairs, rather than take any risk herself.

"Just because you're a widow and single mom, it doesn't mean you're dead," I said gently.

Her eyebrows shot up in surprise before she cleared the reaction. "I know that."

"Do you?" I asked. "Because I know you were pretty young when..." She never talked about her husband. For crying out loud, she still had several years before she saw thirty, but she acted like she was an old crone sometimes.

"I g-get it," Aaron said, dropping in the seat across from Miranda. I hadn't even realized he'd been listening. "When you hold onto control so t-tightly, it's hard t-to let it go. You worry you'll lose e-everything."

"Is that what you do?" I asked him, leaning back. "You always seem so laid back."

A wry smile spread across his face. "I-I'm an alcoholic and a c-compulsive gambler."

Miranda's mouth dropped open while I stared at him in abject horror. "Then what the ever-loving fuck nuggets are you doing working at a hotel on the Vegas Strip?"

Then it all came out. How he'd traveled around the world chasing adrenaline and parties. He'd parachuted in Brazil, ziplined in Spain, and hiked through Japan. All the while playing online poker to fund his travels.

But two years ago, while surfing in Australia, some amateur surfer collided with Aaron and their board slammed into Aaron's jugular. Before then, Aaron never had a stutter, but the trauma seemed to be permanent. His need to chase the next high took a dark turn as he resorted to hitting the bottle and continued betting when he should have folded.

But one day he cleaned up his act with the usual programs and a good sponsor.

I finally understood why Timothy held himself back. Timothy kept things in tidy order, helping Grim control events accordingly. Aaron was chaos by comparison. He loved the thrill and the danger. Even now, he skated along the edge of his darkness by serving java to the people who played in the pits where he used to live. Anyone else would have run far away to stay clean, but Aaron wanted to feel the warmth of the fire.

If the two of them ever let loose, would some beautiful alchemical harmony come about, or would they crash and burn in some fantastic explosion?

Despite all our girl talk—we informed Aaron he was officially one of the girls—we still had airtime to kill. It passed by impossibly slowly while we silently imagined what hell unfolded at Sinopolis in our absence.

When the plane landed, we waited for night to fall so I wouldn't turn into a crispy critter. When Miranda finally gave us the all-clear, I practically blew the door off the hinges to get out.

The air was hot and dry in a familiar yet different way from the Vegas climate. Here I could smell the sand, the history, and spices coming from the nearby town.

A private car in black waited on the tarmac. Timothy arranged for a local guide to meet us and take us wherever we wanted.

Our guide didn't say a word as he drove us to the pyramids of Giza. I sighed, looking out the window as we made our way into Al Haram. Yellow spotlights were trained on the world's wonders, so they could be admired even at night. The complex of pyramids were referred to as the Giza necropolis. Another day I would have loved to get out and walk around and explore the pyramids and massive sphinx. But there was no time. We needed Grim, and we needed him now.

I took a moment to appreciate the sphinx settled in front of the great pyramid. If I needed oxygen, this place would have stolen my breath away. The Vegas edition could not compare to the real deal.

The car stopped, and the guide opened the doors for us. Tourists gathered en masse during the day, but in the dead of night, the place felt downright spooky. And *I* was a blood-sucking vampire.

Our guide led us past all the checkpoints with some wave of the hand since we left the airport. Though Grim was gone, I felt his influence, leading us past all the red tape. The guide stopped at a dark cavern amidst a group of eroded pillars at the back of the largest pyramid. He waved us on, urging us to cross the roped-off entrance. Then he handed over a backpack, which Miranda opened to find bottles of water, snacks, and flashlights inside. It was clear our new buddy had no intention of accompanying us.

"Is it too late to back out now?" Miranda glanced at the dark hole we were about to enter.

"Don't worry, I can see in the dark," I assured her.

"Yeah, but how does that help me?" she asked in a flat tone. She distributed the flashlights and shouldered the rest of the pack.

For the first stretch, Aaron went on about how so many of these tunnels were uncharted and blocked off from the public. He declared it would be all too easy to get lost and die down here. Miranda told him to stop talking, or he definitely would.

We walked in silence for a long time. We didn't have a map, but I could feel my way through the shafts. Whatever

Xander had packed in that kiss, it had given me some kind of pyramid sixth sense.

We took a left, then a right, and another right. It didn't take long to sink into the zone, guided by my gut, no longer noticing where we were going or where we had been.

I led them past taped-off tunnels, and found a hidden entrance in the back of a cave. I'd had to claw away dirt to make enough room for us to squeeze through. In doing so, we stumbled upon cobweb-infested tunnels. I swiped the gauzy nets away as I led our trio deeper into the pyramid.

"I've seen this m-movie before," Aaron whispered, pulling me out of my trance-like state. "D-don't touch any bugs or mummies."

"Or treasure," Miranda agreed.

"Why are you both looking at me when you say that?" Their pointed looks were hard to miss even in the dark cavern.

Apparently, they didn't feel my question warranted an answer. *Rude.*

As if to prove their point, the walls changed as we walked by them, and suddenly glittering green gemstones covered the expanse like wallpaper. It created an almost alien-like passageway that entranced me,

My fingers itched to touch, but two sets of eyes dug into the back of my head, promising murder if I did. "I think we are getting close," I said instead.

Finally, the tunnel opened into a larger cavern. As soon as I set foot inside, torches along the wall sprang to life with flames.

"Sp-spooky," Aaron said, shooting me a nervous little grin. He lived for this kind of excitement, while Miranda remained vigilant and alert.

Depictions of Egyptian gods decorated the walls, the

paint slowly flaking away with time. I recognized the falcon head of Horus, the crane head of Thoth, and wondered if Galina had overtaken Fallon and Timothy. At last, I approached the life-sized depiction of the god with the jackal head. Anubis, the god of the dead. My heart gave a painful squeeze.

"Honey, I'm home," I said, quietly. I reached out to touch a faded portrait.

"Don't," Miranda warned.

"W-what did we say?" Aaron added in a stern tone.

I pouted but lowered my hand.

"Cozy place," Miranda said, cracking open a water bottle and handing it to Aaron. "I bet the archeologists would go nuts over this. To think they are steps away from the secret chamber of actual gods."

My stomach dropped, and a tether connected me down down down to the very center of the earth. At the back of my mind, I heard Xander's whispers again, like when I'd astrally traveled here the first time. The strong tether nourished and grounded me in a way I'd never known before. My spine straightened, and the room sharpened around me. Xander's words guided me, showing me the path.

"What happened?" Aaron asked in alarm. "Why are h-her eyes all white?"

"I'm fine," I said, though my voice came out in airy layers.

My feet started toward the painting, undeterred by the wall. I saw this in my vision. Without stopping, I ran right through the seemingly solid rock, Xander's whispers echoing through my mind all the way.

The shouts from Miranda and Aaron came from behind me, muffled through the limestone. Though I was still in a trance state, I still mused that I'd passed through that wall just like Harry Potter and the platform of nine and three quarters.

Slowly, but surely, the strange, otherworldly feeling faded until it was only me again. There was no door the way I'd come. I'd traveled through the stone itself. Xander had somehow granted me entry. I found myself in an alcove next to a shimmering pool of light. Stacked stones created a rim around the pool, coming up to just below my hip.

I could feel the cells in my body vibrate while matching the ebb and flow of the ethereal matter. Being near Xander had felt like standing by a nuclear reactor, while this was like standing in the middle of one. Like at any moment, the pool could explode and cause eternal chaos, or freeze and create a frozen state of harmony.

And in the depths of that glowing liquid was Grim.

Xander told me how to get here, but I didn't know what to do next.

"Grim," I tried to call, my voice cracking.

The mass of light didn't respond.

"Grim, I know you're in there," I said, trying to sound stern, but my words quaked. I neared the pool, but the atoms of my being shook more violently until I thought I would dissolve, so I backed away. I paced back and forth, struggling to think my way through the situation. Once I'd phased into this room, my phone became as useless as a brick. Zero reception. So I couldn't call Timothy or Fallon for help.

Wracking my brain, I tried to recall all I'd absorbed about the resurrection of Osiris from the books I'd read. It had to be a similar problem, right? Isis, his wife, asked Anubis to help her resurrect her husband and his father. There were accounts of Isis gathering all the bits of the chopped-up god and putting him back together like

Humpty Dumpty. But Grim's body had turned to dust. I didn't know any resurrection spells, and Grim couldn't help me.

Sudden anger spiked in me. I was annoyed that I didn't know what to do. Angry that Xander and Timothy sent me here without telling me what the next step would be. Angry at myself for not asking more specifics before getting on a plane. Angry at Grim for leaving, and angry I didn't tell him I loved him when I had the chance.

I hoped if I showed up, Grim would magically appear. But yet again, my need to jump into things short-circuited my smarts. I hadn't thought this through.

Returning to the wall where I entered, I pressed my back against it and slid down until I was sitting. And the other bad news was I didn't know how to get out of here either. Would Miranda and Timothy give up hope and leave me here? Would I try to chip away at the rock to free myself?

No, I couldn't think like that. I wasn't leaving here without Grim. I just needed to be smarter than I was.

I shut my eyes and tried to think my way through this.

After two minutes, I sighed and rubbed my face. Was that burning smell my own brain?

"This isn't going to work," I said to myself. No one would accuse me of being the brainiest vampire around. But right now, I could really use some smarts to work through this.

The sound of a yip made me jerk. I looked down sat at my feet.

"Cupcake!" I cried in joy. I gathered her into my arms, grateful to have a friend with me. Of course, the little reaper puppy was already incorporeal and could go anywhere.

Still hugging the pup, I spoke to the room as if he were here. "Grim. Anubis," I corrected, feeling like I was talking more to myself than to him. "The world needs you. Your family needs you. I need you."

Then an idea came to me. It might have been a stupid idea, and it was definitely forbidden, but if I worshipped Grim, could he hear me? I set Cupcake down and rolled to my knees. Next to me, my furry companion leaned down while sticking her tiny wagging butt in the air.

I used to do this a lot. For a long time, I'd tried my hand at praying my way out of a house where the hands were too mean or too friendly. It never worked, and I eventually gave up.

I clapped my palms together and closed my eyes. "Anubis, I pray to you."

Something in the room shifted. It was subtle, but I didn't open my eyes, not wanting to lose concentration.

"I didn't bring you gifts. I don't have mummified cats, or treasure to show you how much I adore you. But I can also tell you, no one has ever adored you more than me. I'm calling on you, Anubis, for help. To come back to the mortal world, to protect the souls you care for, and to be with me." The last part came out as a ragged whisper.

Again, something shifted in the room. This time, I opened my eyes. Cupcake sat next to me. Her gaze set on the pool of light.

My prayer turned to a whisper, but I couldn't stop the words from spilling forth. "I pray to you, Anubis. I pray you come back. Come back to me."

Anticipation built up in my chest as the liquid churned and splashed over itself, making waves. They spilled upward in a vertical motion. My jaw dropped as I took in the magic display of swelling glow. I grabbed hold of Cupcake to help ground myself and she didn't fight me.

The liquid turned into a reverse fountain as it rose into

beautiful sheets until it nearly touched the ceiling of the alcove.

A foot stepped through the pearlescent sheets and landed on the stone ledge of the pool, then another broke through, stepping down onto the floor. Familiar bronze skin curved up over muscled calves and legs, and then Grim emerged, standing there before me, whole and alive in the flesh.

Power shifted around him in waves of gold and black. The same sizzle of power I detected from Xander hit the air, but tenfold. And dark hair fell into a pair of deep amber eyes that held no recognition for me.

18

GRIM

I'd been drifting, one with the universe and beyond. Without form, I experimented with the stars, dipped my fingers into time, and tasted the echoing cacophony of sounds that rang throughout all of space. But someone called my name even though I could not remember it.

The call penetrated my formless consciousness, tugging on me like a petulant child. Part of me didn't want to go, but I had to. The prayer, more powerful than any other I'd known, drew me until my atoms rearranged back into solid form. I hurtled up from the center of the universe.

I pray to you. Come back to me.

When my feet connected with the ground, I felt how young it was compared to me. The ever-shifting exchange of life and death churned through and around me. Nothing stayed the same.

My connection to the cradle, to the realms beyond, was too strong. It called me back, throwing off balance. But I was here now. I was Anubis, the god of the dead, and I controlled the souls of this realm. I reached out and pulled the power back to me. Someone else had been holding it for me, but it wasn't theirs. It was mine.

The soft brush of a feather caressed my forearm. Then I felt the souls everywhere, all at once. They cried out for salvation, for order, for guidance. And I would do just that.

The ground moved under me, travelling a thousand miles an hour, but when I looked, it appeared to be still.

The one who called me forth stood at the opposite end of the cradle. The woman's auburn hair fell around her in thick waves and her eyes shone like sea glass at dawn's first light. She wore jeans, and a black buttoned shirt she'd tied at her navel because it was too large for her. Her expression held both expectation and affection.

The alcove held my power, even as it thrashed about me with violence. My body crackled with it. This skin was fresh, as was this muscle. Everything was too new, too raw. I should not have returned like this. Darkness roiled at my center, unstable.

The devotee standing there desired something from me. She likely believed I would be her salvation. Able to grant her wish, whether that meant a boon of crops, or to heal an ailing relative.

But she must not have known who she'd summoned forth.

Death.

And Death answered to a higher power than hers.

"You shouldn't have brought me back," I said. My voice came out in layers and echoed menacingly through the alcove.

"I think you mean thank you," she shot back in irreverence. Though she licked her lips nervously and shifted from one foot to the other.

The woman held a small, onyx-colored puppy who leapt

from her arms and ran up to me. I regarded the little animal. I knew this creature. A reaper. But this pup was too young to reap souls, so I turned my attention back to the woman who summoned me.

Prisms of light danced and circled about her. Her soul was special. No longer transient, the spirit had crystallized. Now diamond hard, it had grounded in her vessel. This was no woman; this was a sekhor.

Fragmented memories assailed me. Blood, war, and loss swept over my mind in horrific waves. Hordes of these magnetic creatures thirsting for freedom, for blood, for power, and I could not allow it.

The sekhor's eyes widened with fear as I advanced. "I need you to remember me, Grim. Please. Remember me," she begged.

The name she used was unfamiliar to me. I was Anubis.

I didn't slow down as I reached for her. The sekhor anticipated my move, rolling out of reach, before popping up behind me.

Annoyance glimmered in her eyes. "For crying out loud, you are going to make this hard, aren't you?" Sand coated half of her body from the tumble. The sekhor's gaze dropped to stare between my legs. "Well, I guess you are pretty hard already."

I lunged for her again, and she tried to dodge my grasp. But this time my hand clasped her throat. I raised her until the sekhor's feet dangled in the air. The reaper jumped at me, yipping in protest, but I paid the pup no mind.

Still, the reaper was insistent. I could hear the small pup going on about forgetting, or remembering, someone named Vivien. Reaching my limit with the distraction, I swept my free arm out and Cupcake careened through the walls and far away to where the other reapers would keep her out of trouble.

Cupcake? What kind of name for a reaper was that?

Was I forgetting something?

"Grim," the sekhor gasped out, even as I squeezed her neck. Though I could rip her head off and be done with the sekhor, I paused. Her crystalline aura intensified, magnetizing me to her.

The permanence of a sekhor's soul called to the gods. Like attracts like. Some part of me wanted to acknowledge that we were meant to pair, to walk into the ever after, united. It was as natural as seeing the missing shape that would complete my own. What a mere child would view as two blocks needing to be clicked together.

Still, blood and screams continued to assail my mind. Were these memories from long ago or had it been yesterday? I couldn't be sure.

I leaned in, examining the sekhor more closely. Bold, fierce passion flared in her eyes like flares off a star. So many allowed themselves to die before they ever crossed the veil. I found the girl herself even more compelling than her soul's aura.

A wave of my own power crashed into me like a wrecking ball. I released the sekhor, stumbling back as my body transformed into my god-likeness. My hands elongated into beastly claws, black fur sprouting along my flesh as I expanded into my full form. Eight feet tall, with dripping fangs, my god-likeness was part monstrous jackal, part man. I struck fear into the hearts of all. In this frame, I could handle the surge as I fought to calm my rioting magic.

Too soon. I'd emerged too soon.

I should have lain in the cradle for several more centuries. Why was I called here? I held out a clawed hand in front of me and tried to focus on it. But the image of my own form vibrated as I attempted to stabilize.

The sekhor's hand pressed against my monstrous one. Her small fingers slid in between my claws, holding on.

"Hey baby, I got you," she cooed, sending me another look full of feeling.

My body melted under her touch. Dark, black fur receded, leaving me in the flesh of a man once more. Our hands remained entwined.

The sekhor stepped forward, running a hand up my cheek.

I should end her. One of my jobs was to eliminate the sekhors, protect the souls of humankind from being petrified in such an immovable form. I needed to keep them from trespassing against my brethren.

But warmth filled my chest at her touch.

"I'm sorry. I'm so sorry." A tear slid over her lashes and down her face.

My hand covered the one she'd pressed against my face in a movement that felt so familiar, yet still entirely foreign.

Before I knew what I was doing, I wrapped my hands around her hips, pulling her against me. Her body, soft and yielding, against my hardness. My heart strained against my rib cage as if reaching out for this creature, though I did not know her.

Then she leaned up and pressed her mouth against mine. My eyes drifted shut when she opened to me. My tongue dipped in, tasting her. Leather and sugar wrapped around me in a drugging haze.

Suddenly, I wanted to know if she tasted like that everywhere. I traced down the column of her neck, licking and sucking, before nibbling on her collarbone. She groaned and pressed her body against mine.

Voice thick with emotion, she said, "I missed you."

My head rose as I regarded her. Need pulsated through me, though I didn't understand. Some unknown sentiment tangled with the knowledge of my duties.

Lust? No. Something more powerful permeated my being, gripping me tight. I wondered if I could blame her prismatic soul for bewitching me?

She searched my face before it crumpled in pain. "You really don't remember me, do you?" She reached into her pocket and pulled out a golden skull ring with ruby red eyes.

Instead of answering or taking the ring, I resumed my exploration of her collarbone. There was something so painfully familiar about the taste of her. Pushing aside the strap of her top, I continued down the swell of her breast. The ring fell from her fingers.

Despite knowing I had to eliminate the sekhor, arousal pounded through me. I wanted inside her. To feel connected to this being, as if it would somehow ground me.

Her hands took hold of my face, bringing me back up to hers. "I know this won't make sense to you right now, but I never had one foot out the door. Even if I couldn't say it then, it was always you."

This time, what felt like a surge of lightning ripped through me. I arched back, gritting my teeth. Still too unstable. Still too new.

Acting off instinct, I grabbed the sekhor, pulling her onto my hips. The radiant woman wrestled with her top, ripping it over her head and throwing it off to the side, revealing perfect breasts. I lost my ability to breathe for a moment, everything in me stilling. This felt so right, though I couldn't say why. Then I laved my tongue against her exposed, most sensitive tips, needing to taste more. We did away with her pants and undergarment in a flurry of movement.

Her weight was nothing as I finally lowered her onto my straining hardness. We moaned in unison. Her exquisite, tight heat surrounded me—like coming home.

Nails bit into my shoulders as she threw her head back. "Grim, oh god."

Grim. That was my name.

The realization was fleeting, suddenly unimportant, as I lay her down on the edge of the pool. One leg balanced on the ground as I drove into her. Need, and that unnamable emotion, both ancient and powerful, gripped me. The atoms in her body turned unstable as I trapped her so close to the cradle. I used my own magic to draw down a protective cloak to shield her from it.

Fangs sank into the space between my shoulder and neck. She drank deeply of my blood. Time felt like an amorphous entity, moving around me, everything happening at once, even as my hips continued to buck. Her skin warmed underneath mine until an inferno blazed where we were joined.

The connection was almost instantaneous, as the blood bond formed. Panic flared in me, then anger.

The treacherous vampire used her wiles on me to get to my blood. The harpy desired a blood bond, or perhaps to drain me until she took enough power to defeat the gods. Either was unacceptable.

And she'd made a fatal mistake. I now controlled her will.

I grabbed her by her hair and jerked her head back until it tilted up and away from my throat. She arched her back to ease the pressure, forcing me deeper inside her. I pinned her against the stone with my weight. A bright red smudge of my blood marked the corner of her lips.

Again, expectation shone in her glassy eyes.

"You deceitful wench," I growled, even as I warred with myself on what to do. My lust demanded I force her to fall apart under me, finishing what we started. But I knew she must die for her transgression against a god.

The expectation in her face gave way to sorrow, as if I'd dealt her a killing blow. Her lips parted, then closed. She accepted her fate. She knew I couldn't let her live. Not when she drank of a god's blood. It was forbidden.

The position I'd trapped her in made her last words raspy. "I'm sorry I couldn't fix this. I love you, Grim."

Feeling flooded my body, though my mind didn't understand. First, a staggering sense of relief, followed by an intensity that made my heart nearly break through my chest.

My gaze fell to the small cupcake charm that lay between her bare breasts. Something about it niggled at the back of my brain. Then the scarred-over, mangled patch of flesh between her neck and shoulder first pulled, then pushed me. New memories mingled in with the years of old, the years filled with sand and blood. It felt like floating into a dream.

The scent of leather, sugar, and her skin.

How I slammed her against an elevator, infuriated, aroused, and needing so much more.

My thumb brushing sugar and flour off the tip of her nose.

The inviting softness of her lips as we writhed against silken sheets, drowning in need and pleasure.

The sound of her small gasps to her keening screams for me. Not for some self-reflective death wish, but the true me.

Sea-green eyes straining for more, even as we pushed and challenged each other.

Love poured through me as our life together returned to me in taste, touch, and sound.

"Vivien?" I asked.

Relief swept across her face. "I love you," she choked out again.

A shudder ripped through my body. I'd waited so long to hear those words from her. Vivien had given me her body, gifted me her will not once, but twice, and at last, I possessed her heart.

I released the tight grip I had on her hair and leaned over to brush my lips against her so gently. "I love you, Vivien, beyond eternity."

Then I kissed her deeply, knowing what a precious being I held in my arms now. We began rocking again until we found our rhythm. The hot friction of our naked skin nearly drove me back to madness. Fire ran through my body as I tried to hold my release back.

I loved her. I left her. I hadn't meant to. Soon we were both gasping. She begged to pitch over that cliff, while I did everything to last just a little longer.

With her will mine once more, I sunk my power into Vivien's skin, letting it caress her inside and out.

"Come for me," I said into her ear and her body arched, knees bending as she succumbed to my command, quaking with impossible tightness around me as she screamed. At another time, I might have been able to hold back, but not now. I let go. Power flared from me in a cacophony of darkness and thunder without sound as my hips stuttered.

When my faculties returned to me, I registered Vivien mumbling into my neck, clinging to me even as I'd collapsed on her.

"I'm sorry, I'm so so sorry," she mumbled in a continuous stream.

"What are you sorry for?" I asked.

"I didn't say it back." Her eyes were shiny with unshed tears. "I knew I loved you when you said it the very first time, but I was afraid. I couldn't be brave then, but I am now. I'll say it a gajillion times to make it up to you. I love you. I love you, Grim. I'm so sorry I hurt you and made you wait. I love you."

My fingers trailed along her jawline, gratitude imprinting into my being.

I'd almost killed her. The difference of a moment could have meant losing her forever, and there would have been no undoing it.

When I finally returned to myself, I would have scoured the earth for the Blade of Bane and run myself through rather than greet the next day without her. But Vivien pulled me back and there was no safer place than in my arms.

"Shh," I hushed, trying to calm her down. "I've got you. And we're together now."

Vivien's expression turned stony. "You're damn right. And we're going to make sure nothing changes that."

19

GRIM

After Vivien apprised me of all I missed, I led her out through the veil separating the cradle from where her friends waited in earnest. Miranda's eyes rounded and Aaron took a step back as they saw me. His gaze bounced between my face and between my legs before his face reddened and he looked away. I adjusted the skull ring on my finger. It was the only thing I wore.

"Yeah, he didn't exactly come out of the cradle with clothes on." Vivien shrugged. "Just like a baby, a big hot baby." She grinned at me, her hair a tousled mess and a flush on her cheeks.

I readjusted my grip on her hand, dragging her closer to me. I craved her, needed her near me. Vivien grounded me, and I needed that more than ever right now. My power still flared around and inside me, testing my control.

"How long was I in there?" Vivien asked, scrunching her nose in that impossibly adorable way. "Is it daylight yet?"

Aaron checked his large-faced sports watch. "About two hours, so no."

"Did it work? Is he the god of the dead again?" Miranda asked, her demeanor cool, as if preparing for the worst.

I rotated my arm and made a fist. The tattoo of Ma'at's feather rose to the surface on my forearm.

"I bet Fallon is relieved," Miranda said, also relaxing her stance. It was then I saw she held the Blade of Bane.

"D-do the others know you are back?" Aaron asked. Then his eyes bounced all over the room as if he weren't sure if he should meet my eye. They had obviously informed him of my divinity and was unsure how to act around me now.

I spoke to him directly to put him at ease. "Other than Fallon, no. The pulse of energy released when I rose may alert some of them, but I doubt it." With that, I nodded to Vivien that we should go.

We made our way to my private jet. Our escort kept his eyes downcast, never looking upon me as he ushered us into his vehicle in the cover of night and drove us back. Vivien refused to release my hand, not wanting to let me go for even a moment.

On the plane, I was afforded the chance to change into my own clothes stored aboard. I donned a pair of slacks and threw on a button-up shirt, but I didn't fasten it. My skin was still too fresh, and the fabric felt too tight.

With Vivien perched on my lap, the trio recounted all I missed while I slumbered in the cradle.

Galina's betrayal stung my pride more than my feelings. I was used to my brethren vying for their own agendas, no matter the cost to others. And Galina played her cards so close to the chest for all these years, I never guessed her secret desire to release her sister upon this world again.

The threesome ended up crashing, having not slept on the way to retrieve me. Miranda fell asleep with her hands folded in her lap, seat still straight up, while Aaron had reclined his. Mouth slack, he snored. Vivien fought to keep her eyes open, but daylight had come. We shut all the windows to protect her, and the dim lights cast a warm glow across her beautiful, yet exhausted, face. I picked her up and carried her to the private cabin at the back of the plane.

"I don't want to fall asleep," she moaned in protest even as she pushed off her jeans. I lay down next to her. I didn't need to sleep, having done so for long enough.

"It's okay," I said, pushing her hair back over her ear. "I'll be here when you wake," I promised.

I was true to my promise, though I cut her rest short, as she awoke to my mouth between her thighs. The desire to taste her was far too strong for me to resist. Her eyes fluttered open as she writhed under me until she fell apart under my tongue and fingers. Immediately after, she clambered on top of me and rode me hard until I feared I'd perish all over again.

Spent and sweaty, we splayed on the bed until I felt the plane descend. We got dressed and emerged just before we had to buckle in.

The limo waited for us on my private landing strip, headlights cutting through the darkness.

"D-do you think they are d-doing okay at the hotel?" Aaron asked.

I'd attempted to call my aide, but there had been no response from Timothy.

Aaron tried to cover up the concern in his eyes and failed. The words he didn't speak rang out all too loudly. Vivien had regaled me with the unspoken love affair between Timothy and the barista. She and Miranda spent a surprising amount of time growing vested in the outcome. While I submitted to listening to their wild conjectures, I'd never broached Timothy about it. But now I could see what Vivien already knew. This man cared deeply for my aide.

We returned to Sinopolis and found caution tape covering the front doors. I ripped it off and entered the trashed lobby. My senses searched for life, for souls, but the hotel was empty of guests. My oasis of plants were uprooted and thrown about. Timothy and Fallon were nowhere to be found and all my staff were absent. I went down into my antechamber of judgement under the hotel to find my friends, but they weren't there. At least Amit, the crocodile god, remained. He had no preference how he got souls and would not pick sides.

But my allies were all abducted.

I traveled through the scale of walls to the afterlife, seeking the council and aid of Osiris. But he was gone, as Fallon had already discovered. Only the ferryman was about, and he was of little help.

Back in the lobby, I stood with my sekhor and two mortals, seething from the audacity of Bast's reach. Vivien changed into leather pants, boots, and a blood-red bustier. She threw Cookie Monster over the outfit.

A cold snake of fear wove through me at the thought I'd almost killed her. This vibrant, bold vampire, who'd do anything to get me back. She had helped guide me back to myself, even though I'd strayed so far away. Vivien proved to be more of a home to me than any other place I'd known. Even the cradle of birth could not compete with the power of my love for her.

"What are we going to do?" Miranda asked, her grip adjusting on the Blade of Bane.

"First off," I said, "you are not to use that weapon on anyone unless I deem it necessary."

Miranda's chin rose. "Excuse me, Mr. Scarapelli, but I'm

off the clock, so I don't have to listen to you. And the sword was entrusted to me, so I believe I'll defer to my own judgment. I do not kill indiscriminately."

I pinched the bridge of my nose as I pushed back another flare of power that threatened to overtake me. "If you take the life of a god, it cannot be undone. We must handle this matter in a manner that does not threaten the balance, and therefore, we must find some other means to subdue Bast other than that weapon."

Miranda practically snarled at me. "You mean the goddess responsible for Jamal nearly dying?"

"Yes," I snapped back, my death mask flickering wildly. Her son had, in fact, crossed the veil, but I did not correct her. Miranda was no stranger to death, and she didn't look away from my deathly visage. Aaron, on the other hand, stepped back and averted his gaze. I tried to maintain a calm tone. "I mean that even she will answer for her crimes, but I intend to send her to the cradle, not to absolute oblivion."

"And how are we going to defeat Sekhmet?" Vivien asked. "Did you find Osiris? Can he come help us spank them back into good little gods?"

I rubbed at my temple. The desire to crack the souls from the bodies of the two mortals near me was overwhelming. My power raged like a stormy ocean. It took all my attention to keep it in check. "Unfortunately, what you mentioned Fallon said is correct. Osiris is gone. He could be anywhere, for any length of time. We cannot rely on him to act. That is why he put me in charge of this realm."

Vivien licked her lips, her brow furrowed. "Now is the time to give up the big secret we've been dying to get to. How did you defeat Sekhmet? Because mommy vampire needs to go down."

"I..." I had never revealed how I defeated Sekhmet to anyone. It was a long-guarded secret. "It won't work again."

"Well, tell us what you did," Vivien urged, "and we can at least use it as a jumping-off point."

I looked away by reflex.

"Grim, it can't be that bad," Vivien said, coming to hold my hand. I turned and studied her adoring face, knowing her sentiment would be fleeting once she learned the truth.

"I bound her by blood," I said.

Vivien stiffened, then her hand slowly pulled from mine. I instantly missed her touch, but I didn't reach for her.

"You said you've never created a blood bond before," she said, her voice and shoulders now stiff.

"Not to a sekhor, no," I explained. "For as bloody and gruesome as the war had been against the sekhors, the way I subdued Sekhmet was far simpler." My skin tightened over my bones as I prepared to confess everything. "I invited Sekhmet to partake in some ale with me. She expected, after we imbibed, we would enter our own showdown and the loser would submit to the other's power. Instead, I slipped my blood into her ale."

Vivien's eyes rounded, her mouth parting as she shook her head and took a step back.

"I wasn't even sure it would work," I went on, "but the blood bond was instantaneous. And I used that connection to put her into a deep slumber. And there I kept her all these years."

"So not only did you lie to me about never having a blood bond before, but you drugged her in the same way I was by the master vampire who turned me. All so you could control her?" I saw in her eyes that she wanted me to change the story. Tell her I hadn't done the very thing she detested.

I stepped forward, reaching a hand to touch her, but

Vivien flinched. Something inside me fractured as she did so. A crackling sound came from behind me. Aaron and Miranda took a step back, while Vivien barely glanced at what I'd done. The glass of the hotel's front entrance spider-webbed in a thousand small cracks. Then a thunderous crack echoed through the lobby as a fissure shot from the doors and up the slanted pyramid wall.

Fantastic. If I didn't get ahold of myself, I could bring the entire place down.

I rolled my shoulders, coming back to myself. "It had to be done, Vivien. Humanity was at stake. Sekhmet's thirst only grew. Everyone she sinks her teeth into turns into a sekhor. And those turned violent, razing a bloody path through any and all in their mission to kill the gods. The protectors of humans, like your friends here," I said.

"Don't bring my peeps into this," Vivien snapped, then took a few steps back.

Darkness flooded me from the overflow of power and the emotion churning inside. I hurt the woman I cared most about. But the omission had been necessary. The bond formed between Sekhmet and me was literally ancient history and had become so unconscious I almost never thought of it.

"Vivien, the bond with her, it is nothing like what I have experienced with you," I said in a soft voice.

When she turned back around, she wiped away at her eyes. Her words came out business-like. "You don't want to run Galina through with the Blade of Bane, so how do you plan on defeating her and Sekhmet this time? Because I doubt Sekhmet will take another roofie-colada from you."

"Roofie-colada?" Aaron asked Miranda in a quiet voice, with a confused look.

She explained in an equally low tone. "Like a pina colada but with roofies? You know? A roofie-colada?"

I hardened at Vivien's coldness and focused on the path forward. "We are going to do what they did to me. We'll discover Galina and Sekhmet's secretum mortis and send them back to the cradle."

"And do you know what exactly their Achilles' heels are?" Miranda asked, glancing at Vivien as if trying to assess the damage done to our relationship at the same time.

"No, but I know who does," I said.

20

VIVIEN

G rim and I pulled into a run-down casino past the Strip. It was one of the countless dives I never thought to take notice of.

Cars littered the parking lot, some likely here since last night or before. This is where the true gamblers went, the ones who showed up day after day with a cup full of quarters and a hunger for that next win that bordered on sickness.

The supernatural war had not yet spilled over onto human turf. But that wouldn't last much longer if we didn't do something about it. Grim wove through the lot until he rounded the back of the building. He stopped near the employee entrance by the dumpsters.

The morning sun blazed down, but Grim stepped out of the UV-protected Bugatti and opened my door. If I got out of the car I'd burn to a crisp. Maybe this was his idea of ending a fight.

I crossed my arms over my chest, hunkering down in my seat. "I guess I'll stay here." My teeth ground against each other. To say I was pissed about Grim lying to me about being blood bound to another and drugging another god was an understatement.

He tried to insist it was the olden days or some bullshit. That the fate of humanity relied on him, and it solved a violent altercation. But I had been drugged the same way, and my life had been ruined.

An unwanted voice popped up in my mind.

Has it been ruined? Or have you gone from being alone to having Grim, who has loved you like no other? Not to mention you have friends who literally travel to the ends of the earth with you.

I swatted the thoughts away like the irritating irrelevant bugs they were. There was absolutely no way I was cool with this behavior. I didn't care if it was five thousand-years ago, he should never have drugged a woman. Even if it was to save the world a rocking, bloody fight, and keep countless humans safe from her unending hunger.

Okay, maybe he had a point, but I was still too damn human, and proud of it, to accept this bullshit.

Grim held out a hand for me. Did he mean to pull me out into the daylight so I'd burn up? His power flared out in shadow that bent over his head to the car, creating an extensive and godly umbrella. The death mask flickered across his face, reminding me of his unstable state.

My mouth twisted in displeasure, though I took his hand and let him lead me out, under his faux shade.

"Best to stay close," he murmured, pulling me to him. "I don't want you getting singed by the sun." His deep amber eyes sparked with gold flecks of barely restrained power. The silent plea there was unmistakable. He wanted me to understand, to forgive.

I hated the way my body betrayed me as I pressed against him. He still hadn't bothered to button up that black shirt and the urge to slip my hand under it to skim down his sculpted abdomen was strong. I fisted my fingers instead.

I loved him. There was no taking that back now. But I feared the path before us.

Instead of parking through the front doors of the casino, Grim had taken us around to the employee entrance at the rear. He easily opened the lock, slipping in a bit of dark mist into the keyhole until it clicked. The godly shade dropped once the door closed behind me, as there were no windows. I'd expected some fantastic bizarro secret waiting inside. Instead, I found exactly what one would expect. A bunch of banged-up orange lockers, and a paper-covered desk under a white board outlining everyone's shift schedule. The place was empty, as everyone was likely working on the casino floor, leaving just us in the back room.

Grim regarded the numbers on the lockers before stopping in front of locker sixteen. He ripped the lock off it with a screech of metal before opening the door. I peered over his shoulder. Hot damn, it was a secret entrance down a dark tunnel.

There was the bizarro I'd been waiting for.

Before we entered, Grim turned to me. "Let me do the talking."

"No," I shot back on autopilot.

"Vivien." He sighed. "This is a tricky situation, and I need you to be on my side if we go down there. I can't focus if I'm fighting from all sides. Apep is incredibly dangerous, and bringing you along is a tremendously bad idea. I expect we will see disturbing, dark things in his lair. Things that will provoke you. And I know even if I tried to leave you behind, you would follow me down anyway."

"Damn right I would," I said with a nod.

"Remember what we are here for. Do not antagonize or

attack him. We need him for information. He's the only one who knows Galina and Sekhmet's *secretum mortis*. They battled long ago and after Galina sent him back to the cradle, he slithered out many centuries later but remained under the radar. I doubt even she knows he has returned to this realm. I suspect he has taken precautions and gathered information against Galina to make sure she could not defeat him again. He's our only chance to stop Galina and Sekhmet from turning more people and making an unstoppable army. You must remember that above all else."

I stuck a hand on my hip. "I've faced scumbags before, Grim. It's like you think I'll lose my shit at the first sign of trouble."

His eyes searched mine for a moment. "I trust you, Vivien. More than anyone. Please trust me."

The tiny men running my brain raced to meet.

"Jenkins, what's the hold up?"

"I'm not sure she trusts him anymore, sir."

"Don't be ridiculous, Jenkins. She loves him, so she must trust him."

The other man checked the control panel and shook his head. "Not true, sir. These readings are erratic, not to mention conflicting."

The man in charge slapped Jenkins upside the head. "They always are, you idiot. We don't have time to sort this out, so we press on."

Jenkins shot a skeptical look at his boss but pushed a lever forward.

"Let's go," I said, pushing past Grim into the secret entryway. I ignored the ache in my heart.

Why did feelings have to be so complicated?

Dark stone tunnels led us on a downward slant, taking us under the casino. The echo of something dripping surrounded us. The lit candelabras along the walls made me feel like Scooby Doo trotting through a monster's den. The urge to say Ruh Roh was overwhelming, but I somehow kept my mouth shut.

At last, the tunnel opened up into a large stone room. Grim stepped in front of me, as if to prevent me from going first. He gripped my arm in warning, worried I would react and do something stupid.

Taking in the scene, I realized that's exactly what I wanted to do. Something incredibly stupid and reactive. Because what I saw both outraged and made me sick to my stomach.

We'd entered a monster's lair. On top of a stone dais sat a god atop a throne of bones. Unlike Grim's antechamber, this hole in the ground reeked of pain and debauchery. It revolted me to be down here.

A jewel-encrusted crown perched askew on the god's head. Only wearing an open green robe and burgundy underwear, his thinly muscled frame lounged in repose. His jaw was unshaven, and silver streaked the long black hair that flowed over his shoulders. Down here, the sun likely never touched his skin. His impossibly pale complexion appeared even more sickly because of his red-rimmed, dark eyes.

"Apep," Grim acknowledged. "I see you have been busy." He nodded, referring to the barely clothed vampires positioned about the room. Two male sekhors stood behind him, while two women sekhors kneeled on all fours, chained up to the throne like dogs. And apart from the black leather masks covering the top half of their faces, they were naked. I could tell by their rigid stance, this monster had all of them under his control.

There was no need to chain them up with the blood

bond. He did it simply to degrade the vampires. My stomach churned.

Grim's hand squeezed me a little tighter. If he didn't have a hold on me, I would have absolutely flung myself at the god to pummel him into a bloody pulp. This was beyond sick. These were people. I mean, they were vampires, but so was I. And it was like looking into my worst nightmares. The ultimate expression of abuse of power.

If Grim hadn't been so adamant before we came down here that we needed information, this situation would have gone differently.

"Grim," Apep acknowledged in a lazy, Romanian accent, bowing his head. The crown somehow stayed in place. Was this the guy that everyone based Dracula off of? Because he fit the bill, seeming more vampiric than me by a long shot.

"Indeed, I was delighted to discover these sumptuous sekhors, wandering on their own. Ripe for the taking. I'd surface for nothing less." His red-rimmed eyes swiveled to me. "But I'd never turn down a delivery. Did you bring me a gift?"

"She's mine," Grim said in a vicious growl, black power exploding around him in one terrifying second before disappearing back into his body. He turned his head away, as if working to maintain control.

I had brought him back too soon, and he struggled to not go supernova.

Apep flicked his fingers in the air, though interest glittered in his eyes. "Apologies, sire. I did not realize you would take advantage of the new...opportunities."

Grim nodded his head. "Yes, well, sometimes change is for the best. My duties have become tiresome, and I find myself surprised by the refreshing turn of events.

One of the sekhors in chains suddenly snapped to attention before scrambling over to the god. She lay her head in his lap, nuzzling between his legs. Then reached inside and pulled out his soft member before taking it into her mouth.

My forehead tightened and burned with fire. I was going to be sick. That poor woman was a slave, and somewhere she was trapped inside his thrall, fighting to break free. I wanted to fly at him and rip the god's dick clean off.

Again, I wondered why the fuck I hadn't brought the Blade of Bane? Why hadn't I brought Miranda so I could have her chop his little prick into bits before stabbing him through?

I had a knife tucked inside Cookie Monster, so I'd have to suffice with that if I chose to inflict any damage.

"Oh really?" Apep glanced at me, and I could see how skeptical he was that Grim had changed his tune. Forcing his sekhor to suck him off in front of us was a deliberate one to test both Grim and me. It was meant to provoke, and I was more than provoked. I was fucking incensed.

Grim was a terrible liar, which was a big part of why the secret he'd kept about Sekhmet had been so shocking. But if Grim planned to show up as an ally to pump this god for information, we would not get anywhere like this.

I did the hardest thing I'd ever done. I reined in my raging emotions, knowing we had to stop Sekhmet. Who knew how many vampires were being made and forced into a blood bond with evil gods like Apep who treated them like slaves? I had to do something and beating him wouldn't help.

I emptied my expression, trying to make it look abrupt. I nuzzled Grim's neck, sliding my hand into his open shirt. Even as I licked up his delicious column of throat, I maintained an empty, doll-like expression. Grim stilled underneath me.

I caught the surprise flicker in Apep's eyes. He still wasn't convinced. It had to look like Grim took hold of my will. I turned around and grabbed Grim's hand. I sucked his long index finger into my mouth, pulling it out slowly, then I repeated the motion to his middle digit. I kept my dead stare on Apep as I did so. Then I guided Grim's hand into my top until his wet fingers traced over my nipple.

Feeling warred inside me. Though Grim's rough, strong hands on my breast sent desire flooding downward, the horror sitting on the throne of bones chilled my blood.

Come on, Grim. Work with me here.

Grim finally massaged and gripped me before burying his nose in my hair, inhaling deeply. "Yes, well, there is only so long one can be all work and no play. But I confess, I'm surprised you're okay with Bast's new reign."

"Bast doesn't care to reign." Apep's eyes remained glued to my breast, as if hoping Grim would push down the cup and reveal more. All the while that poor vampire had to choke down his repulsive dick.

Grim choked out a laugh. "You're kidding yourself if you don't believe Bast has plans. Why else would she unleash her sister on the world?"

"All the better, more playthings for us," Apep said, watching me too carefully. "And I'm still surprised to find out you play at all. In fact, I heard dear Bast sent you back to the cradle."

Shit. He knew more than we thought. I needed to keep him entertained, and my eyes empty, or we'd blow this operation.

Ew. I fought a grimace. I did not mean to make that pun.

"Oh, I can play," Grim said, his hand coming to grip my ass. "After an eternity of work, I'm sent back to the cradle to miss all the fun? That's exactly why I had to come back."

"You've always been against sekhors roaming this earth, Grim. Don't fuck with me," the god said, pushing the sekhor away from his lap, now vested in the conversation. My insides relaxed slightly with relief on that poor woman's behalf, though he eyed me with renewed suspicion.

Crap. I removed Grim's fingers from my top and turned around to face him. Out of view, I shot Grim a look that told him he'd better make this worth it. I slid down his body, my fingers and lips trailing down his exposed skin. I sank to my knees and unclasped his belt, pulling out the prize.

I knew what this god got off on. And I'd make it appear Grim liked to play, too. I wrapped my lips around Grim and sucked and licked in earnest. Though I knew Grim well enough to know this was completely out of his comfort zone, he began to harden in my mouth. His hand went to my hair, but I could tell it was to steady himself.

Grim said, "Apep, you have missed so much in your hole down here. Did you not hear that Osiris made special compensation for my toy here? I've found these creatures... enjoyable." He paused as I did that thing with my tongue that he liked. I could feel the heat of his glare on the top of my head for a moment before he continued. "And I've come to see the truth: if all the humans become sekhors, there will be no souls left to reap. I won't be a slave to humanity anymore. You think I want to work every day as Osiris's lapdog?" He gripped my hair with sudden force, to help make his point, forcing me to choke on his fully hard length for a few seconds. I rolled my eyes, but knew Apep probably got the message better.

I picked up the speed of my motions, feeling Apep's intent gaze prickle along my back. Grim kept talking. "But I need Bast out, so I can help lead us into the new dawn. I'm the only one who can handle Osiris if he comes back, and I can protect you. Protect this new world. Bast is as unpredictable as a cat who pushes a glass off a counter, just for the hell of it."

A strange gasp sound came out of Apep and it took me a minute to recognize it as a laugh. I continued to work on Grim's straining length, though I did not care for this setup at all. Granted, I was usually more than enthusiastic about deep-throating Grim's incredible, mortal-defying size. But I was not a fan of the audience or the location. I deserved an Oscar for this stupid performance. Or what was the Oscar equivalent for a porn star? A Blowie? Did I just make that up?

"Tell me," Grim urged, finally pushing me away. He tucked himself in his pants but didn't zip back up. He took a few steps toward where Apep still sat. "Tell me what Bast's secretum mortis is. Don't deny you know what it is. Share with me, and you won't have to stay in the shadows unless you want to. Hell, you can have her domain, her hotel, for all I care. Cover it in darkness, fill it with sekhors to do your bidding."

To make him look good, I crawled over next to Grim on all fours, sticking my butt up in the way Apep had his sekhors. Keeping my eyes blank was the hardest thing I'd ever done. I watched him out of my periphery.

Wait. Just a little longer. We've almost got it.

Apep leaned in, pressing his elbow into the arm of his bone throne. Hunger sparked in his eye. He wanted everything Grim offered. "Venom."

"Whose venom?" Grim demanded.

"Mine," he hissed.

"Now?" I asked.

"Now," Grim agreed.

I sprung at the god, pulling the knife from my coat.

21

GRIM

When I confirmed the time had come, I'd been of the mind that Vivien would take the cue to stop her far too convincing subservient act. I hadn't counted on her launching herself directly at Apep. A blade gleamed in her hand.

Before Apep knew what was happening, Vivien slashed the knife across his face. Blood sprayed the floor next to his throne.

She stabbed him in the chest several more times, his body jerking under her assault. The crown hit the ground and rolled around in a circle.

Apep activated the vampires, sending the two in chains at Vivien, and the two sentries behind him at me. Despite their eyes being hidden under leather masks, they knew exactly where we were. Before they got to me, I gripped the two vampires in my power and threw them across the room, where they slammed into the wall. Their skulls cracked, and when they hit the ground, they didn't get back up. It would take time for them to regenerate.

My power. It was so much more than before. I hadn't known my own strength, and I still didn't.

The chained sekhors clawed at Vivien, trying to rip her off their master. My hand shot out, and the two of them stilled as I gripped them even from a distance. I jerked them back from Vivien, their bodies hanging in midair before I slammed them into the floor. This time, the crunch came with blood pooling around them.

A shriek of pain cut through the room. Black and gold swaths of magic shot out, surrounding me.

Vivien.

My heart pumped faster, but before I could do anything, something flopped on the ground. Apep's most prized appendage. "You monstrous piece of crap," Vivien screamed. "If you want your dick sucked, do it your goddamn self."

When I drew near, I found Apep's features had mottled and swollen. Stuck halfway, turning into his god-likeness of a snake monster, but Vivien had nearly cut all the way through his throat, stopping his transformation.

His pale flesh turned rubbery, and his now-red eyes bulged unnaturally. His massive fangs elongated, too big for his mostly human face and dripping liquid.

Blood covered Vivien's cheeks and her expression bore down on Apep with a ferocity that rivaled any god's power. Since the moment I met her, she'd been a force to contend with.

Despite myself, a tendril of arousal curled in my stomach, not allowing my still-hard length to soften. Though I'd prefer not to have her take me in her mouth in such a place, her tongue and lips could bring me to my knees under any circumstance.

She was more powerful than even she knew.

"So, we just rip off one of his fangs?" Vivien snarled. "Or

do we have to milk him like a venom cow?"

Without waiting for an answer, she ripped a fang out. Apep's scream came out half muffled with her hand in his mouth.

As Vivien investigated the tooth, red eyes rolled over toward me. Apep shot me a look of pure hatred, then it smoothed into an expression that communicated a silent message.

Payback's a bitch.

Panic crept along my skull as I searched for the source of his smugness.

While one of his legs appeared to be a boneless piece of melted wax, the other had elongated into a serpent's tail with a large spike on it. In one quick move, he slammed his tail up against Vivien's back, spearing her.

Vivien stiffened under the blow even as a strangled gasp came out of her mouth. Apep wrenched his tail free, and she jerked with the movement. Before she could fall back, I caught her. Panic raced through me. A spike that big. He could have decimated her heart beyond a vampire's regenerative capabilities.

"Vivien?" I asked, anxiously searching her face, feeling her blood coat my arms.

Her eyes rolled toward me, and her pallor turned ashen. She struggled to get her words out in between harsh gasps. "I'm o-okay. I just need a minute, i-if that's alright." He'd likely destroyed her lungs, but it looked as though her heart hadn't been damaged too much.

I dropped a kiss on her forehead, and gently set her down so she could sit upright against a wall, since there was no seat available. I held her hand, assuring myself she wasn't going anywhere.

A gurgling sound caught my attention. I stood and

turned to see the skin of Apep's throat knitting back together. The energy it required to heal himself forced him back into human form.

Reactive emotion took hold of me. Black clouds exploded around me, skulls pushed their way out before receding into the mass. Apep's red-rimmed eyes blinked, fear written on his face.

"You touched my mate." My words came out in a low, sonorous layer of voices. "You hurt her. And now, what she's done to you will be the least of your pain." My fist clenched shut as my entire being vibrated with outrage.

My death mask flickered, then remained. I wanted him to see who he was dealing with. He would learn why Anubis stood on the right side of Osiris.

With the flick of my finger, the black magic surrounding me shot at him, careening into every orifice of his face, eyes, nose, mouth, even his ears.

He jerked like a marionette with tangled strings. Something resembling a scream tore from Apep's throat as he continued to feel the brunt of my darkness ripping him inside out over and over again.

Then I stretched out my hand, calling back the darkness from his body. It formed into the scythe that so many came to associate and fear with my presence. With one swing, Apep's head flew across the room.

The scythe disappeared from my grip in a puff of smoke.

I shrugged off my shirt, and crossed back to where Vivien sat, transfixed. With my shirt, I wiped away some of the blood on her face, a mix of mine, hers and Apep's.

Vivien's rounded eyes were fixed on Apep's head; his eyes continued to blink in dismay. His body flailed behind me, searching for his missing parts.

I'd make sure they would be separated for a long time.

22

VIVIEN

To say Grim was more powerful than he had been before was an understatement. The beheading of Apep with the almighty scythe had me shaking in my booties, and that was my boyfriend.

Though part of me had never felt so safe, watching daddy death go loco over me. If it were possible to fall more in love with him, I did.

After assuring Grim I needed a little longer of a time-out slumped on the ground, he grabbed Apep's head. He left to throw it in the trunk of the Bugatti, leaving Apep's body stumbling around in the cavern. When he returned, I was on my feet, though a bit wobbly. Then the vampires regained consciousness.

Still set on attack mode, they went right back to trying to rip us to shreds. We quickly discovered Apep had an adjoining dungeon room—which first off, ew—that could be secured from the outside. We rounded the sekhors up and locked them up. I scrounged up clothes for the vampires and left them inside on the ground. The naked sekhors were too busy trying to murder me to pay attention to their lack of dress, but maybe they'd want to get clothed after we'd gone.

I took the time to kick Apep's dismembered wang under a massive, ornate bureau. After stomping on it a couple times, of course. Good luck finding that, dickless.

Back in the employee break room, I stood a couple feet back, so the sun wouldn't burn my skin when Grim opened the door.

I gripped Apep's fang, knowing it was the key to sending Galina to the cradle. Maybe it would also work on Sekhmet because they were sisters.

Grim activated his dark shadow shield and walked me back to his car.

We drove up to Sinopolis and Grim got the door for me before rounding to the trunk and grabbing Apep's head. Hate filled those red-rimmed eyes, but without his vocal cords, he couldn't say a damn thing.

With head in hand, we found Aaron and Miranda still waiting for us in the penthouse.

Grim dropped Apep's head in the kitchen sink.

"Whoa," Miranda said. "Did that thing just blink?"

"Sure did." I wrinkled my nose in disgust. "And while I got away with my life, Cookie Monster was not so lucky." I clutched my ruined coat. There was no saving my big blue friend as Apep left a massive, blood-soaked hole in it from his spiked tail.

"I'm so sorry for your loss," Miranda said, touching my shoulder.

"Sh-should we throw a funeral later?" Aaron asked jokingly.

"I think we should," I answered in all seriousness. Aaron looked back and forth between Miranda and me to see if I'd break. I didn't.

I'd wear black. Say a few words. Maybe sprinkle some cookie crumbles in the grave over my beloved accessory.

"Did you get what you needed?" Miranda asked, bringing things back to the present.

"Yeah," I said, nodding toward the kitchen. "We are going to keep Apep's head on ice, though. In case we need him to grow another fang."

Grim came to stand next to me and laid his hand along my lower back. I loved how he always touched me. "The venom in it is Galina's secretum mortis. I daresay it could be Sekhmet's too."

Aaron edged closer to the kitchen to get a look at the head, but quickly backed away. I can only assume Apep shot him a scathing glare.

Aaron stuttered and muttered to himself about how trippy life had become. Then he asked, "Sh-should we be talking in front of...uh...whoever this is?"

"His name is dickless," I supplied in a flat tone. "And unless he can grow back his body, I think he's pretty harmless in the sink until we decide what to do with him."

Grim shot a disapproving glance at the sink. "Apep is a blight upon this earth and had long outgrown his usefulness. I plan to spread the pieces of him out across the land in boxes, as was done in the old days. Or perhaps use a more permanent means to remove him from this plane." His eyes swept to the blade in Miranda's grip.

"So what's the plan now?" Miranda asked, shifting her grip on the weapon.

"I go in with the fang and try to end this quickly and quietly with Galina," I said, casting Grim a glance. That was the best-case scenario. "Things are even worse than we thought," I added, then explained to my friends about the vampires.

Miranda's cheeks grew more drawn as I described the naked vampires in chains, while Aaron listened with open disgust on his face.

"Who knows how many other gods are out snatching up vampires to be their sex slaves and worse," I finished, still hugging my brutalized jacket.

"Yes, cleaning this up will be quite the task," Grim said, his thumb rubbing up and down my spine.

I turned to look up at him. "Wait, what do you mean clean up?"

His whiskey-colored eyes dipped down to meet mine. "We have to kill them, Vivien. All of them."

He said it as if it were the most obvious thing in the world. My stomach dropped, like the two-hundred-foot plunge of an amusement park ride.

"No, what? We can't kill them," I said, hearing the panic rise in my voice.

Grim used a gentle yet firm tone. "Vivien, we have to. It's the only way to preserve the balance. As it is, all of those souls will never gain entry into the afterlife. They are lost."

I took a step back. "They aren't lost. *I'm* not lost. My soul may not travel to heaven, but I'm willing to stick out this immortality business. I bet my left boob most of those who were turned also don't want to forfeit their life just because this was forced on them. No, screw that. I bet my right boob, too."

Grim closed his eyes and for a moment I thought I'd bored him to sleep, but on closer inspection, he seemed to be warring with himself. Ozone permeated the air, and I realized his power was spiking.

"How about you two take a minute to go get changed," Miranda offered, seeing as we were half dressed, and covered in blood, and clearly about to have a fight. I nodded and dragged Grim off to our bedroom.

Grim got control enough to speak. "Vivien, this is exactly what happened in ancient times. The vampires did not take kindly to the hierarchy. They too will turn on my brethren, and eventually humanity itself will be at stake."

I couldn't believe he was saying this after all we'd been through. "Stop. Just stop judging for one second. It's your job, not who you are."

A muscle in his jaw jumped. "That's where you are wrong. I am the god of death, and I am tasked with keeping the balance."

I poked his chest. "Bullshit. If you were still in the cradle, Fallon would be the one in charge."

His eyes flashed this time. "And you regret bringing me back? Because he would know how to use the power better than me?"

"No." I clutched at my heart, searching for the invisible knife he ran through it. "I want you here, with me. You know how much I love you. But that doesn't mean I will ignore what's right. And if you start killing vampires"—I took a step back, drawing a line in the sand—"you might as well kill me, too."

Grim turned and stalked to the other end of the room, before walking back and stopping in front of me again. Power whipped wildly in his eyes, but I wouldn't back down.

"What would you have me do?" he demanded.

"This is what I was afraid of," I said softly. "That love would mean I have to sacrifice my character if I want to be with you."

"That's not what I'm asking you to do," he argued.

"It is," I shot back. "You want me to stand by your side

and help you kill innocent people, vampires? You are making me choose you or my race!"

"And what about you? You would have me choose between you and keeping the entire world in balance." It came out on a roar as his death mask flickered.

Anyone else would have backed up from his unstable power state. So of course, I took a couple of steps closer to get in his face.

"Well, your idea of balance sucks, and it isn't balance at all. It's time to change that. And yes, I may continue to love you, but I can't stay with you if you plan to uphold this bull-shit simply because you are too ancient and stuck in your ways to think outside the box."

Silence fell over us in a smothering blanket.

I couldn't let it go. My intensity wasn't optional, and if he wanted me, he had to know by now, it was the rule, not an exception.

My vision swam from unshed tears as I vibrated with feeling. I took a moment to steady myself before I spoke in an even tone. "If you could have seen that girl before she died. How scared she was...She wasn't the enemy. She didn't have grand plans to overthrow the gods or drink all of your blood. She was a woman with a life. And she had her choice ripped away from her when Sekhmet turned her. I learned to want this new existence. Why shouldn't she get the chance? Just because I'm dating someone who can protect me, and she doesn't have a godly ally?"

This time his words came out low and raspy as if from the effort it took to keep his magic in check. "You want me to change the entire world order? You want me to defy the decree of Osiris?"

I touched my face. "I didn't say it was easy. I'm just telling you, it's the right thing to do."

He pulled my hand away and turned from me. The space between us expanded.

"Then that settles it," he said with all the finality of a nail in a coffin.

The floor dropped out from under me, though I seemed to be miraculously standing there still. This couldn't be it. Could it? I didn't need to breathe, but I felt suffocated. My core froze, adrift on an icy ocean.

We went from being to enemies to lovers, and I feared we were on the precipice of being enemies once more. But even if we went to war over this, I'd never stop loving him. I couldn't if I tried.

Turning back toward me, he smoothed back the hair that had fallen in his eyes. "You're going to have to marry me."

My jaw dropped. "Wh-what?" My mind spun wildly, trying to figure out what was happening.

"Immortality, and favoring tradition, has made me blind to certain aspects of this world, and obviously the only way to rectify the situation is to make sure I have you by my side. Since you are the only one who isn't afraid to show me a different and much-needed perspective."

Then I squinted an eye at him. "You want to marry me because you want me to be your politically correct officer for the rest of time?"

He grabbed me, kissing me so thoroughly he didn't let go until my hair was mussed, lips swollen, and I was left dazed. Desire struck me hard and fast, riding the waves of my rage and fear. How could he do that? Affect me so completely.

Resting his forehead against mine, he said, "I want to marry you because I'm madly, deeply in love with that smart mouth of yours and everything attached to it."

"We are already stuck in an eternal blood bond," I pointed out in a husky whisper.

We'd never discussed marriage. Who needed to? We were bonded for all time. So then why did his proposal send feelings rocketing through my entire body?

He smirked, eyes sweeping down to my lips. "Call me old-fashioned, but my essence craves the public declaration that comes with a wedding and marriage."

I opened and closed my mouth.

Doubt flickered across his face as he pulled back. "Do you want to marry me?" The way he stilled told me he was bracing himself for whatever my answer would be. If I said no, it would devastate him. But he'd likely take it with the stiff upper lip of an ancient god.

I wasted time before, and I knew better than to hold back now. "Fuck yes, I do."

He crushed me against him, kissing me, evoking liquid heat to flow through my body. His hands roamed, stoking the fires inside me. I was hungry again, and for more than just his blood.

When our kiss broke, I said, "Okay, but if you think you can wriggle your way out of a fight every time by proposing, you got another thing coming."

"The only thing I care about is if you are coming," he whispered against my lips.

My brain fritzed right out. Okay, so he had more in his arsenal than a proposal to throw a girl off her argument.

Then he dropped to one knee and removed the skull ring he wore and slipped it onto my finger.

It was far too big for me, but he closed his hand around it, warming the metal. When he pulled away, it melded perfectly to my size.

"Just for now," he said.

Emotion swelled in my chest as I looked at my hand in his. "No, it's perfect." Then clearing my throat, I said, "Well, if we are going to get hitched, we better spring our friends out of whatever prison Galina has them trapped in. It won't do to have a wedding party of zero."

23

VIVIEN

G rim and I were engaged. My mind still struggled to wrap around that fact, but I'd dig into it later. Right now, I had an opportunity to deal with this issue quickly before anyone else got hurt.

I strode up to the Martini Hotel. No one stopped me. I had a standing invitation. The fresh air of early dawn surrounded me.

Vegas felt so quiet. It unnerved me. The stakes of the supernatural battle were dangerously high, but the humans were likely sleeping off their hangovers or a night of partying on the Strip. The world was on the precipice of spiraling out of control and they had no idea.

It neared four a.m., and the hotel was closed, but I had no trouble letting myself in. The corridor lined with shops led to the center attraction. Innumerable swaths of crystals surrounded the floating bar at the heart of the hotel. It hung so anyone from at least five floors could look out over the ledge and view the chandelier-like installation. The soft yellow lighting made it feel like being inside a giant glass of champagne.

I followed a winding path of pink crystal flooring to the entrance.

I can do this. I can do this one thing without making an absolute mess of everything.

The men who ran my brain were oddly silently but intently paying attention to my every move.

Galina sat at the bar, sipping on something steaming in a white mug. Stylish horn-rimmed glasses rested on her face, and she wore flowing, white-linen loungewear. Her dark hair was slicked back. In this repose, she could have modeled for either the cover of *Forbes* or *Vogue*.

Cats covered every spare chair and tufted seat in the bar. Her envoys surrounded her. Some paused licking themselves to look up at me. They watched me with unerring intensity. Galina seemed absorbed in the magazine she flipped through, only looking up when I stopped ten feet from her.

Neither of us spoke for a long moment. I adjusted the leather duster around my shoulders. I missed Cookie Monster something fierce, but this would do.

Finally, she said, "I thought you'd come."

I rocked back on my feet. "Yeah, well, some things you said to me have begun to penetrate, so I thought we should have another chat." I shrugged and tried to count how many cats were around me. Forty, maybe fifty? The cat goddess was literally the mother of all crazy cat ladies.

A nearly Cheshire grin curled her mouth. "Then you see how much better everything is?"

"Where is Sekhmet?" I asked, trying to sound casual as I neared her.

"I almost worried you would hold Grim's demise against me," she went on, without answering.

"Is she feeding?" I didn't want the Original vampire

goddess sneaking up behind me with what I was about to do.

Galina removed her glasses and set them on top of her magazine. "My sister was...overwhelmed, so I put her away for a little while."

Finally, I stopped next to where she sat. "Put her away? She's not some toy that goes in a chest."

"Being asleep for so long..." Galina trailed off, seeming to go somewhere else in her mind. A pinch formed between her brows. "This world differs greatly from the one she lived in. And now she has an excess of energy I am helping her cope with."

She removed her glasses, setting them on the counter. Galina arched an eyebrow, scanning me from top to bottom. "There is something different about you."

Could she tell my renewed calm came from having Grim back? I couldn't risk messing this up, or I'd end up on the ground with a broken back again, except this time, I'd doubt she'd let me live to change my mind.

I tried to keep my tone airy. "You could say my attitude has changed. I have a whole new outlook on life."

Suspicion lurked under her perfect bone structure, so I looked down at myself as if searching for the same thing.

Galina seemed to shrug off whatever bothered her, and I internally sighed in relief.

"So now what?" I asked. "Are you going to tell me what the big master plan is?"

As Galina opened her mouth, I pulled Apep's fang out from under my coat and stabbed at her chest.

Before the tip could meet her flesh, something flew into my face, sending me careening backward. Whatever attacked me, sent me to the ground. I blinked and found myself covered in hissing, pissed-off felines. I recognized the

Maine coon from before, with wild, electric green eyes. He'd eat my nose and ears just for the fun of it.

Fuckity fuck nuggets. I missed it. I missed my chance for the clean kill and things would only get uglier.

I did my best to brush off the angry horde of cats, but even as I tried to scoot back and get away, they clawed and jumped on me like a cat version of the horror movie *The Birds*.

"You've seen Apep?" Galina asked in a disgusted voice, eyeing the fang I still gripped in one hand.

I would have responded, but I was a little busy at the moment trying to bat off fifty felines. I knew they were Galina's envoys, but I also didn't consider myself to be the kind of vampire to kill cats.

You are a mega badass vampire, you can handle a fluffle of cats, I insisted to myself, even as they continued to barrage me in a violent mass.

A tiny yip penetrated through the hisses and cat screeches. Cupcake stood on the ground nearby. She yipped again with all the ferocity she could muster. My heart swelled with emotion as she charged the cats and yanked one back by the scruff of its neck.

A sweet attempt, but Cupcake still didn't even the odds.

Then a reaper dog appeared at the entrance to the bar. Then another. Then five, ten, thirty more.

A thunderclap of power boomed through the room. Grim strode in through the pack, decked out in his finest suit. Black smoke curled around him, filling the room and creating a deathly parade. His eyes were live fire.

For once, Galina's cool demeanor broke. Her mouth went slack with surprise, eyes widening as if she couldn't believe what she was seeing. "No," she whispered.

Grim's eyes narrowed and the pack leapt forth. A sea of

onyx fur rose as the reapers attacked the cats. Half of my feline aggressors dispersed while the other half took their chance, fighting the reapers. I let out a sigh of relief, feeling like a twenty-year-old scratching post removed from a crazy cat lady's home. Cupcake yipped at my feet, warning off any other cats from attacking me. I reached down and petted her head in thanks. Someone was getting extra ear scratches tonight.

As the kerfuffle died down, Grim walked forward in a confident stride until he arrived at my side. My hand readjusted its grip around the fang. I'd tried to do this the easy way, but now we were going to take the hard way.

"You brought him back," Galina said. Her coldness had returned. "Though it's forbidden."

"What with you bringing your sister back, turning sekhors, and crossing the other gods? I'd say everyone is making the naughty list this year," I shot back.

Galina's expression smoothed as she caught sight of something behind us. "Looks like it's two against three."

Before I even turned around, the hairs along the back of my neck rose. A familiar ancient drum beat in my head. The fang slipped from my fingers and hit the ground. Sekhmet had arrived, Idris backing her up. Suddenly my body was not my own. Mama vamp had me under her thrall.

Grim reached for the fang, but green light blossomed around him as Galina zapped him with a power that singed my nose hairs.

I could do nothing to help. I was merely an avatar for Sekhmet as she plunged inside me, taking over. A vicious thirst plagued me. Unlike any thirst I had known before. Like an endless black hole, I knew that hunger would never be satiated. The pain made existence pure agony.

Next to me, Grim burst free from the green energy in a

swirl of dark clouds. Death filled the air. He stalked toward
Galina.

Her skin erupted into inky fur as she grew several feet,
her limbs lengthening until she transformed into her god-
likeness. A giant cat beast with glowing emerald eyes,
complete with claws and fangs. Despite her monstrous
visage, she carried an elegance in her god-likeness.

Grim crashed into her, not bothering to transform. They
ripped into each other, snarling, biting and clawing at each
other.

Pulling all the strength from the pit of my being, I fought
against Sekhmet's presence in my mind. I was no ordinary
vampire. I'd drank from a god, and I knew how to give as
good as I got.

Sekhmet's eyes widened as she realized what I was
doing. My fingers twitched. I had control over them again. I
bared my teeth, pushing harder, using all I had in me.
Seeing as I was a willful bad bitch, I took a step forward.
Then another step. I rolled my neck as I shook the rest of
her off me.

"Not in my house, bitch," I hissed as my fangs elongated.

In those mad eyes, I saw a glimmer of respect.

I added with a sly smile, "And your sister is wrong. It's
four against three."

Sekhmet whirled around just as Miranda barreled into
the party, ready to run Sekhmet through with the Blade of
Bane. Sekhmet grabbed her wrist, and was about to plunge
her fangs into Miranda's neck, but I blurred forward and
shoved Miranda. Both she and the god-killing blade went
spinning across the room.

While Sekhmet and I traded blows, Miranda scrambled
to her feet and lunged for the weapon. Idris stepped in
the way.

The demigod looked down at her. "What do we have here? Little mortals getting involved in business that isn't their own?"

To show him, she punched him right in the nose. Idris didn't react. He simply narrowed his eyes at her. Then, as he wound his arm back, ready to smack her down, Aaron snuck behind him. He kicked Idris behind the knee, sending the demigod to the ground. Then Aaron proceeded to lay down some seriously impressive martial arts moves that kept Idris distracted.

Miranda pulled out her handgun and put three slugs right into Idris's forehead without even blinking. He looked up at her in befuddled offense. Like he didn't understand why they were picking on him.

Something about his expression tugged that thread in my gut. I still couldn't help but think in another world, Idris and I could have been friends.

Idris hit the ground, unconscious, and blood oozing out of the holes in his brain. He wouldn't be out for long, but I appreciated them taking him out of the game for any amount of time.

Sekhmet and I were stuck alternately trying to squeeze the life out of each other's throats, but seeing as we were both undead, that wouldn't work. I kicked her kneecap with all my might and it loosened her grip enough that I got free.

Snarls and roars emanated through the room, and I spotted Apep's fang on the ground. I raced toward it. I needed to stop this before someone I loved got hurt.

As my hand wrapped around the fang, a shadow cast over me. I looked up and found Sekhmet holding the Blade of Bane. She ran the blade through my chest, ripping it straight through my heart.

24

GRIM

I tossed Galina across the bar, pitching her through the curtain of jewels and over the edge where she fell down several stories of the hotel. I turned around in time to watch Sekhmet run Vivien through.

Blood exploded from Vivien's mouth as she made a choking noise, stiffening under the blow. The sword stuck out through her back, speared straight through her heart. Sekhmet ripped the blade out, and Vivien's body jerked with the motion.

Panic detonated inside of my brain like sizzling fireworks. Power burst out of me as it had with Apep, slamming into Sekhmet, sending her shooting across the floor and crashing through the glass doors of the hotel, careening far away. The Blade of Bane clattered to the ground.

Confusion, pain, and anger filled Vivien's eyes before she wobbled.

I caught her in my arms.

I kneeled, holding her to me. Vivien looked up at me, confused. As if she still didn't understand what happened.

"No, it's going to be alright," I assured her, though the panic in my voice said anything but.

She shot me an apologetic look, knowing the blow to be both permanent and fatal.

My insides howled in pain, and I wondered how the whole building did not come down around us. My power flailed with wild abandon. Feeling and energy swirled inside me with such force I could not see straight. The booming typhoon in my brain nearly pulled me under.

All I knew was Vivien was dying and there would be no resurrecting her if I lost her.

Muscling past my own raging powers until I could think, I knew there was only one possible way I could save her now. And even that was uncertain.

I elongated my fingers into claws and sliced my other wrist before putting it to her lips.

"Drink," I urged.

Vivien's eyes rolled and her lids fluttered. "Drink," I said louder.

Still, she didn't obey. The bond between us unraveled, and my soul clawed to keep it near. The weight of her body lightened, as I knew I was losing her. Soon, she'd turn to dust.

Drink. I commanded, taking hold of the last threads of her will. Vivien's lips pressed against my wrist, but her fangs failed to latch on.

Drink, damn you. I sank all the volatile power from the cradle into our fast-dissolving thread.

Vivien's eyes snapped open. They turned into the black sucking holes of my own deathly visage. Fangs finally cut into me and she drank.

Hope and fear warred inside me. Vivien continued to

suck while I cradled her head. Then she brought her hands up to my arms, pulling me closer.

Every part of me focused on her until she sat up, continuing to drink. The weight of her body grew stable again, but not quickly enough.

Needing to feel closer still, I readjusted her in my arms, bringing her to my neck. She bit down instantly. Our tether strengthened as her body regenerated from my blood.

After a while, her hands pushed at my chest. She'd had enough.

But I'd commanded her to drink, and I couldn't let her stop. I needed her to have more. I needed her to be strong, to be unstoppable. I could never lose her.

Dizziness swirled inside my head. She was drinking too much. If I hadn't just emerged from the cradle, I'd be close to true oblivion.

But I didn't care. No one would take away the only woman who made me laugh, who wasn't afraid of my intensity, who would go to the ends of the earth to find me, then still call me out.

There would be more cupcakes, and sex, and surprises that leapt from her mouth.

The tether holding us together strengthened into a golden chain. We bathed in the intensity of our connection. It grew brighter until it glowed impossibly bright. A pulse beat between us, and the heat of our shared divinity warmed me. But my essence waned as she drank.

Vivien pressed harder against me, but still she could not stop sucking my blood. Her hand smacked the backside of my head, but I couldn't let her stop.

Perhaps I'd lost all sense, but I forced her to continue.

Another futile smack against me as she continued to drink.

Blackness crept in the edges of my vision.

The golden chain forged between us exploded into fragments.

Vivien's palms slammed into my chest as she broke free from me. Sea-glass eyes wide, she stared at me in utter panic. Not only did her crystallized soul sparkle, her skin glowed a golden color like mine. She was magnificent.

"What did you do?" she asked. Her hand drifted down to her heart, touching the spot where the wound had closed. Disbelief shone in her eyes.

A new pulse of energy throbbed.

"I couldn't let you die." I swallowed hard.

Thump.

"What did you do?" she demanded, nearly shouting, reminding me of when she first drank my blood. She was just as scared, just as unsure as she was now.

Thump. Thump.

The pulse wasn't mine or ours. It was Vivien's. And it was the sound of her heart beating again.

She consumed all the unstable energy I carried from the cradle. I felt weakened, as though I'd been battling for months.

If I'd not just emerged from the well of power, I would have died under her fangs.

Horror etched in her eyes as she stared up at me. She asked a third time, as I gently wiped at her cheek. "What did you do?"

Unable to look her in the eye, I turned away. With only a slight stagger, I grabbed Apep's fang off the ground. "I set you free. You'll never bond with anyone again."

25

VIVIEN

T*hump. Thump.*
My heart beat in my chest.
What the ever holy-loving fuck nuggets?
This was impossible.

My time for reflection was interrupted as the monster cat version of Galina clawed her way back up into the bar. Though once she landed on her feet, she melted into her human form. Clothes decimated from the change, she was naked now.

A blur sped past me as Sekhmet hit Grim like a furious rocket.

I grabbed the fang and ran toward Galina. I'd send her to the cradle, and Grim and I could handle the rest.

Something slammed into me, and I felt the fang wrenched away from me.

Idris lay on top of me now. "I'm afraid I can't let you stop the nice cat lady."

He tossed it to Galina. As the tooth fell, she stretched out her hands in glowing green light. When she clapped them together on the fang, it disintegrated on impact.

As did my hope for defeating her and Sekhmet.

A gasp caught in my throat like a gang of razorblades.

We didn't have time to go back and get Apep's other fang.

Idris wailed on me with his fists and showed no signs of letting me up. My ribs cracked as my torso got pulverized by his onslaught. I remembered how he tried to trick me into drinking his blood so I'd be bound to him, but Grim just said I was free. Grabbing the back of his neck, I hauled him down and bit into him. He yelped as I sucked his blood. Like Grim said, no bond formed. I was my own vampire, and I was quickly downing the god's blood, absorbing his power and energy.

Idiris cried out in pain, ripping away from me. He covered his neck with a hand, trying to staunch the bleeding. Stumbling back, he regarded me with new wariness. Blood spattered his white attire from Miranda's shots and my bite.

I rose to my feet, squaring off against him. Energy thrummed through me. Grim had brought me from the brink and Idris's blood served as jet fuel. I'd be happy to give him a taste of his own medicine.

A beat passed between us.

Then Idris turned and ran away with his tail tucked between his legs.

Out of the corner of my eye, I saw Miranda hovering over Aaron. He lay on the ground, his face pale. I could hear his heart beating, but it was too slow. They got caught in the crossfire and I didn't see how it happened. Too much was happening too fast.

I felt a tingle at the base of my neck. Sekhmet was trying to take over my mind even as she fought Grim. She wanted to send me after him, too.

But I was fueled up on not one but two gods, and I wasn't ready to be put in time-out. I pushed back on the invisible force, easily brushing it off. Then I went for her mind. Perhaps I could control her the way she controlled me now that I was a super vampire.

Next to the Original, I could feel the drop of blood that connected us. The one I'd drunk that turned me into a vampire. I tumbled inside her head and right into hell.

To be this close to her was to be dropped into madness. I felt her rage, her restlessness, her thirst. Always thirsty, she never had a moment of peace.

But Sekhmet had found tranquility in her slumber. I felt the part of her that longed to return to slumber. She knew she didn't belong here in this new world. She didn't want to look after her children; she wanted to dream of sunshine and flowers.

Grim and Sekhmet traded blows that made the building shake. But I'd weakened him, and she was pounding him down steadily.

So much energy, stored over too long of time. It would take an ocean of blood to calm her. Always seeking the next fix exhausted her, but she could never stop.

Reaching out again, I met Sekhmet on her level. "Bite him," I urged. Closing my eyes, I pressed into Sekhmet's mind and worked to suppress the beast inside. It wasn't as hard as I thought. She wanted to submit too badly that I helped guide her past the violent madness.

Sekhmet's fangs sunk into Grim's arm. Blood gushed from where she punctured his flesh. Surprise shone from his glowing eyes. The blood bond formed instantly, and he wasted no time.

Grim's death mask flickered as he accessed his power.

"Sleep," he commanded in a layered voice.

Sekhmet's face cleared of the bloodthirsty rage long enough to send me a look of gratitude. Grim caught her before she could hit the ground. Once again, her face reverted to a peaceful expression, as I knew she'd returned to the slumber she truly desired.

26

VIVIEN

Galina cried out as she reached for her sister. But she was too late.

Sekhmet bit Grim, and the only way to free her sister was to kill Grim again.

Everything quieted now. Galina's fingers slowly curled into her palm as I watched something in her break. I discovered Miranda at my side, holding the Blade of Bane out at Galina, in warning.

"She didn't want to be awake. I saw into her mind," I said to Galina. "She slept most of her life away and in that place she'd found peace. Here she was hungry. Always hungry. Nothing was ever enough, and she wished for peace."

Galina straightened, her expression emptying. "I would have given her whatever she wanted."

I opened my mouth to say the price was too high, but I closed it when I looked at Grim.

I'd do anything to bring him back, and I did. My heart felt her pain. We really weren't that different. I could tell myself that this world needed Grim. But the truth was, I did.

"You can't change the beginning, but you can change the ending," I reminded Galina of her own message. Even if the new course didn't include her sister, there was a way forward. Granted, she'd have to pay for all the damage she'd done, but I sensed no fear in her.

"You're right," she said, eyes turning down in thought. Then, with lightning quickness, she reached out and yanked Miranda's elbow up before impaling herself on the Blade of Bane.

"No," I screamed, but it was too late. The sword cut through her heart.

Galina shot me a wry smile. "To live an eternity without the love you crave is no way to live at all."

I understood her perfectly. I thought I'd lost Grim, but I went to the edge and back to get him. To live one lifetime without someone you love is a terrible thing. To live for an eternity without them would be interminable torture.

Miranda's eyes flew wide with shock. Then she stared down at the sword as a purple light surrounded the blade, before it wound around her wrist and then traveled up her arm before disappearing into her skin. She pulled the blade out, expression panicked.

Galina rested a hand across her heart before she sunk to her knees, then leaned back into a seated position. Grim walked over to her, his face solemn. He laid Sekhmet down next to Galina, and Galina embraced her sister one final time. Her legs curled in and her head fell to the side in a beautiful repose as her eyes turned white and the last breath left her.

It was done.

27

GRIM

With Galina and Sekhmet gone, I soon discovered how they'd been able to hold my brethren. A magic cage, once used to contain the monstrous titans who reigned terror many millennia ago, had been refashioned to trap the other gods.

Taking a page from my book, Galina fashioned the prison below her hotel in a custom-built basement she'd clearly been preparing for some time. Though the massive enclosure had been well stocked with luxury furniture to accommodate comfort, it still grouped together a bunch of highly pissed-off gods.

I found the key in one of Galina's books. A first edition of C. S. Lewis's *The Lion, the Witch and the Wardrobe*.

Fallon grinned as I unlocked the gate. "I knew she could do it." He clapped me on the back as he exited.

Bianca's reaction had quite a different tone. Her face grew drawn and pensive. Still, she hugged me to let me know she was glad to see me, but she said nothing.

"Sire," Timothy said in a stilted voice, nodding his pleasure at seeing my return. Before he knew what was happening, I grabbed him and pulled him in for a hug. Shocked, he stilled for a moment before returning the embrace.

When Qwynn emerged, she stared at me with equal parts relief and pain. Then she looked past me to Vivien. With a nod, she accepted the truth. Vivien would always be the one for me.

"Thank you," I said, with genuine gratitude. "I was told what you did. How you tried to stop them."

A seductive smile flickered across her face. "I only did it because it served my needs." Then she gave a little sniff as if it had all been a terrible inconvenience.

But I could see through the bravado. I leaned down and kissed her on the cheek. "Perhaps we can be friends?" I asked.

An arched eyebrow rose. "Friends? Absolutely not." She turned to go. She got only a few steps before she paused and swiveled around. "Maybe in another eternity, darling." Then she was gone.

Miranda escaped mostly unscathed, though Aaron had a concussion and suffered some internal bleeding. Fallon laid hands on Aaron, healing most of his traumas. Timothy fussed over Aaron, going on about needing a doctor. Aaron shut him up by grabbing his head and kissing Timothy speechless.

"Y-you give me strength," he said when he broke away.

Timothy's eyes darkened as he framed Aaron's jawline with his hand.

While I looked elsewhere, to afford them privacy, Vivien cooed in happiness while squeezing my arm.

"Did you see what happened when the blade cut through her?" Miranda asked me and Vivien, her tone somber.

I nodded. A supernatural power arced off the sword and

sunk into her body. "Looks like the weapon has attuned to you."

"What the hell does that mean?" she asked.

"It means there are magical properties that have opened up to you and only you."

Miranda snorted. "I don't know how to use a sword. Why couldn't it have been a firearm?"

I nodded. "We'll see that you are well trained if you are to be the guardian of the Blade of Bane."

Something tugged at my gut. A familiar, yet rare sensation. I knew it would come. I just didn't know when.

"Vivien," I said, holding my hand out to her. "We must go."

At first she started to say something smartass, by the twinkle in her eye. But she held her tongue when she saw my expression. She slipped her hand into mine.

It took no time at all to return to Sinopolis, to the antechamber of judgment. The massive wall of scales behind my throne melted away, and I led Vivien into the bright daylight of a sun that would not harm her.

We stood on the threshold to the glorious Afterlife. Where all worthy souls would cross over to the next eternal realm where they would exist in paradise.

Hraf-haf waited on the ferry as usual. When the crooked, graying man set his ancient, watery eyes on Vivien, they widened. He could instantly see her newly gained divinity. Normally, the grizzled old man never failed to launch into a tirade about his back pain or how thankless his job was when I was around, but the ferryman was unusually silent.

Vivien stepped into the boat with me and shot him a smile. He only lowered his eyes. Her lips wilted into a frown.

The journey across the river felt infuriatingly slow. I

knew why we were here. The last time we'd come, Osiris ordained that Vivien could stay by my side until the conspiracy among the gods had been sorted out. He made no promises about afterward.

And now Vivien had ascended by my blood.

I had no choice but to come when he called, but if he thought I was about to let him take her from me, he would have another thing coming.

We stepped out of the boat and began the climb to the massive palace of Osiris. Paintings of our history adorned the grand columns, and the scent of lush reeds and fresh grasses filled the air. Entering this place usually instilled me with serenity, but even the egrets flying overhead did nothing for my nerves.

Vivien and I exchanged a hard look at the threshold.

"Do we have to go in?" she asked. "Maybe we could get a doctor's note and say we couldn't come."

I softened at her joke. How I clung to her levity in times of strife. "There is no escaping his reach when he calls. Best to go voluntarily."

She nodded and straightened her shoulders. We'd faced so much together already.

Through the doors, the sunshine flooded in through the antechamber that lacked a ceiling. A moat of water wove in through the room, butting up against the sides of the throne made of gold and rare gemstones.

Osiris sat there, still as stone with ice blue skin. Eyes, entirely the shade of lapis lazuli, watched us with unerring focus, so much that I couldn't be sure if he was looking at us or through us.

I'd long ago learned there would be no containing Vivien, even if I advised her not to speak before being spoken to.

"We've done what you asked," Vivien said, breaking the silence. "We found out who was trying to upset the balance and the world order and stopped them."

Those alien-eyes scanned over to Vivien. She stilled as if struck frozen by his very gaze.

His words came out in layers of voices that filled the room. "And in the course of this action, changed the balance yourselves."

I answered this time. "Perhaps some change is necessary after all."

Osiris's head tilted ever so slightly to the left. Fear rippled up my spine. The god was old, unpredictable, and more powerful than I could comprehend. Even the slightest movement could signal a danger I would not see coming until it was too late.

When he did not speak again, I informed him of Galina and Sekhmet's activities until I put the Original back to rest and Galina hurled herself onto the Blade of Bane.

"My child is dead," Osiris said without blinking. I thought I almost detected a hint of sadness, but it could have simply been a statement of fact.

"She changed everything," Vivien said softly. "She brought back her sister, and they turned humans into vampires. But those people did not ask for it. And many, if not most, will want to live their lives, even if that means being undead."

Osiris suddenly stood before Vivien. I hadn't blinked or seen the movement, but there he was. Vivien jerked ever so slightly but held her ground. She stared back up at the towering god. Over eight feet tall, his white robes gently swayed in the breeze.

Osiris did not speak. A buzzing filled the room. Was he

reading her mind? Weaving some kind of magic? Was he about to hurt the woman I loved?

Vivien did her best to straighten, but I saw her tremble in his wake.

Just as I was about to intervene, Osiris lifted a hand, his blue fingers hovering over her cheek. "The gods grow unruly, restless with time. They need protectors." Still not touching her, his hand fell until it hovered over her chest. "You were his gift."

My heart smacked against my ribs with heavy pounding beats.

I knew it. I felt as though I'd known it all along, even if I wanted to fight it in the beginning. I'd been curled up into a tight ball, but she opened me up like a night-blooming water lily under the nourishing moonlight.

That was why he let her live. The first time I brought her to him, he looked into my mind. I could feel him, but I didn't know what he'd found. He'd only said, "I see."

Indeed, he did before me.

I wondered if he knew Vivien saw me as a child and promised to walk with me in this life. Had it all been a destiny he'd known, or perhaps even designed? I could never tell with him.

"And your gift..." Osiris said to her, trailing off. Again, the thrum of some magic brushed against my skin as it filled the room.

Her words came out in a whisper. "I just want them to have the same chance as me."

"So be it," Osiris said.

Suddenly he was over by the water, though I didn't see him move. His hand rose, and over his open palm a glowing blue ankh appeared. "But you shall be their shepherd. Prevent the war between sekhors and gods. Keep the balance. Seek out your fellow sekhors and guide them into harmony and ethical existence. And if they cannot abide by the truce..." Osiris crushed his hand into a fist and the ankh disappeared into wisps of smoke. "You do what must be done."

Vivien swallowed hard and nodded slowly.

Osiris didn't move toward us, but an invisible force pulled my hand until it joined with Vivien's.

"As Anubis serves this world," he said to Vivien, "so shall you."

My fingers interlaced with Vivien's and as I caught her sea-glass eyes, I fell into them. Osiris's voice seemed far away now. "Allow me a wedding gift..."

The ground dropped out from under me, and nothing existed except the two of us. The surroundings blurred, but I heard footsteps across a marble floor, the chatter of people. I inhaled the familiar scent of freshly opened lilies and dark roast coffee.

We were back in the lobby of Sinopolis. My employees were bustling about, guests checking in with their luggage or heading out to dinner. The cracks in the building, miraculously erased away.

A line formed between Vivien's brows, her lips parted in wonder at the cacophony we were suddenly amidst.

"What a wedding present," she said in a low voice.

I was thankful she didn't notice the wicked smile I did my best to suppress. My hotel being restored was generous, yes, but that wasn't Osiris's gift. If Vivien tapped inward, she would discover his wedding present to us, but she was too lost in wonder.

I decided to leave it as a surprise.

"So you're shepherd of the souls, and I'm shepherd of the sekhors," she said with a thoughtful frown.

I wrapped my arms around her, dipping down to catch her lips in a kiss. "As long as you are by my side, I'll readily and willingly face whatever comes."

"Even if it's a wedding?" she asked, her eyebrows creeping up, tone uncertain.

I grinned at her. "Absolutely. Are you up for it?"

A twinkle entered her eye as I blatantly challenged her.

"You betcha, buttercup," she shot back.

EPILOGUE

VIVIEN

Miranda stepped into the room, wearing a slinky black dress, holding deep purple lilies in one hand.

We were in the elegant, royal suite at Isis's hotel since Grim and I were getting married in her ballroom in front of every god and supernatural creature. And my two best human friends, of course. I asked if Jamal could come, but Miranda wanted him to stay away from all the immortal heavy hitters, and I couldn't blame her. But the reception would be held at Wolf Town, and Jamal would celebrate with us then. That little dude already promised me a dance.

Miranda's sleeveless gown highlighted her incredibly shapely shoulders and arms. Her brown skin was dewy and the smoky makeup accentuated her catlike eyes. The purple lipstick on her full lips took her from wow to holy-wow-I-might-be-gay-for-this.

"Whoa, hot mama," I exclaimed.

"Me?" Miranda said, giving me the up and down. "Look

at you." Her eyes grew wide as saucers, almost as if she were trying to drink me in.

I was torn between pushing away the attention and basking in it.

The men in my head piped up. "Sir, what do we do?"

Jenkins kicked up his feet from where he drank a coffee and read the paper in his seat. "Nothing. We worked hard to get here. Let's take a five-minute break and allow the moment to come as it will."

"But the wedding!" the other cried.

"Yes, yes, we'll be punching levers and hitting all the right buttons to make sure she doesn't do anything weird as she walks down the aisle but take the damn coffee break while you can." Then he muttered, "I haven't had one of these since she was six."

I spun for Miranda. The black lace dress flared out above my hips into a romantic, flowing gown. One would have to look closely to realize that netting underlaid the lace and beading that gave it an extra sultry look without looking trashy. The sleeves covered my arms until the little hoops at the end wrapped around my middle fingers. The fancy dip of the dress at my breastbone curled up, framing and exposing my shoulders, making me appear elegant beyond anything I'd ever worn.

My auburn hair had been pulled up, but large wisps fell down, adding to the romance of the overall image I presented.

I wore a single tear-shaped red ruby, dark as blood around my neck. A crown of onyx gems stuck out of my hair in little spiky peaks. I felt like a vampire goddess. And I truly was, since I'd broken the blood bond with Grim by drinking so much of his blood.

I spent the last few months tracking down all the vampires

Sekhmet made, trying to help bring them to terms with their new life. A lot of them had moved into Sinopolis, so I could help them and use Grim's wealth of resources to get them blood and comfort and afford them time to adjust. Only a few hadn't been able to cope and either ran off or tried to fight me. But in Sekhmet's absence, I found I could control their will.

I did so carefully, and with as much compassion as possible, trying to sink peace into their bones. I knew it wouldn't always work, but that was a later problem. Right now, I was about to get married.

"It took Timothy's team of sadists, err, I mean stylists, about two hours," I complained, even as I continued to swish my dress, overly pleased with my appearance. Though sitting still that long nearly killed me.

Yip. Cupcake barked at my feet. She was just as excited as I was for today, if not more so.

Miranda ignored the invisible reaper dog as she walked around me, taking in the detail of my gown.

"So, are Timothy and Aaron..." I trailed off, expecting her to fill me in on the juicy bits. Miranda and Aaron were my bridesmaids, though Aaron got to wear a suit. Timothy and Fallon were Grim's groomsmen.

She pursed her lips. "They are still dancing around each other. Something about there being too many complications to the situation since Timothy is a god. Though the way they look at each other..."

"Hot enough to melt metal." I nodded. "Did you see the tower at Wolf Town?" I asked, letting giddiness get the best of me.

"How could I miss it? The tower of cupcakes is unlike anything I've ever seen. The press is going nuts over it, taking all the footage they can before they get kicked out for the ceremony. I think every food channel host and vlogger is down there dropping bricks right now."

I grinned. The mass of cupcakes was compiled to create the image of an even more massive cupcake. It was the biggest cupcake display in history and would go into the Guinness Book of World Records.

"Knock knock," a familiar deep voice interrupted from the doorway.

Miranda's brows shot up as she grabbed my arm. "He can't be here." Then she faced the door. "You can't be here," she called out. "It's bad luck to see the bride before the wedding."

I waved her off, though my stomach somersaulted. "We've both died, or almost died, a bunch of times. I think we paid our bad luck up front."

Then I remembered Bianca approaching me after we released all the gods. I knew she would be displeased I'd resurrected Grim, but it had been more than that. She said her vision of potential futures had always been clear, but now they turned dark and fractured at points she'd never seen before. We'd all have to be careful. The balance had been broken too many times. I hugged her and told her we'd handle whatever came. She seemed appeased, but the worry lines didn't disappear from around her eyes.

Grim stepped into the suite, taking my thoughts away from impending doom. Even after all this time, he stunned me. A luxury onyx suit coat lay over a silken black shirt that opened past his pectorals. His skin shone as if he had oiled it. And then I remembered Timothy saying something about Grim needing to be anointed for the ceremony. The exposed strip of his tantalizing caramel skin made me swoon. A golden ankh lay on his chest. His whiskey-colored eyes drank me in while flashing heat so scalding, I felt it hit my sternum and then blaze down between my thighs.

"Gods," he growled, and I knew my appearance hit him good. I'd never heard him take the namesake of his own kind in vain.

Miranda muttered something I didn't hear and left us alone, closing the doors behind her. Cupcake trotted out too, disappearing through the solid door.

"What couldn't wait?" I asked, trying to flash him a flippant, flirty smile. Though every part of me wanted to lose the cool and rip off his clothes and see if all of him got oiled up.

My inner bits purred at the thought. *Yum.*

It almost made up for the fact our broken blood bond didn't allow him to play with my body the way it used to. Almost...

"I have a gift for you," he said, still looking me up and down like a wolf smacking his chops, ready for a meal.

"Doesn't that come after the wedding?" I teased.

"After the wedding, we shall be lost in the crush of party guests and embroiled in celebration. I wanted to take my moment with you while I could."

"There is still time to elope. We could tie the knot at an Elvis wedding drive-through."

I'd actually pitched that idea frequently in the last couple months, but Grim promised we'd do that for a vow renewal.

He reached out to run one of my softly curled hair tendrils through his fingers. "No," he said, voice now husky. "I want everyone to see you, to worship you, to know you are mine for all eternity."

My knees turned to rubber, and any smart-mouth come-back died in my throat at his intense sincerity. The love radiating from his eyes was positively bone melting. Before him, I'd thought I'd been better off on my own, but knowing the warmth of his love allowed me so much more in this life than I could have imagined for myself.

I belonged. I belonged with him. And I'd always be safe, respected, and desired.

"Are you ready for your present now?" The mischievous tilt of his lips had me curious.

I closed my eyes and held out my hands. "Ready."

He set something in my palms that felt like a phone. It better not be a phone. I already had one of those.

"Open your eyes," he said.

I did, and then frowned. It *was* a phone. Wait, it was his phone. A video played, showing a shop in the Sinopolis lobby, covered up by a big curtain.

"Now, please," Grim asked, and I realized we were on a live video call. A woman walked over to it and tugged at the fabric.

I gasped as I read the shop's name. "Bite Me: Cupcakes and Desserts" was next to a logo with fangs biting into a cupcake.

"It's yours," Grim said. "You can run it, let others run it for you, do whatever you like. But I remembered how intently you desired this to be a part of who you were. Now it can be."

Then I saw a petite woman standing at the edge, smiling up at the sign.

"Wait, is that..."

"Cheri," Grim nodded. "Your friend who owns the Cupcakery. She agreed to help get the shop off the ground, and depending on what you two set up, I'm sure she can find happiness running both storefronts."

I clutched at my now-beating heart.

Cheri waved at the camera, and I could only blink. My heart exploded. I was going to perish moments before my own wedding. Not cool.

Grim turned off the phone and put it away in his pocket.

"I don't deserve you," I croaked.

The full-body laugh that escaped him shocked me out of my stupor. "No, my darling sekhor," he said, stroking another strand of my hair before trailing a finger down my neck and exposed collarbone. "I do not deserve you. But let's not get in a game of deserving. There are far more interesting and pleasurable games to play."

"Like what?" I dared, stepping into him. My hands smoothed down the ridges of his exposed muscle. My mouth watered. I wanted him. I didn't care that we needed to get married in a little bit. I wanted him now. Hard, fast, and dirty. I licked my lips, slow and deliberate, until his attention was arrested on my mouth.

Then Grim turned me around, so I faced the mirrored vanity. He put my hands on the countertop. "Don't tease Death," he warned, even as he nuzzled into my neck while shooting me a dark look in the mirror.

"It's only teasing if I don't intend to follow through," I shot back. His hands molded down my sides until he gripped my hips. Then I found my words coming out breathy. "Like you said, after this, it's all about the party and socializing. Maybe I can give you a gift before we go out there and say I do."

The smile on his face turned the place between my groins positively liquid. "Oh, I have one more surprise for you. The wedding gift from Osiris."

Without ever moving his hands, dark smoke curled around my dress, melding into it while lifting the back of it, until he exposed my thighs and backside. I wore strappy garters and a complicated undergarment that more framed my womanly bits than covered.

A growl emerged from his throat.

"I thought the repair of Sinopolis was his gift?" I said, even as I felt the velvet hardness press against my already slick center.

"No, he must make sure the operation of souls is not compromised." Grim waved it off. "That was business. The gift was more for...pleasure."

Then he entered me and I cried out, my fingernails biting into the wood. The friction sent sizzles along my every nerve ending as he stretched me. Grim's death mask flickered as he stroked in and out of me.

Despite the hot sensations rioting through me, I feared getting my hair messed up. Timothy might try to set his stylist hounds back on me. But Grim left my updo alone.

A phantom pressure blossomed on my sensitive bud, though Grim's hands were nowhere near that, still gripping my hips.

"Wh-what is—?" I started to ask, but the phantom pleasure grew sharp and insistent, cutting me off.

Grim fought to get his own words out between clenched teeth. "Though our blood bond is broken, Osiris forged a new tether. One for both of us to...play with."

Nothing made sense, but I didn't care if it did. It felt like Grim's tongue was playing me like a fiddle, though he still drove into me from behind. I crested over my orgasm with surprising quickness, dissolving into shudders and incoherent moans.

"That's a good girl." Grim dropped a kiss on the back of my neck, though he never stopped pushing into me.

The fog of post-orgasm brain settled around me, even as he stoked the pressure and need in me again. Then I felt it.

The invisible tether Grim spoke of. I hadn't noticed it before, but I could...feel him. I could also play with him.

I tossed a devilish smile his way as I wriggled on him more and sent my own shot of sensation, directed right at the base of his hardness. Grim's head fell back and black clouds exploded out of him as his growl rattled the room. Still, he managed to keep his control and not release into me.

When he righted, the death mask flickered wildly. "You think you can play with Death?"

"Oh yeah," I said, squirming and pushing back and against him faster, needing more.

"Beg me for mercy," he said.

"Never," I shot back.

"It's your death wish."

"Absolutely," I agreed.

His silken command gripped my body. "Then feel the kiss of death."

I exploded into a million pieces of pleasure as I melted on his hardness, crying out his name.

Then I grabbed the tether again, ready for retribution. I wanted to bring him to his knees.

I vaguely hoped we wouldn't miss our wedding. But they could wait. We had eternity. And I loved flirting with death.

Not ready to be done with this series, we're going back to the deep dark underbelly Sinopolis to visit a certain crazy, feral God.

Visit www.hollyroberds.com and download the bonus epilogue now!

WANT A FREE BOOK?

Join Holly's Newsletter Holly's Hot Spot at www.hollyroberds.com and get the Five Orders Prequel Novella, The Knight Watcher, for FREE!

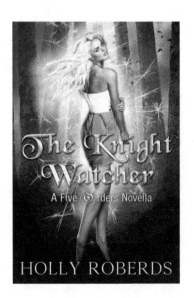

Plus you'll get exclusive sneak peaks, giveaways, fun lil' nuggets, and notifications when new books come out. Woot!

A LETTER FROM THE AUTHOR

Dear Reader,

Thank you for reading!

I loved writing this story and have so much more in store for Grim and Vivien as they discover the cancerous root amidst the gods and learn the limits of trust and love.

Loved this book? Consider leaving a review as it helps other readers discover my books.

Want to make sure you never miss a release or any bonus content I have coming down the pipeline?

Make sure to join Holly's Hotspot, my newsletter, and I'll send you a FREE ebook right away!

You can also find me on my website www.hollyroberds.com and I hang out on social media.

Instagram: http://instagram.com/authorhollyroberds

Facebook: www.facebook.com/hollyroberdsauthorpage/

And closest to my black heart is my reader fan group, Holly's Hellions. Become a Hellion. Raise Hell. www.facebook.com/groups/hollyshellions/

Cheers!

Holly Roberds

ABOUT THE AUTHOR

Holly started out writing Buffy the Vampire Slayer and Terminator romantic fanfiction before spinning off into her own fantastic worlds with bitey MCs and heart wrenching climaxes as well as other errr climaxes...

Holly is a Colorado girl to her core but is only outdoorsy in that she likes drinking on patios in Denver.

She lives with her ever-supportive husband and is searching to recruit two new house rabbits to supervise this writer, to make sure she doesn't spend all of her time watching Buffy reruns.

For more sample chapters, news, and more, visit www.
hollyroberds.com

Printed in the USA
CPSIA information can be obtained
at www.ICGtesting.com
LVHW011042030724
784559LV00014B/565

9 781960 961044